The Faber Book of Northern Legends

by the same author

for Children
THE CALLOW PIT COFFER (Macmillan)
THE EARTH-FATHER (Heinemann)
THE FIRE-BROTHER (Heinemann)
THE GREEN CHILDREN (Macmillan)
GREEN BLADES RISING: THE ANGLO-SAXONS (André Deutsch)
HAVELOK THE DANE (Macmillan)
KING HORN (Macmillan)
THE PEDLAR OF SWAFFHAM (Macmillan)
THE SEA STRANGER (Heinemann)
STORM AND OTHER OLD ENGLISH RIDDLES (Macmillan)
THE WILDMAN (André Deutsch)
WORDHOARD (*with Jill Paton Walsh*) (Macmillan)

Poems
THE DREAM-HOUSE (André Deutsch)
THE RAIN-GIVER (André Deutsch)
THE BATTLE OF MALDON AND OTHER OLD ENGLISH POEMS
(*translations; with Bruce Mitchell*) (Macmillan)
BEOWULF (*translation; with Bruce Mitchell*) (Macmillan)

Travel
PIECES OF LAND: JOURNEYS TO EIGHT ISLANDS (Gollancz)

as Editor
RUNNING TO PARADISE: AN INTRODUCTORY SELECTION
OF THE POEMS OF W. B. YEATS (Macmillan)
WINTER'S TALES 14 (Macmillan)
WINTER'S TALES FOR CHILDREN 3 (Macmillan)

The Faber Book of
Northern Legends

EDITED BY
KEVIN CROSSLEY-HOLLAND

illustrated by Alan Howard

FABER AND FABER
3 Queen Square London

First published in 1977
by Faber and Faber Limited
3 Queen Square London WC1
Printed in Great Britain
by W & J Mackay Limited, Chatham
All rights reserved

Illustrations © Faber & Faber Ltd., 1977

British Library Cataloguing in Publication Data

The Faber book of northern legends.
1. Legends, Germanic   2. Tales, Germanic
I. Crossley-Holland, Kevin
398.2'0917'43   GR139

ISBN 0-571-10912-8

for
RICHARD AND HELEN BARBER

Contents

9

Contents

Sources and Acknowledgements

"The Apples of Iduna" is taken from *Thunder of the Gods* by Dorothy Hosford, published by The Bodley Head, London, and Holt, Rinehart and Winston, New York. "The Curse of Andvari's Ring", "Loki Makes Mischief" and "Ragnarok" are taken from *Myths of the Norsemen* by Roger Lancelyn Green (Penguin Books, Harmondsworth; pp. 76–83, 138–142, 203–208 © Roger Lancelyn Green, 1960, reprinted by permission of Penguin Books Ltd.). "Dietrich of Bern" comes from *German Hero-Sagas and Folk-Tales* by Barbara Leonie Picard (Oxford University Press, London, 1958). "Balder's Doom" is taken from *The Children of Odin* by Padraic Colum, by permission of the Executors of Padraic Colum's estate and the publishers, George G. Harrap & Company Ltd.

"Thor goes Fishing with Hymir" is translated by Brian Branston in *The Lost Gods of England* (Thames and Hudson, London 1957. Reissued 1974); "The Lay of Thrym" comprises part of *The Elder Edda* translated by Paul B. Taylor and W. H. Auden with notes by Peter H. Salus (Faber and Faber, London, 1969, and Random House Inc., New York); "The Expedition of Thorfin Karlsefni" is taken from *The Norse Discoverers of America: The Wineland Sagas* translated by G. M. Gathorne-Hardy, 1921, reprinted by permission of the Oxford University Press; "Authun and the Bear" and "Thorstein Staff-Struck" both come from *Eirik the Red and Other Icelandic Sagas* selected and translated by Gwyn Jones © Oxford University Press, reprinted by permission of the publishers; "Gestumblindi's Riddles" are translated by N. Kershaw (Nora Chadwick) in *Stories and Ballads of the Far Past* (Cambridge University Press, Cambridge, 1921); "The Burning of Bergthors-

11

Sources and Acknowledgements

knoll" is taken from *Njal's Saga* translated by Magnus Magnusson and Hermann Pálsson (Penguin Books, Harmondsworth, © Magnus Magnusson and Hermann Pálsson, 1960). "Beowulf fights the Dragon" comes from my own translation of *Beowulf*, reprinted by permission of Macmillan, London and Basingstoke.

Acknowledgements are due and gladly given to the holders of copyrights listed above for their kind permission to include material in this anthology.

The following stories in the anthology are out of copyright: "How Thor went to Jotunheim" from *Heroes of Asgard and the Giants of Jotunheim* by Annie Keary (Macmillan, London, 1857); "The Battle of Stamford Bridge" from *The Heimskringla, or Chronicle of the Kings of Norway* translated by Samuel Laing (Longmans, London, 1844); "How Sigurd awoke Brynhild upon Hindfell" from *The Story of Sigurd the Volsung and the Fall of the Niblungs* by William Morris (Ellis and White, London, 1877); "The Hauntings at Frodriver" translated by Walter Scott in *Illustrations of Northern Antiquities* by Henry Weber, R. Jamieson and W. S. (Walter Scott) (Edinburgh, 1814); and "The Making of the Worlds" from *Norse Tales* by Edward Thomas (Clarendon Press, Oxford, 1912).

I am especially grateful to the three writers who have prepared stories specifically for this anthology: Penelope Farmer ("Wayland Smith"), Ursula Synge ("The Building of the Wall of Asgard") and Jennifer Westwood ("Walter and Hildegund"). It seems to me that their versions have no betters.

I must also make a few personal acknowledgements. My editor, Phyllis Hunt, has kept me on my mettle with her own knowledge of the Northern legends, and has been most patient and supportive. I have had the advantage of being able to discuss with Richard Barber the background to this anthology, its thrust and some of its constituents. The staff of the British Museum Reading Room have been unfailingly courteous and helpful. Finally, my wife Ruth has brought her own experience of books for children to bear in her detailed criticism of this anthology and has helped me to keep at it and complete it.

*And they sat on the side of Hindfell, and their fain eyes looked and
     loved,*
As she told of the hidden matters whereby the world is moved :
And she told of the framing of all things, and the houses of the heaven ;
And she told of the star-worlds' courses, and how the winds be driven ;
*And she told of the Norns and their names, and the fate that abideth
     the earth ;*
And she told of the ways of King-folk in their anger and their mirth ;
And she spake of the love of women, and told of the flame that burns,
And the fall of mighty houses, and the friend that falters and turns,
And the lurking blinded vengeance, and the wrong that amendeth wrong,
*And the hand that repenteth its stroke, and the grief that endureth for
     long ;*
And how man shall bear and forbear, and be master of all that is ;
And how man shall measure it all, the wrath, and the grief, and the bliss.

—WILLIAM MORRIS
The Story of Sigurd the Volsung

Foreword

It is almost two thousand years since the Roman Empire was at its zenith; and since innumerable tribes—Angles, Saxons, Frisians, Jutes, Franks, Goths, Ostrogoths, Vandals, Amelungs, Burgundians and many others—jostled for position in North-West Europe, on the fringes of that Empire.

These tribes had been heading slowly westward from the over-populated south Russian steppelands, land-hungry and loot-happy, for even longer than the time that divides us from them. Their group name is the Teutons and they were only one of a series of human waves—Balts, Slavs, Illyrians, Celts—all of them Indo-European, that rolled westward during what is known as the Age of Migrations. In a wide sense, therefore, the Teutons were tied by a blood knot, like one unwieldy family. As they moved west, they fought each other; they grabbed one another's land; they traded; they intermarried. To some extent, they shared one experience.

Whatever the later contact between the Teutonic tribes (between, for example, the settlers in England), it is their common origin and shared experience that explains why the substance and mood of their stories so often resemble each other. The storytelling poets went their separate ways; the stories were passed by word of mouth from generation to generation, until they were finally written down by different people at different times speaking different languages in different places. But look and see, they are like buckets of water drawn from the same well. So, for instance, the dragon guarding a cursed gold hoard that Beowulf kills in the eighth century Anglo-Saxon poem of that name and the dragon guarding a cursed gold hoard that Sigurd kills in the *Volsunga Saga*, composed in thirteenth

15

century Iceland, are the *same* dragon. The difference is only in their clothing, not in their meaning.

To identify the common imaginative strain of the Teutons, and incidentally to illustrate how that strain was coloured by the geography of the places in which the various tribes finally settled: that is the purpose of this anthology.

The twenty-two stories in this volume are drawn from the three sources that together constitute the heroic literature of the Teutonic peoples: Germanic heroic legends, Icelandic sagas, and Norse mythology.

The Germanic heroic legends were not composed in one place, at one time. They were the history, actual and imaginary, of the North-West European tribes, the record of great men, great dynasties, and great deeds and misdeeds passed down by word of mouth from grandfather to father to son. That is why the oral poet was so important a figure in any pre-literate culture: he was, and in a few very remote places such as the Amazon basin and the Phillipine rain forests still is, the repository of times past, a living memory. Some of the heroic legends were ultimately written down by the twelfth century Danish historian Saxo Grammaticus and by anonymous writers in twelfth and thirteenth century Iceland; bits and pieces of other legends appear in the great body of Anglo-Saxon poetry which also boasts, in *Beowulf*, the earliest surviving Germanic heroic poem (the fact that the action takes place in Denmark and Sweden is striking evidence of the shared inheritance of the Teutonic peoples); the great medieval German poem, *Nibelungenlied*, is based on traditions that predate it by at least one thousand years. But however much survives, much more has been irretrievably lost—stories in manuscripts that have not escaped the rapids of time, and stories that were not written down at all.

Iceland was discovered and colonised by the Vikings towards the end of the ninth century. It is thought that its medieval population never exceeded 60,000 or 70,000—the size of a town like Carlisle or Lincoln, High Wycombe or Maidstone—but in the twelfth and thirteenth centuries its people produced a remarkable harvest of poetry and saga, recognised as one of the great bodies of world literature. The Icelandic sagas are prose narratives; they are conscious works of art, a distillation of separate oral tales into epigrammatic, ice-bright, immediate prose; and they vary in length from stories as short as "Authun and the Bear", which nevertheless takes in Greenland, Norway, Denmark, and Rome into the bargain, to the great *Heimskringla*, or "Lives of the Kings of Norway", by Snorri Sturluson (1179–1241). There are family sagas that tell of the lives, loyalties, dilemmas, and feuds of individuals and families during what is known as Iceland's heroic age around AD 1000; there are sagas about saintly Bishops and historical sagas (like *King Harald's Saga*, from which "The Battle of Stamford Bridge" is taken); and there are sagas about the Norsemen's insatiable appetite for exploration and settlement; drawing on earlier sources, they all combine historical accuracy and imaginative interpretation in varying degrees. No fewer than 700 manuscripts survive from this period. A contemporary scribe noted:

> With sagas one man can gladden many an hour, whereas most entertainments are difficult to arrange; some are very costly, some cannot be enjoyed without large numbers of people, some only entertain a very few people for a brief time, and some entail physical danger. But saga entertainment or poetry costs nothing and holds no dangers, and one man can entertain as many or as few as wish to listen; it is equally practicable night or day, by light or in darkness.

Snorri Sturluson, the leading politician, historian, poet and saga writer of his age, Saxo Grammaticus, and the poems preserved in the *Elder Edda*, a collection made in Iceland in about AD 1200, are the principal sources for our knowledge of the religious beliefs to which the pre-Christian Teutons subscribed, as revealed through the Norse myths. For, as Hilda Ellis Davidson has written:

> The mythology of a people is far more than a collection of pretty or terrifying fables to be retold in carefully bowdlerised form to our schoolchildren. It is the comment of the men of one particular age or civilisation on the mysteries of human existence and the human mind, their model for social behaviour, and their attempt to define in stories of gods and demons their perception of the inner realities.

17

Norse mythology begins at the beginning, with the creation. In the great chasm, Ginnungagap, ice and fire meet and engender life. In time a race of gods emerge, and they create nine worlds—notably Asgard (Kingdom of the Gods), Midgard (Middle Earth) for men, Jotunheim (Land of the Giants), and Niflheim (Land of the Dead). The entire universe is bound together by the roots of the mighty world-ash, Yggdrasill.

Led by Odin, the gods prosper for a time. They are confident, and ward off the forces of evil in the shape of the giants and malicious dwarfs. Indeed, they seem unassailable despite the machinations of one of their number, the god-giant Loki, who is forever scheming against them, and who fathers three appalling monsters, Fenrir (a ravening wolf), Jormungand (the World Serpent) and Hel (Queen of the Dead). A series of highly dramatic myths record the interrelation between the worlds and the derring-do of specific gods, giants, humans and dwarfs; there are contests of many kinds (strength, fleetness of foot, wits, in the smithy, drinking ability); there are prodigious fishing expeditions; single combats; thefts (of the mead of inspiration, the apples of youth, and so on) and recoveries; unexpected love matches.

But Odin has already learned the future, after terrible sacrifice; he knows it is the destiny of gods, giants, men and dwarfs alike to be immolated at Ragnarok (Destruction of the Powers). Slowly the enmity of the various worlds becomes more destructive, more self-defeating. The innocent god Balder is slain through the devilry of Loki, and Loki it is who prevents his return from the dead. This act presages the onset of Ragnarok, and in one fearful battle involving all creation, the world is destroyed.

But this most fatalistic of all mythologies (the only one that culminates in cataclysm) allows a shaft of light to penetrate the darkness. Odin also learned, through drinking at the well of wisdom, that there would be a new cycle in the history of the world. And so it turns out. Balder and other, lesser gods and two humans are seen to have survived Ragnarok. They return to Asgard and Midgard to repeople the worlds once more. The end is a beginning.

There are many strains that recur again and again in early Teutonic or Germanic literature; I can only briefly suggest some of them, with reference to stories in this anthology. Predominant is the sense of fate that governs the lives of gods and men, giants and dwarfs, from the day on which they are born until Ragnarok. The Anglo-Saxons called it *wyrd*, the Norsemen *urðr*, "what will be". Fate manifests itself in virtually every story in this book. It is the relentless force of the inevitable. But for all that, as I have written elsewhere, the *way* in which a man lived his life was up to him; he could ride the tide of events, face life with spirit and dignity, and be remembered and honoured for it; or else he could crumple before a seemingly meaningless destiny, and be forgotten in the dark drumroll of years.

In a heroic society, the principal bond was between man and man. Physical and moral courage, loyalty, a willingness to take vengeance—these were the important qualities in a world where men slept with their swords beside them. The hero Beowulf, represented in "Beowulf fights the Dragon", lived a life that epitomised all the virtues of the Germanic heroic code, and so won the coveted *lof*, the "fame" and good name that would live after him. Bravery and loyalty are the leitmotifs of the story of "Dietrich of Bern"; almost reckless courage leading to a loyal bond is the satisfactory outcome of "Thorstein Staff-Struck"; it is divided loyalty that is Hagen's dilemma in the story of "Walter and Hildegund"; and it is, of course, Loki's growing disloyalty to his fellow gods in Asgard, culminating in "The Death of Balder", that precipitates Ragnarok.

Thor was the very embodiment of physical courage, and he was never slow to take vengeance; "The Lay of Thrym" demonstrates this. The story "Wayland Smith" shows how a man overcame the terrible wounds inflicted upon him and was able to exact, all too literally, an eye for an eye and a tooth for a tooth. But the vengeance that leads to "The Burning of Bergthorsknoll" is more complex. After endless family feuding, Flosi is hopelessly compromised. In the words of Gwyn Jones, "This is the familiar tragic dilemma of the Germanic hero: he has a choice not between right and wrong, but between wrongs, and cannot renegue."

It is true that there are also great romantic love stories in

Northern legend, such as "Walter and Hildegund" and the ill-fated love of Sigurd and the Valkyrie Brynhild, part of which is retold in "How Sigurd Awoke Brynhild upon Hindfell". The superstition of the omen-ridden pre-Christian Germanic peoples is well expressed in "The Hauntings at Frodriver"; their ironic wit is on parade in many of the Norse myths and Icelandic sagas; their predilection for the aphoristic and enigmatic in "Gestumblindi's Riddles"; their tendency to melancholy in "Beowulf fights the Dragon" and "The Death of Balder"; their restless spirit of adventure (what an Anglo-Saxon poet called *ut-fus*, "out-eager") is at the heart of "Authun and the Bear" and "The Expedition of Thorfin Karlsefni"; and their keen sense of wonder at the natural world, and their identification with it—ice and fire, unpredictable ocean, and tracts of desolate land—are evident everywhere, and nowhere more so than in the story of the creation, "The Making of the Worlds". Fatalism, courage, loyalty, superstition, cunning, melancholy, a sense of wonder, curiosity about all that's new: these are, I believe, the most pronounced strains in the make-up of the Germanic heroic peoples, as revealed through their prose and poetry.

It is the function of an anthologist to provide variety within unity. I have suggested some common factors in these stories but what I have also aimed for has been difference, difference of event, tone and length. I have tried to indicate the very considerable range of the Northern legends and the way in which that range has been interpreted and translated since the beginning of the nineteenth century. No disc is any good if it sticks in the same groove.

In my opinion, the Northern legends are less well known than they should be. Since the Renaissance began in fourteenth century Italy, with its revival of interest in classical learning, artists working in all disciplines have regularly derived inspiration from the south. Relatively few artists, on the other hand, have turned to North-West European models or traditions for stimulus, although it is true that in the last few decades a number of highly influential writers—notably W. H. Auden and J. R. R. Tolkien—have excited new interest in the northern world, perhaps especially amongst writers for children. Nevertheless we are still as used to the clement

20

lapping of the Mediterranean as we are unused to the bracing floes of the Baltic.

It is entirely proper that we should be acquainted with the great bodies of classical myth. The paradox is that, geographically and temperamentally of the north, we should not be at least equally well acquainted with our own great traditions enshrined in the Northern legends. This matters; it matters very much indeed. We all need to understand the nature of our own roots, our own belonging—we all need to know the stirring and sometimes tragic Northern legends because the fundamentals they embody are dressed in clothing we may immediately recognise *as having something to do with us*. By reading them, enjoying them, coming to terms with them, we are learning about our own forebears; and in meeting qualities that seem especially pronounced in the North-West European make-up, we are learning more about ourselves. The Norse gods, the monsters, and our Teutonic ancestors, are nearer to us than we know.

KEVIN CROSSLEY-HOLLAND
Greenwich, 1976

The Making of the Worlds

Long ago, in Iceland, there was a king named Gangler who was famous for wisdom and for magic, and there were few things which he could not understand. One thing alone always astonished him, and that was the fact that whatever the gods willed came to pass. He did not know whether this was due to their own great wisdom or to that of some even mightier gods whom perhaps they themselves worshipped as men did them. This question returned to his mind again and again, even when he was old.

One day while the king was thinking about this power of the gods he rode far away from his palace without looking at the road, and leaving his horse, which was a new one, to take him wherever ti pleased. For he was thinking very hard. He did not know even that he was hungry. He did not know that what he was seeing was not the things around him, but those in his own brain. He was thinking about the gods and their palace of Asgard, and he could see them as plain as his own warriors and his own house; in fact the gods were very much like his warriors, and the palace of Asgard very much like his house, except that they were larger and looked as if they must last for ever. It was not until the horse stumbled that he saw anything else but gods and Asgard. He slid gently off on to the ground, and the young horse, glad to be free, walked on, turned round, and galloped away.

As Gangler followed the horse with an indifferent eye he saw that he was far up on the side of a stony mountain. It seemed as huge as the sky, especially as the pale stones scattered about it resembled the flocks of white clouds when those flocks are at their smallest and highest in the blue. Though he had never before been on this mountain or any like it, he was in no way surprised or alarmed. It was, in fact, just such a mountain as he had been seeing with his mind's eye for some time. At the top of it was a palace such has he imagined the gods' palace of Asgard to be. With untired step he went on up the slope towards it. It did not seem to him a wonderful thing that he should have come in this short time to Asgard.

The first thing he saw was a mansion huge as a hill, roofed with golden shields instead of tiles; and a man stood at the entrance tossing up and catching seven swords to amuse himself.

"What is your name?" said the man. "Gangler," said he; "I have come a long way and should be glad of a night's lodging. Pray tell me whose house this is." "It is the king's," said the man, and led him into the hall. He saw room after room, and many people in them, some drinking, some at play, others fighting. He went without fear, yet very carefully, through the crowd, from room to room, until he came to one where he saw three thrones one above the other, and three crowned men like brothers sitting on the thrones. "Who are these?" asked Gangler. "The one on the lowest throne is a king, and his name is Har; the second is equal to him, and is called Jafnhar; the highest is Thridi, and he also is a king." Now Har himself spoke to Gangler, asking his errand and telling him that all strangers were welcome to eat and drink in his hall. "But first," said Gangler, "I should be glad to know if there is any one here famous for wisdom." Har smiled: "Unless you show yourself the wisest, O man, I fear you may not return in safety. Stand below, and here sits one who will be able to answer your questions."

Gangler bent down before the lowest of the thrones and began to ask his questions.

"Who is the first or eldest of the gods?" he asked.

"All-Father," answered Har, in a voice like thunder, "but he has twelve names."

"Where is this god? what is his power, and what are his works?"

"He has been from the beginning," answered Har, "he reigns everywhere: all things obey him."

And Jafnhar said in a voice like the sea: "He made heaven and earth and air, and all that dwells in them."

Thridi also spoke, and his voice was like wind in the forest: "He made man, and gave him a soul that cannot die."

"But where," asked Gangler, "where was this god before he made heaven and earth and air?"

"He was with the frost giants," said Har.

"And what was before that?" continued Gangler.

"In the beginning," said Har, "there was no earth, no sea, and no heavens. There was no grass; there was nothing but a yawning chasm such as no man can imagine and such as would make the gods dizzy even to think of."

"Long before the earth," said Jafnhar, "a cloud world was made, called Niflheim, a cold world of everlasting fog, rain, and sleet."

At these words Gangler felt himself upon a ship, as once he was in his younger days, sailing over an unknown sea after a storm. He saw before him the dim rocks and the dim marshland on the shore of an island where he could find no men, and nothing alive but sea-birds all crying together as they flew round about in the mist. It was between a wet autumn and a bitter winter. The coast of that un-inhabited island seen through the sea-spray, the mist, and the low grey clouds must have been like Niflheim. He remembered yet another scene. He had just stepped out of his house after a night of rain and wind. The rain and the wind had beaten round the walls all night, so that as he lay awake, the only man awake in his hall, he seemed to be on a ship. And as he stepped out in the morning he thought at first that he was in the middle of the sea. Below him was the steep hill on the top of which stood his house, but the hill was blotted out by mist. Through the mist he could see mountains which he had never seen before, but either they, or he and the house, were moving. He dared not take another step lest he should fall into that strange sea. Then as he stood still thinking, he saw that the mountains were clouds. His house and the little piece of ground where he was standing seemed to be all that was left of the earth. The night's storm had washed away all the rest, and there he was shipwrecked in a sea of clouds and mist, rocking and swirling round about. This sea must have been like Niflheim.

"But before Niflheim," said Thridi, not noticing Gangler, "there was a world in the south called Muspellheim. It is a flaming and burning world, too bright and too hot for any one, man or god, who was not born there. It is guarded by one with a flaming sword seated at its border. His name is Surt, and at the end of the world he will go forth with his flaming sword and harry and overcome the gods and burn the world."

"Tell me more," said Gangler, "of the chasm between this burning world and Niflheim."

Thridi answered him: "One half of the chasm was fog and frost from Niflheim, the other bright because of the sparks and flakes of fire of Muspellheim; and in the middle part the frost was melted and the drops of the vapour rising from it grew into the shape of a man. This was Ymir, the ancestor of all the frost giants."

"Where did he live?" asked Gangler, "and how did he live?"

"A cow also was made out of the drops of the melted frost," said Har, "and four rivers of milk flowed from her teats, and Ymir lived on the milk."

"What did the cow feed on?"

"The cow fed on the salty hoar-frost that she licked from the stones. At the end of the first day hair like a man's appeared on the stone that she had licked; at the end of the second there was a man's head; on the third the complete likeness of a man. He was fair to see, big and strong, and his name was Buri. He begot a son named Bor. This son begot three sons, Odin, Vili, and Ve. These were gods."

"And how did the sons of Ymir agree with the sons of Bor?"

"The sons of Bor," said Har, "slew the giant Ymir, and his blood drowned all his children except one called Bergelmi, who saved himself and his wife in an ark. The gods made the earth out of Ymir's body in the midst of the chasm. His flesh was the land, his bones the mountains, his blood the sea."

Here Jafnhar spoke: "The blood ran out of his wounds in a great ring encircling the earth. On the shore of this ocean dwell the giants."

"Ymir's skull," said Thridi, "made the heavens above the earth. They set a dwarf at each of the four quarters, North, South, East, West. With the sparks and flakes of fire scattered from Muspellheim they made stars to move in the heavens, to give light, and to mark the days and nights, spring and summer, autumn and winter."

"Do the giants not seek revenge?"

"They are kept out by a great wall," said Har. "Inside this wall is Midgard, the abode of men."

"But where did men come from to dwell in Midgard?"

"As they were walking on the sea-shore, these sons of Bor found two trees, and taking them up made them into men. Odin gave them breath and life, Vili gave them the power to know and to move, Ve gave them speech, hearing, and sight. They gave them also clothes and names. The man was called Ash and the woman Elma, and these two were the first parents of all mankind living in Midgard. Then the gods made an earthly city for themselves called Asgard, in the centre of Midgard but high above the homes of men. Highest of all in Asgard is the solitary seat of Odin, called Lidskialf. From there he can see all the world and all that men are doing therein. One of Odin's names is King of Lidskialf. Odin and Frigg, his wife, are parents of all the gods. Rightly, therefore, is Odin named All-Father."

For a little time Gangler was silent. Then suddenly he asked: "What is Night?"

"Night," said Har, "is a giant's daughter, and like all of them she is dark. She married one of the gods, and they had a son whose name was Day. This child was as bright and beautiful as his father. Odin took him and his mother Night, and gave them two chariots and two horses, and gave them the heavens to drive in, first one and then the other. Night's horse is Rimfaxi; when he has run his course he stands still, champing the bit; his mouth is covered with foam and this falls to the earth, where men call it dew. Skinfaxi is Day's horse, and as he runs light is shaken out of his mane over earth and the heavens."

"And who guides the sun and the moon?"

"Once there was a man who had two children so beautiful that he called them Sun and Moon. This angered the gods, and they snatched up the two children and set them in the cars of the sun and moon to guide them across the sky for ever—until Ragnarok."

Gangler had never heard the word Ragnarok. If he thought at all about it, he supposed it was only a muttering, an oath of some sort, in the throat of Har. "Why," he asked, "does the sun always go on? It is as if she were flying in fear from some one."

"She is in fear. Some one is pursuing her, and he is not far behind."

"Who is it?"

"A wolf named Skoll, and one day he will catch her and devour her. Another one named Hati follows the moon and one day will devour him. They are two of the children of the old giantess living in Iron Wood on the east of Midgard. She has many children."

Gangler thought for a little while of Iron Wood, and an old giantess with a beard there in the darkness, and a herd of her children who were wolves, some of them running out from under the trees of Iron Wood to look for Midgard. Gangler had never seen Iron Wood, but when Har spoke of it he saw clearly the edge of a great wood. He was hunting a bear, and had left all his companions far behind; and it was the end of a winter's day. The bear had gone into that wood, and though he was not afraid yet he stood still, leaning upon his spear and looking at the wood. The trees were oak-trees, twisted, bare and black, and he could not see far into the wood. All was black except one tiny blot of orange on a low branch of one oak-tree. All was silent except one tiny song which came from that blot of orange. It was a robin singing, and he stood watching it. Nothing was moving inside the wood. Suddenly the light was gone, and the robin turned, flitted, and was silent. He watched for it, but in vain. Long after he had ceased to expect the bird or the song, he remained standing still with his eyes towards the forest of black oaks. It was useless now to follow the bear. Slowly he turned back and wearily retraced his steps, so that not until the night was half gone did he enter his house. Several times afterwards he turned the hunt that way in the hope of finding the forest and going into it. But he never could. Years went by, and he forgot the forest. Now he remembered it, and shuddered at the thought of the old giantess and her wolf children that would some day devour the sun and the moon. It seemed to him that the oak forest where the bear had disappeared was Iron Wood.

When he had come back from this wandering of his mind, Gangler tried to hide his thoughts by asking:

"Which is the road from earth to heaven?"

Har laughed:

"Have you never been told how the gods made a bridge from earth to heaven, called Bifrost? You have seen it, if you did not know what it was. Perhaps you call it the rainbow. It is a most mighty bridge, and yet if—and yet when the sons of Muspellheim ride over it they will break it down."

"The gods cannot have made such a bridge in earnest. They might have made one that could not be broken down."

"You are but a man. The gods are not to blame. Bifrost is a good bridge. It is the best of all possible bridges; it cannot resist the sons of Muspellheim, nor can anything else. Why, then, should the gods have tried to make a better bridge, when they had made one which would keep out any one and anything save the sons of Muspellheim? It keeps out the giants."

It would have been easy to annoy Har still more, but Gangler asked him:

"What did the All-Father make after Asgard?"

"He formed a council to govern Asgard and Midgard. They built themselves a temple of gold for the high seat of the All-Father and the twelve seats of the other gods. It is the best and the biggest house on earth, and its name is Gladsheim. They built another beautiful palace, called Wingolf, for the goddesses. They built also a smithy, and there they worked at the forges with hammer and tongs. They made things of metal and gems and wood, but above all they made things of gold. Everything in their houses was of gold, and this was called the age of gold. It was destroyed by the coming of women from Giantland.

"While they sat on their thrones the gods remembered the maggots in the dead body of Ymir, and they gave them the shape and the understanding of men, and homes in the earth and in the rocks. These were the dwarfs, and though small they had often much wit.

"At one time it happened that a dwarf, named All-wise, took the shape and size of a god, and by a trick persuaded the gods to promise him Freya for his wife. After giving orders to the servants to deck his cavern and make ready a feast for the bride, he hurried off merrily to fetch her home. He had now returned to his true shape, and outside Valhalla he was met by Odin, who said to him, seeing his wedding attire:

"'Who are you? why are you pale about the nose? You look a sorry sort of bridegroom.'

"'My name is All-wise,' answered the dwarf. 'My home is in a cave under the earth. I have only come here to fetch my bride, and I hope you are not thinking to break your promise.'

"'But I am,' said Odin, 'I am the bride's guardian, and she can do nothing without my consent. I was not at home when she was betrothed.'

"'Who are you, then, to be guardian to the lovely maid?' asked the dwarf, contemptuously.

"'I am the Wayfarer, Longbeard's son. Nevertheless, the maid cannot make a match unless I consent,' said Odin.

"'If that is so, I would rather have your permission, though you are a wayfaring man. I will not lose the snow-white maid by any scruples.'

"'She shall be yours, All-wise, if you can answer all my questions. Tell me first, you who probably know everything, what other names has the Earth?'

"'The gods call it the "Field"; giants call it the "Ever-green"; elves the "Growing".'

"'What are the names for Heaven?'

"'Gods call it "Warmer"; giants "High-home"; elves "Fair-roof"; Dwarfs "Drip-hall".'

"'What are the names for the Moon?'

"'It is the "Whirling-wheel" in Hell; the "Hastener" among giants; "Sheen" among dwarfs; "Year-teller" the elves call it.'

"'And the Sun?'

"'It is "Dwales-doll" among dwarfs; "Ever-glow" among giants; "Fair-wheel" among elves.'

"'What is the Wind?'

"'It is the "Waverer" of the gods; the "Whooper" of the giants; the "Soft-gale" of the elves; in Hell they call it "Whistle-gust".'

" 'What is the Sea?'

" 'The gods call it "Level"; the elves "Sea-blink"; the dwarfs "Deep".'

" 'And Fire?'

" 'It is called "Greedy" by giants; "Furnace fire" by dwarfs; in Hell it is the "Destroyer".'

" 'What is Night?'

" 'It is called "Unlight" by giants; "Sleep-joy" by elves; "Dream-fairy" by dwarfs.'

" 'What is Ale?'

" ' "Beer" among Gods; "Clear-beer" among giants; "Mead" in Hell; "Good cheer" among dwarfs.'

"And thus by many questions, which could only be answered after much thinking, Odin wasted the dwarf's time.

" 'I never met one man,' he said, 'who knew so many different names. But your wit has been too much for you. The sun is now up, or, as dwarfs call it, the "Dwales-doll"; and the sun is too much for dwarfs; they cannot endure its light.'

"The hall was full of sunshine, and All-wise was turned to stone; and for a stone to marry a bride is impossible."

"Which, then, is the chief abode or most holy place of the gods?"

"Under the ash-tree, Yggdrasill. There they hold their court every day," answered Har. "Yggdrasill is the greatest and best of trees. It stretches out over the world as a common ash-tree does over a cottage. The roots of it are in Heaven, in Giantland, and in Niflheim. A dragon is always gnawing at the root which is in Niflheim. Many other serpents also gnaw at the roots; four harts nibble the buds; and the bark is rotting. An eagle who knows many things has its perch among the branches of Yggdrasill, and a squirrel named Rata-tosk runs up and down, telling the eagle's words to the dragon and trying to make strife between them. Under the root in Giantland is Mimir's brook, whose water gives wisdom and understanding. The All-Father himself once went to the brook for a draught, but Mimir would not give it unless he left an eye for a pledge. Under the third root is Weirds' brook, and beside it the gods sit in judgment. Every day they ride up over Bifrost bridge to Weirds' brook. These are the names of their horses: Gleed and Gylli,

Gler and Skidbrim, Silvertop and Sini, Hostage and Fallow-hoof, Goldcrest and Lightfoot. Only one of the gods may not ride over Bifrost, and that is Thor. If he were to ride over it in his thunder-chariot he would set it on fire. So he must walk, wading through the deep waters of Kormth and Wormth and the two Charlocks every day.

"Many fair palaces have been built in Heaven. One standing close to the Weirds' brook is the home of three maidens, Urd, Verdandi, and Skuld. These are the Norns; they water Yggdrasill with the water of Weirds' brook, and they make men's fates. They dwell alone except for two swans in the brook. There are many other Norns. One or another of them comes to every child that is born, and decides what is to be its fate. Such Norns are of the race of gods. Some Norns belong to the race of dwarfs, others are elves. Of elves there are two kinds. The elves of light, dwelling in Elflheim which is in Heaven, are as bright as if sunlight flowed in their veins for blood; but the dark elves who live down in the earth are blacker than pitch."

Gangler hardly listened to this about the two sorts of elves. "If these Norns," he said to Har, "give men their fates, good or bad, their gifts are very different. They are not like a good farmer who gives equally to his cattle that all may thrive, but like a bad mother who gives good things to one child and bad or nothing at all to an-other. Some men are fortunate and rich, others poor and in every way unfortunate; some live to be old, others are cut off in childhood or in their prime."

"Good Norns," said Har, "make good fates for men, but evil Norns make bad ones, and they alone should be blamed for them."

Gangler was silent and not glad. He could see these Norns too plainly to speak. They were three black-haired sisters living alone in a large dark house beside the brook. They never spoke to one another, but seemed to understand without speaking as they went to and fro in the long rooms, weaving. They wove just as if they were working at clothes for some one else. They had no joy in it, but went on and on. They did not care what they had made, when once it was done. They were like slaves who have too much work to do for a master whom they never see. One was as pale as any living thing can be, and sighed continually as she went from one web to another: she was too tired to leave off her toil. One of her sisters seemed to have more spirit, for now and then she clutched at the web and tore it in anger; but she was angry with herself, not with what she had made, and so she began another immediately, and the only effect of her anger was that her hand trembled and her lips were touched with foam. The other was neither sad nor glad. She never smiled or sighed, but worked as if she were asleep. It was so easy to her that she closed her eyes. Yet, like her two sisters, she laid down her work at the very moment when her day was over, and never began before it was time. And as Gangler watched them he said to himself: "If these three women make men's fates, somebody has made theirs for them long ago. If they were to die it would not be easy to find three other such sisters among the slave women who are no longer young." But he was still silent.

Therefore Har continued:

"Many other fair mansions stand in heaven. There is Breidablik, and Glitnir, and three most beautiful of all, brighter than the sun, which will stand when heaven and earth pass away, and there in the glittering ale-hall under the golden roof built upon the hills of the moon just men shall dwell for ever. Some say that this is now the palace of the elves of light, but we do not know. We have only heard tell of it."

Gangler was tired, and would have fallen asleep but for those three kings. To his half-dreaming eyes they seemed to be gods. He was afraid that they would disappear if he slept, and that they might send him away if he asked no more questions. He asked, therefore, why it was that summer was hot and winter cold.

"A wise man," said Har, "would never ask that, and any foolish one can answer it. The reason is that the father of summer was of a sweet and kindly nature, and summer took after him; while the father of winter was grim and chill, and his son likewise."

In spite of his fear and his good intentions, Gangler fell fast asleep while Har was speaking.

35

The Building of the Wall of Asgard

When they had slain the giant Ymir and created Middle Earth to be the abode of men, the gods built Asgard for themselves. Here Odin sat in his great hall, Gladsheim, and sometimes, when he grew weary of feasting, he would cross over to Middle Earth to see for himself how men were faring or to remind some little king that even kings are mortal.

Odin was the chief of the gods and he was called All-Father but he had other names too; men called him the One-eyed, and God of the Hanged, and Father of Battle, and they shared the spoils of war with him, hanging slaves and axes and gold rings in the branches of a tree to do him honour. Of the other gods Thor was the strongest; he struck thunder from the sky with blows of his hammer, Mjollnir. And there was Balder the Bright-faced and Tyr the Victorious who lost his hand when the wolf, Fenrir, was bound. And Bragi the Poet and Heimdall who was the son of nine maidens. There was Ull the Archer and Forseti Oath-keeper and Hoder the Blind. And there was Loki.

For the most part the gods looked sideways at Loki for he was a trickster and, moreover, kinsman to the giants. He had a way of mocking at serious matters, he was a shapeshifter and not to be trusted. Yet Odin trusted him.

"Then Odin is a fool," said Heimdall. "The giants seek for ways of overthrowing Asgard. When it comes to war, on which side will Loki stand?"

"When that time is here we shall know," said Odin. "But they will not find us sleeping while you, Heimdall, guard the bridge."

Loki turned away to laugh, making such a show of politeness that Heimdall reached for his axe.

"Do not think I doubt you," said Loki, wiping the laughter from his eyes. "Bifrost Bridge could have no better guardian. Who beside yourself can see wool growing on a sheep's back though that sheep grazes at the far distant edge of the world? Who but Heimdall can hear grass piercing the earth?"

Heimdall let his anger cool.

"Nevertheless," said Loki, "what can a guardian do but warn us? It is not enough. Asgard should have a wall to protect it."

"Na!" said Heimdall. "We are well enough as we are. A wall is a small thing to keep out a horde of giants if they've a mind to get in."

"That is for a council to decide," said Loki. But it was no easy matter to reach agreement.

"It would need to be a strong thick wall indeed," Forseti said. "And how long would such a wall be in the building?"

Loki shrugged. "Am I a mason? Four years—perhaps five. Yet behind such a wall we would sleep sound. Even Heimdall might close those sharp eyes of his and let the grass grow a while without being overlooked."

"Too long," said Forseti. "If the giants came while we were busy heaping stone on stone, our weapons would be strangers to us. A spear does not leap lightly from a blistered hand. We will think no more of it."

Yet the thought was in their minds. Asgard rose unprotected above the plain of Midgard; it was a prize worth taking and could be stormed from any side.

"These are unworthy fears," said Odin. "They have made us like old women who dare not leave the hen-yard lest a fox get in. There is not one of us who sleeps now more than an arm's length from his spear. I tell you I have been about in the world and I have heard no news of giants abroad—so let us hang up our shields again and remember that we are gods."

"Ah," said Loki, behind his hand, "but would they arm themselves in the clear light of day so that any travelling packman might count their spears and sell his knowledge at a high price?"

"Have done," cried Odin, "or, by the blood of Kvasir, I swear I may remember again the time before you were my brother."

"And indeed," said Loki hastily, "Heimdall guards the bridge."

Yet it was Heimdall, not Loki, who brought the mason to the gate of Odin's hall.

"Odin," he said, "there is a man outside who calls himself a worker in stone, well able to build such a wall as would keep the frost giants out."

"What manner of a man?" asked Odin, setting down his ale-horn. His thumb itched and he bit it to stop the tingling.

"He seems a civil enough, well-spoken fellow," said Heimdall. "And ready to bargain over the price. Will you speak with him?"

"I can do that, at least," said Odin and he left the hall, the other gods crowding behind him.

In the yard a man walked, pacing slowly with his arm through the reins of a great white stallion. The man had a decent, quiet bearing but the horse skittered and danced so that sparks flew from his hooves.

"Ho!" called Odin. "Are you the man who says he can build the wall?"

"I am," said the man, turning and looking the god straight in the eyes as though he were his equal. "It is no small task, Odin All-Wise, yet not beyond my prowess, and I swear that I will build it as strong, as high and as thick as ever you could wish."

"How long would it take?" asked Odin, and bit his thumb again.

The man thought a moment, looking all around him, measuring with his eyes the distance to left and right.

"Three years," he said. "No longer."

"And your price?"

"A fair price for the work. Your oath that, when the work is done, you will give me the Lady Freya to be my bride. Aye! and the sun and the moon as well, to make the balance equal."

"You jest," said Odin and gave a shout of laughter.

"I do not jest," said the man. His eyes were cold and there was no hint of merriment in them.

"Then you may take yourself off," said Odin, "for Freya is not to be given to such as you. And better the frost giants should trample Asgard into the ground than that the sun and the moon be taken from the sky."

"You may have decided otherwise by tomorrow," said the man and he mounted his horse and rode away.

That night at meat Odin toyed with the food on the dish before him, then flung down his knife as petulantly as a child.

"The fellow stays in my mind," he said. "What meant he when he said I might think otherwise by morning?"

"Perhaps he bargains in riddles," suggested Bragi. "Not Freya—but Freya's necklace. Not the sun and the moon but so much gold and so much silver."

"Riddle or no," said Odin, "he has had my answer and will get no other."

"Yet we should not be too hasty," said Loki.

Heimdall glared at him. "The day that Loki is not hasty I shall be as blind as Hoder. If you have anything to say, then say it, Loki. Your mind runs too fast for mere gods to follow."

"It is this," said Loki. "Such a wall as would protect Asgard would take us, who are gods, five years to build—and we have Thor to break the stone. But this man, this mortal man, says he can build it in three. Therefore he has a secret."

"He may keep his secret," said Odin. "The price is too high."

Loki leaned across the board. Lightning played behind his eyes and his shadow leapt like a dark flame on the wall at his back.

"Tell him he may have what he asks if he can build the wall in one year," he said. "I think he is a proud man and will not refuse the challenge."

"In one year!" said Heimdall. "And what then?"

"No man could do it, whatever his secret," said Loki. "The year will pass and so much of the wall will be built, the foundation and perhaps ten courses. Hardly more. We shall have the work well begun—and nothing to pay!"

The gods sat silent while each one of them tried to find a fault in Loki's plan.

"Can you be sure that he will take the challenge?" asked Odin.

"He must," said Loki.

Thus it was agreed between them all. And when the man returned to Asgard on the following day, Odin went out to greet him. "We have considered your offer," he said.

The man sat aloof, astride his fine white stallion. If his heart quickened at the promise of his payment, he did not show it.

"And you shall have what you ask," said Odin. "That is a fair price for the finished work."

The man neither smiled nor spoke.

"He works in stone and he has a stone face to go with it," said Bragi.

"But three years is a long time," said Odin. "I cannot wait so long. Finish the wall in one winter and you shall be paid. But if by the first day of midsummer there is any part that remains to be done, you will get nothing. Is that understood?"

"It is understood," said the man. "But I must have the help of my horse, Svadilfari. Is that understood?"

"Why," said Odin. "I would be a niggard indeed to say no to that. You will need the help of a horse to haul the stone."

And a little feeling of unease crept along Loki's scalp, raising the hair. He felt a prickle of fear at the base of his neck and he would have put a stop to the bargain there and then had it been possible. But already Odin and the stone-worker had clasped hands on it, and it was too late.

The next day the work began and all the gods turned out to watch—even blind Hoder was there, leaning on Bragi's arm. "Tell me how it goes," he said, "for it is a lonely thing to be always in the dark."

"It goes well," said Bragi. "And it goes ill too. For that horse is a devil on four strong legs. He hauls as much stone in an hour as any ordinary horse could haul in a month."

"Then surely he will tire," said Hoder.

But it was not so. Each day the horse went to and fro between the quarry and the growing wall, and with every journey he brought enough stone to occupy a hundred stonecutters for a day. In the quarry the man, his master, hacked and hewed at the rock so that the great white horse never had to wait for his load. And every night he dressed and squared the stones and laid them side by side

and one above the other, so that each day began clear, with no work left lying from the day before. And the wall lengthened and grew. And the winter passed through its darkest time when the sun stayed low above the rim of the earth, rising late and setting early. And the wall grew higher, first to the height of a man's knee and then breast-high. And the winter days lengthened.

"Summer is in the air already," said Hoder the blind. "I can feel its breath on my face. A man might wade through the streams now without losing his legs to the frostbite. How goes the wall?"

"Too well," said Bragi. "We must say goodbye to Freya before long. And when the light of the sun has gone from us, and the light of the moon, we shall all be as blind as you, Hoder."

"Then we had best hold council together," said Hoder. "Perhaps Loki will know what must be done."

"We have trusted Loki too far already," cried Heimdall in the council-hall. "Who wanted the wall? Loki wanted it. Who thought to have it built without cost? Loki thought. Perhaps this master stonecutter is his kinsman."

"Yet it was you, Heimdall, who brought him into Asgard," Forseti reminded him.

"I do not need you to tell me that, Forseti Oath-keeper," said Heimdall. "Loki is no friend to me but I will not lay the finding of the mason at his door. That is my sorrow. But the blame for all else is his. And he must set it straight—if he can."

Loki stood alone in the doorway. He was as proud as fire and as dark as death.

"By my father, Thunder-Smiter," he said, "I think you are a parcel of sheep who rule in Asgard and call yourselves gods. You knew as well as I that what this mason undertook was impossible. You did not argue then that no good would come of it. Am I to blame because I did not guess the man had magic powers? Neither did you guess. Yet now it is Loki's fault and Loki must set it right."

"I had no knowledge of it," said Thor. "I was not here . . ."

"Would you have been wiser?" Loki snapped at him. "Would you have raised your voice against mine, and against Odin's voice, and against Bragi's? No, Thor, you would have bleated with the rest, 'Clever Loki!'"

"Must I stand by the agreement?" asked Odin. "Must we lose bright Freya and the light of the heavens too because I made a bad bargain in a hasty moment?"

"You must stand by it," Forseti said, "for a breaker of oaths wears a wolf's head for ever."

"You hear him, Loki. There is nothing we can do."

"There is always something," said Loki. "We can prevent him from finishing the wall."

"Is that so easy?"

"It is not too hard, perhaps. But no! I have brought you trouble enough already with my schemes. Better not listen to Loki, he will only cheat you."

"I have not said so, brother," said Odin. "And it is true you have more cunning than all of us together. Use it well, Loki, and use it quickly for it wants but three days till midsummer morning."

"You trust me?"

"We trust you."

"Do *you* trust me, Heimdall?"

"Aye," said Heimdall, grudgingly. "But not too far."

Loki laughed at that and made a kissing face at him which made Heimdall bare his teeth in a snarl.

"Fail and I will cleave your head with my axe," he said, "though I should have to grope five days in the dark to find you."

The wall was high now—a fine, great, curving wall with watchtowers and gate-houses—and it was nearly done. The gods could not keep away from it. It drew them as the North Star draws the lodestone. Each night they walked its length and felt their hearts grow heavier with each step.

Below them on the plain of Midgard they saw the builder's moving light as he led his stallion, Svadilfari, in from his day's last journey. The horse shone through the evening like a white mist. All day he had toiled between the quarry and the wall yet there was nothing weary or plodding in his gait, he was still as fresh as he had been at sunrise.

"I would I had bargained for his beast and not his wall," said Odin.

"If we but knew what Loki has in mind—" said Tyr. "Though I doubt neither his intent nor his courage I would be happier if he were less close."

"Close?" raged Heimdall. "By death! he is far enough away by now. Who has seen him since he left the council hall?"

The moon rose. The man and the horse came nearer, almost to the shadow of the wall. In the white light Svadilfari's eyes were like stars, his hooves were like silver. The man looked up to the watching gods and smiled. There was no warmth in his smile, it crept along his mouth as ice creeps down a crevice in a mountain.

"But look!" cried Bragi, and pointed. From a little wood nearby stepped a mare, white as sea-foam and gay as a blown leaf. Her neat hooves clattered on the stones as she frisked and pranced in the moonlight. She tossed her mane and neighed to Svadilfari, a high, imperious call. Svadilfari reared and neighed in answer, reared higher and higher, beating the air with his hooves. His eyes rolled and his nostrils smoked. Again and again he reared and plunged, and all the time the small white mare danced in front of him, flirting her head and calling. Svadilfari, maddened, lunged forward and broke the traces that held him; he overset his load of stones and dashed away in pursuit, the broken harness strap trailing behind him.

"My money's on the stallion," said Odin.

"And mine's on the mare," said Bragi. "Not even the wind could catch her!"

She was as fast as fire, her mane and tail streamed behind her in the wind of her flight. And the great stallion pounded after her. And after him ran the master-mason, wasting his breath in curses. Then clouds hid the moon and all three were lost in the darkness.

The sun rose on the last day of winter and neither the white mare nor the white stallion returned. The stones lay scattered at the foot of the unfinished wall and the mason was nowhere to be seen.

"It was foolish of him to follow the horse," said Thor. "See, he has neglected a night's building."

"But without the horse he could get no stone to complete the work," said Odin. "Either way he has lost his prize."

All day they watched the plain and saw nothing and that night, the last before the first day of summer, the mason came limping across Bifrost Bridge. Alone.

"If you've come for payment, you're out of luck," said Odin. "It's a good enough wall, as far as it goes, but incomplete."

"Because I was cheated," said the mason, grimly.

"Come, those are hard words," said Odin. "A bargain was struck and *you* would have held me to it, had matters gone the other way."

"I'll not deny it," said the man. "And I worked right well and willingly. It's a sorry thing that the gods should cheat a man of his just reward."

"If you speak of cheating," said Heimdall, "what of your magic horse?"

"Aye," said Tyr, reaching for his knife. "There was a crooked clause in your bargaining."

"It was agreed," said the man and he put his hand on his own knife.

"It was agreed," Forseti said. "Let none of us here—nor you neither—speak of cheating."

"And as for you, Forseti," stormed the mason. "Who made you judge in this matter? Forseti Oath-keeper, they call you? Oath-breaker, I say, like all the rest—"

Rage choked him. Anger swelled his throat, his hands, his frame. He grew in stature and in ugliness and evil, showing himself at last in his own true shape—that of a frost giant from icy Jotunheim, an enemy.

The gods fell silent. Even Heimdall's ruddy colour left his face. "Now make a song of this, Bragi, if you can," he said. Bragi moistened his dry lips with his tongue, but a song needs more than a voice to sing it and this seemed no time for juggling with words.

"What is amiss?" begged Hoder. "I smell evil here and feel a cold that belongs to a different season."

"Hush," said Bragi. "There will be warm work soon."

"We clasped hands on a bargain," said Odin to the giant. "Let us keep to that. 'The wall must be finished in a year,' said I. 'So be it,' said you, 'if I may have my horse to carry for me.' That I granted without argument, and before witnesses, though it was obvious before long that I would be the loser. It was *your* horse that failed you—and the bargain stands. Surely there is honour, of a sort, even in Jotunheim?"

"Dare Odin speak of honour?" sneered the giant. "That is a point we might argue until Doomsday. But you have gained a fine wall, Odin All-Wise, a wall to keep the giants out—" He laughed so hugely that even the air trembled. "To keep the giants out! Yet here am I—a giant—in Asgard! Heimdall the Guardian brought me in and before long I shall be welcoming my kindred to the hall where Odin himself bade me welcome. It is a good jest."

"We are many against your one," Forseti reminded him.

"There will be blood shed before you take me," said the giant.

But Odin, looking up, had seen the stars pale and a golden glow lighting the rim of the world. And he remembered what power lies in the rays of the midsummer sun, something the giant had forgotten.

"Let us be fair," he said, pleasantly. "We are not wolves to fight in a pack against a single foe, be he man, god, or giant. We will stand against you one after the other and, as each of us falls, so let another take his place."

As he said this he raised his great shield Svalin, holding it against the eastern sky so that the sun might not reveal itself too soon.

"When I cast down my shield, then begin," said Odin.

"Who will try my blade first?" demanded the giant, hefting his axe in his hand and looking fiercely about him. "You, Heimdall, guardian of Bifrost? You, Bragi Word-spinner? Na—you have little to say now, it seems. Or you, Thor? They tell me you are a strong fellow in your way. Will you test your strength against mine?"

And then he faltered for, watching Odin's arm that he might see it drop, he saw the rays of the risen sun bright round the shield's edge, and he thought too late of what he should have remembered earlier—that the midsummer sun is death to a frost giant. Its touch turns him to stone.

He sprang away, thinking to vault the wall and find safety in the shadow beneath but, even as he sprang, Odin lowered his shield to let the sun be seen blazing in the sky. In his very leap the giant was defeated. The halls and palaces of Asgard patterned a chequerboard of shadow on the paving—a step to right or left would have kept him safe for at least a little while. He might have dodged and parried the shifting sun till the end of its day's journey and been safe for ever. But he leapt too soon, as he had triumphed too soon and, between the wide plain of Midgard and the high arch of the sky, there were no shadows at all to protect him. It was a stone giant that was dashed to pieces against the scattered stones below.

Thus the wall of Asgard was built at no cost to the gods. The sun drove her chariot across the sky by day, and the moon drove his at night. Freya was spared. But where was Loki?

"Hiding from our mockery," said Heimdall. "For where was Loki when we needed him? It was chance, not Loki's doing, that called the stallion from his duty."

It was some months before Loki returned to Asgard and he brought with him a fine grey foal, a gift for Odin.

"His name is Sleipnir," said Loki. "And see, he has eight legs. He will be the swiftest horse in the world."

Odin looked and wondered. "How came you by this foal, brother Loki?" he asked.

Loki Shapeshifter tossed his head and made a little whickering noise that reminded Odin of something he had heard before. He looked into Loki's quicksilver eyes and saw in the depths of one a fleeing mare, and in the other, the white stallion, Svadilfari.

"Bragi put his money on the mare," said Odin.

"Then he lost it," said Loki. "But the foal is better than its sire."

Loki Makes Mischief

Loki deserted Sigyn, his wife in Asgard, and married the giantess Angurboda with whom he had three ghastly offspring. Odin condemned the first, Hel, to become Queen of the Dead and threw into the sea the second, the serpent Jormungand, where it grew and grew until it encircled Midgard and bit on its own tail. Loki's third child, the terrible Fenris Wolf, defied the gods until the dwarfs gave them a magic chain, Gleipnir, fashioned from six things—the sound of a cat's footfall, the beard of a woman, the roots of a rock, the sinews of a bear, the breath of a fish and the spittle of a bird. Thor and the other gods were then able to bind the Fenris Wolf (at the expense of Tyr's hand). Loki was so angry that he immediately sought vengeance.

In the morning when Thor strode home to his great palace of Bilskirnir, the Storm-Serene, his beautiful wife Sif met him in tears, with a cloak muffled tightly round her face.

"What has chanced?" cried Thor, his eyes flashing.

Weeping and with eyes downcast in shame, Sif slowly drew back the cloak and let it fall.

Then Thor cried out in grief and rage, for all her lovely golden hair had gone, and her head was as bald as the stubbly cornfield after the harvest has been gathered in.

"A thief came in the night while I slept," she sobbed. "When I woke this morning all had gone—all, all."

Then Thor strode through Asgard, his eyes flashing like lightning, his red beard bristling with rage, roaring with fury until the thunder rolled upon the hills of Midgard and distant Jotunheim.

48

"Loki, son of Laufey!" bellowed Thor. "Where is that spawn of the giants? He alone could have done this thing. Show me Loki the mischief-maker so that I may break every bone in his body!"

Loki had stayed in Asgard, thinking that no one would suspect him, and knowing that the Æsir would not allow any harm to befall him there. But when Thor grabbed hold of him, roaring that he would carry him to Jotunheim and there break him into little pieces, he grew frightened.

"Let me go," he begged. "I will make you any recompense you like. I was angry and did not think what I was doing."

But Thor only shook him until his teeth rattled, and went striding across Asgard shouting:

"Unless you can put back the hair which you have cut off, so that it grows again upon Sif's head, I'll break your bones and crush you under a mountain, so that you can work no more mischief!"

"I will! I will!" cried Loki. "Put me down, and listen to me."

Thor set him on his feet doubtfully, but did not let go his hold.

"Well," he growled, "how will you replace the hair you have dared to cut from Sif's head?"

"The three dwarfs who made the chain Gleipnir!" cried Loki eagerly. "Those three sons of Ivaldi who live in Svartalfheim can make new hair if anyone can! Let me go to them, and I will also pay a fine for all the trouble I've caused. If you break my bones, Sif will never get her hair again; but if you let me go now to Svartalfheim there is every chance that she may. You will lose nothing by letting me try—but may lose everything if you don't."

Slow-witted Thor took a little while to see this. But when he did he flung Loki from him, shouting:

"Go to Svartalfheim then, and do your best with the sons of Ivaldi. But don't think to escape me if you fail. Wherever you are, I'll find you!"

Loki picked himself up, muttering curses on Thor under his breath, and set out from Asgard towards the land of the dark elves.

Over the Bridge Bifrost he went, and through Midgard to the high, lonely mountains, in the gloomy caverns beneath which dwelt the dwarfs and their cousins the dark elves.

Down into the caves went Loki, by winding passage and steep

stair, until he heard in front of him the clink of hammers on anvils, and saw the red glow of the forges.

At last he came out into the cavernous underworld where the dwarfs were at work, digging the gold, the iron, and the jewels from the rocks and working them into beautiful swords and cups and necklaces, armour, and other treasures.

Loki found the sons of Ivaldi, and when he had told them what he wanted, the master-craftsman, Dvalin, exclaimed:

"This will bring us great honour and glory among the Æsir! Let us set to work at once, my brothers, and show them how great is our skill."

So they put gold into the fire, and began to work, while the bellows roared and the sparks flew up the chimney like the molten breath of a volcano.

And first clever Dvalin made the spear Gungnir as a gift for Odin. This is the best of all spears and never fails to hit its mark.

Next they made the ship Skidbladnir as a gift for Frey, lord of the winds. This is the best of all ships, for it can sail over land as well as sea, and through the air also, no matter which way the wind is blowing. It can carry all the Æsir, with their steeds, at one time! and yet fold up small enough to be carried in one hand or in a warrior's belt.

Last of all Dvalin spun golden thread finer than ever was drawn from a mortal spinning-wheel, and made from it new hair for Sif.

"If this is placed on her head," he told Loki, "it will grow there at once just as her own hair did. And I have put into it a charm so that it may never again be stolen by force or cunning."

Loki was delighted, and certain that he was safe now from Thor's vengeance and the anger of the Æsir.

"You are the greatest of all smiths," he cried to Dvalin. "Not in Midgard nor in Asgard, nor even here and among the Black Dwarfs, is there any other who could fashion such cunning, such wondrous gifts for the Æsir."

Now it chanced that another dwarf named Brok heard Loki's words, and he sprang up in a great rage.

"That is not true!" he shrieked. "My brother Sindri is a far better smith than Dvalin. I'll wager my head on it!"

"I'll take your wager!" cried Loki indignantly. "My head against yours that Sindri cannot make three gifts for the Æsir rarer and more wonderful than Dvalin's."

"Good," answered Brok, grinning evilly. "I shall be cutting off your head before night. . . . I must ask Sindri to make me a special weapon for that purpose!"

Then Brok led the way to Sindri's smithy, and the dwarf smith grinned and nodded when he heard of the bet.

"Yes, yes!" he cried. "I'll do better than Dvalin, son of Ivaldi, ever did. Gungnir, Skidbladnir, and hair for Sif! Bah, wait till you've seen my gifts for the Æsir!"

Then Sindri mingled his metals and poured in his charms. When this was done he set a pig-skin bellows on the hearth, and told Brok to blow until he came back.

"Blow hard," he instructed his brother, "and do not cease for a moment—no, not even to mop your brow—not even to draw breath: for if you pause for anything whatsoever, that which lies in the fire will be spoilt."

Then he went into another cave, while Brok blew at the bellows. But Loki, with a sly look in his eyes, stole quietly out of the smithy in the opposite direction.

Presently, as Brok worked at the bellows, a gadfly came and stung him on the hand until the blood came, but Brok never even paused to dash it away.

Sindri came back a few minutes later and drew from the fire a boar with golden bristles and mane of gleaming gold.

"Good," said he. "Gullinbusti is complete. Now blow at the bellows again, and do not stop for a moment, or my next work will be spoilt."

With that he laid more gold in the hearth, and went out of the smithy again. Presently as Brok toiled at the bellows the gadfly came again and stung him on the neck until the blood came. But Brok never even paused to dash it away.

Sindri came back a few minutes later and drew from the fire a glimmering ring of gold.

"Good," said he, "Draupnir is complete. Now work at the bellows again, and do not stop for a moment, or my last and greatest work will be spoilt."

51

With that he laid a great mass of iron in the hearth, and went out of the smithy again.

Presently as Brok worked at the bellows the gadfly came once more and stung him on the eyelid until the blood came. Then Brok grabbed at the gadfly as swiftly as he could and swept it from him and dashed the blood out of his eye. But the bellows grew flat for a moment as he did so, although a moment later he was working away at them as hard as ever.

Sindri came back and drew from the fire a great iron hammer.

"Alas," said he, "Mjollnir came near to being spoilt. See, it is a little too short in the handle. Yet even so I am certain that you will win your wager, brother Brok. So take our three gifts, and hasten to Asgard to lay them before the Æsir for their judgement."

Loki had come back to the smithy in his own form by this time, and he looked scornfully at Brok's gifts, though already he was beginning to feel anxious about which the Æsir would consider the best.

However, he set out for Asgard with Dvalin and Brok, and when they arrived the Æsir assembled and Loki explained the presence of the two dwarfs by telling of the wager.

Then Odin, Thor, and Frey sat down in the seats of judgement, and Loki advanced with Dvalin behind him.

First Thor took the hair and set it upon Sif's head. And immediately it grew there as if it had never been lost, and she tossed back her head and smiled once more like the bright earth when summer returns after the bareness and cold of winter.

Then Loki handed the spear Gungnir to Odin, explaining how it could never miss its aim, nor be stopped in its thrust, whatever came in its way. And finally he gave the ship Skidbladnir to Frey telling him how it would speed over land or sea with a favourable breeze as soon as the sail was raised, yet could be folded like a napkin and thrust into his belt.

The three Æsir admired their gifts, and Odin said:

"Dwarf Brok, it will indeed be hard for you to surpass these three, for never before did I behold such workmanship."

Brok, however, stepped forward with a confident bow; and first of all he gave to Odin the ring Draupnir.

"There, my lord, is the gift of greatest wealth," he said. "Keep that ring well, and on every ninth night shall fall from it eight rings of equal value."

Then he gave to Frey the boar Gullinbusti, saying:

"There, my lord, is the gift of greatest speed. Keep this boar well, for he can run through air or water better than any horse. Moreover, such a glow of light comes from his mane and bristles that you can never be lost in the dark, even though you pass through deepest Niflheim itself."

Last of all he gave to Thor the hammer Mjollnir, and said:

"There, my lord, is the gift of greatest strength. Keep this hammer well, for it shall never fail you. You may smite with it as hard as you will and break whatever you hit. And if you throw it at anything, it will hit that at which you fling it, and return to your hand however far it goes. Yet it is so small that you may carry it in your belt. But I must tell you that there is one flaw in its making: the handle is a trifle short."

After this the three Æsir discussed the gifts among themselves, and then Odin gave judgement:

"We feel," he said, "that the hammer Mjollnir is the most precious of all these works, since in it is the greatest defence we have against the giants our deadly enemies. Therefore we give this sentence: the Dwarf Brok has won his wager, and Loki must lose his head."

"If you want my head, you must take it!" cried Loki with desperate bravado, and in an instant he was far away, leaping through the air on his shoes of swiftness.

"I'll bring him for you!" shouted Thor, and in a moment he had leapt into his chariot drawn by the two goats Gaptooth and Cracktooth and was whirling away across Midgard in a huge black thundercloud.

Before long he was back again and flung Loki out of the chariot on to the stone floor of Valhalla.

"There!" he cried, as the thunder rolled away in the distance. "Now, Dwarf Brok, you may exact the penalty."

Brok at once produced a sharp axe and advanced gleefully upon his victim.

53

"One moment!" exclaimed Loki, and the dwarf paused. "I readily admit that you have won the wager, and my head is forfeit. But will you not allow me to buy it back from you—which I would far rather do before you cut it off than afterwards, when it would be of little value to me?"

"No," cried Brok. "You have nothing to offer which I value. We have far greater treasures of rings and gold and weapons in Svartalfheim than all you Æsir have, with the wealth of Midgard and Jotunheim added. And that is all we dwarfs care about—except revenge. . . . That gadfly which stung me as I blew the bellows was remarkably like you, crafty Loki. But this time your cunning shall avail you nothing."

"Yes, I confess myself beaten," sighed Loki. "So if you will not spare me my head, you must come and cut it off. Here I stand waiting for you to strike. . . But of course you will remember that it was only my head that I wagered: that belongs to you, certainly—but my neck is still my own. So be very careful when you cut off my head that you do not touch my neck, for every scrap of it is mine, and I forbid you to touch it. . . . And of course when I wagered my head, I meant the whole of it, so you must take it all in one piece and leave none behind."

There were a few moments of silence; and then a great gust of laughter swept through Valhalla, while Brok stood swinging his axe and looking extremely foolish.

"I will not cut off your head," he said at length. "But just to warn you against boasting in future, I'll sew your lips together. . . . You talk far too much, as I am sure these noble Æsir will agree, and a little silence will do you no harm."

Loki agreed thankfully to this, for it was a small matter compared with the loss of his head.

"If your skill as a tailor is as great as your skill as a smith," he said, "you'll sew a seam that I shall be proud to wear across my face."

So Brok set to work, but found that his sword was too blunt and clumsy to pierce the flesh of one of the Æsir.

"I wish I had my brother Sindri's awl here!" he cried.

Even as he said the words, Sindri's awl appeared suddenly,

piercing Loki's lips, and Brok made the holes without any difficulty and laced them together with a thong.

Then all the Æsir laughed at Loki standing dumbly there without one of his usual jests to throw at them.

"Take a horn of mead with us, Loki!" they cried. "Sing to us, Loki—sing a rousing catch of love or battle! Tell us some tale of your triumphs over your enemies!"

Loki endured all this mockery with downcast eyes; and when the Æsir were tired of their sport, and the two dwarfs had departed from Asgard, he went quietly to his own palace and tore away the thong.

But ever afterwards his lips were scarred and uneven, and his smile was wicked where it had been only cunning before.

The Apples of Iduna

Odin often travelled forth from Asgard to take part in the affairs of men and to see what was going on in all the wide expanses of the world. One day he set out on such a journey, taking Loki and Hoenir with him. They wandered a long way over mountains and waste land and at length they grew hungry. But food was hard to find in that lonely country.

They had walked many miles when they saw a herd of oxen grazing in a valley.

"There is food for us at last," said Hoenir.

They went down into the valley and it was not long before they had one of the oxen roasting on a fire. While their meal cooked they stretched out on the ground to rest. When they thought the meat had cooked long enough they took it off the fire. But it was not yet ready. So they put it back over the embers and waited.

"I can wait no longer," cried Loki at last. "I am starving. Surely the meat is ready."

The gods scattered the fire once more and pulled forth the ox, but it seemed as though it had not even begun to cook. It was certainly not fit for eating.

This was a strange thing and not even Odin knew the meaning of it. As they wondered among themselves, they heard a voice speak from the great oak tree above them.

"It is because of me," said the voice, "that there is no virtue in your fire and your meat will not cook."

They looked up into the branches of the tree and there sat a huge eagle.

"If you are willing to give me a share of the ox, then it will cook in the fire," said the eagle.

There was little the gods could do but agree to this. The eagle let himself float down from the tree and alighted by the fire. In no time at all the ox was roasted. At once the eagle took to himself the two hindquarters and the two forequarters as well.

This greediness angered Loki. He snatched up a great pole, brandished it with all his strength, and struck the eagle with it. The eagle plunged violently at the blow and whirled into the air. One end of the pole stuck fast to the eagle's back and Loki's hands stuck fast to the other end. No matter how he tried he could not free them. Swooping and turning, the eagle dragged Loki after him in his flight, flying just low enough that Loki's feet and legs knocked against stones and rock heaps and trees. Loki thought his arms would be torn from his shoulders. He cried out for mercy.

"Put me down! Put me down!" begged Loki. "Free me and you shall have the whole ox for your own."

"I do not want the ox," cried the eagle. "I want only one thing—Iduna and her apples. Deliver them into my power and I will set you free."

Iduna was the beautiful and beloved wife of the god Bragi. She guarded the most precious possession of the gods, the apples of youth. Unless they might eat of them the gods would grow old and feeble like mortal men. They kept the gods ever young. Iduna and her apples were priceless beyond words.

"Iduna and her apples! Such a thing cannot be done," shouted Loki.

"Then I will fly all day," screamed the eagle. "I will knock you against the rocks until you die." And he dragged Loki through rough tree branches and against the sides of mountains and over the rocky earth. Loki could endure it no longer.

"I will do as you ask," he cried. "I will bring Iduna to you, and her apples as well."

"Give me your oath," said the eagle. Loki gave his oath. A time was set when Loki should put Iduna in the eagle's power.

The eagle straightway made Loki free and flew off into the sky. A much-bruised Loki returned to his companions and all three set off on their homeward journey. But Odin and Hoenir did not know the promise which Loki had made.

Loki pondered how he could keep his word to the eagle, whom he now knew to be the giant Thiazi in disguise. When the appointed day came Loki approached Iduna.

"Iduna," he said, speaking gently, "yesterday I found a tree on which grow wondrous apples. It is in the wood to the north of Asgard. They are like your apples in colour and shape. Surely they must have the same properties. Should we not gather them and bring them to Asgard?"

"There are no apples anywhere," said Iduna, "like to my apples."

"These are," said Loki. "They are very like. Come and look for yourself. If you bring your apples we can put them side by side and you will see."

So Iduna went with Loki to the wood, taking her apples with her. While they were in the wood the giant Thiazi swooped down in his eagle's plumage and carried Iduna and her apples off to his abode.

The gods soon missed Iduna. And they knew her apples were gone, for the signs of old age began to show among them. They grew bent and stiff and stooped.

Odin called a hasty council of the gods. They asked each other what they knew of Iduna.

"Where was she last seen?" asked Odin.

Heimdall had seen her walking out of Asgard with Loki. That was the last that was known of her.

Odin sent Thor to seize Loki and to bring him to the council. When Loki was brought the gods threatened him with tortures and death unless he told what he knew of Iduna. Loki grew frightened and admitted that Iduna had been carried off to Jotunheim.

"I will go in search of her," he cried, "if Freya will lend me her falcon wings."

Freya was more than willing. When Loki had put on the feather dress he flew to the north in the direction of Jotunheim.

He flew for a long time before he came to the home of Thiazi, the giant. Then he circled slowly overhead and saw Iduna walking below. She carried in her arms her golden casket of apples. Thiazi was nowhere to be seen, for he had rowed out to sea to fish. Loki quickly alighted on the ground beside Iduna.

"Hasten, Iduna," he cried, "I will rescue you." And he changed

Iduna into the shape of a nut and flew off with her in his claws.

Loki had no sooner gone than Thiazi arrived home. At once he missed Iduna and her precious apples. Putting on his eagle's plumage, he flew into the air. Far off in the distance he saw the falcon flying. Instantly he took after him. The eagle's wings beat powerfully, making a deep rushing sound like a great wind. Thiazi drew nearer and nearer to Loki. Loki flew with all his might, but the eagle was bearing down upon the falcon just as the towers of Asgard came into view. With a last burst of strength Loki hastened toward the shining battlements.

The gods were on watch for Loki's return. They saw the falcon bearing the nut between his claws, with the eagle in close pursuit. Quickly they built a great pile of wood shavings just outside the wall of Asgard. As Loki came near he swooped down low over the shavings. Thiazi swooped down too, hoping to seize the falcon before he reached the safety of Asgard. Just as the eagle came close to the pile the gods set fire to the shavings. Instantly the fire blazed up, but Thiazi could not stop himself. He plunged into the flames and the feathers of his wings took fire. Then he could fly no more and the gods slew him where he was.

There was great rejoicing within the walls of Asgard to have Iduna safe once more. And the gods grew young and bright again.

The Lay of Thrym

The Hurler woke, went wild with rage,
For, suddenly, he missed his sacred Hammer:
He tore his beard, tossed his red locks,
Groped about but could grasp nothing.
Thus, then did Thor speak:
"Loki, Loki, listen well.
Unmarked by men, unmarked by gods,
Someone has stolen my sacred Hammer."

Fast they went to Freya's quarters.
Then said Loki, Laufey's Son:
"Freya, will you lend me your feathered cloak
To fly in search of the sacred Hammer?"

"I would give it you gladly, were it gold not feathers,
Part with it now, were it pure silver."

Then Loki flew—the feathers whistled—
Out of the door of the Hall of Gods
On and on to the Hall of Giants.
There, on a howe, Thrym sat,
Braiding gold collars for his kennel of hounds,
Unteasing the manes of the mares he loved:
'How fare the gods? How fare the elves?
What brings you on this journey to Gianthome?"

"Ill fare the gods, ill fare the elves.
Have you taken and hidden the Hammer of Thunder?"
"I have taken and hidden the Hammer of Thunder

Eight miles deep, way under the ground:
Henceforth no god shall get it back
Till you fetch me Freya for my future bride."

Then Loki flew—the feathers whistled—
Out of the door of the Hall of Giants
On and on to the Hall of Gods.
Meeting him there in the middle court,
Thus then did Thor speak:
"Do you come with a message, not mischief only?
Stand where you are. Let me hear your tidings.
He who sits is seldom truthful,
Who stretches at length a liar always."

"I come with a message, not mischief only.
Thrym stole your Hammer to hide it away.
Henceforth no god shall get it back
Till we fetch him Freya for his future bride."

Fast they went to Freya's quarters.
Then said Loki, Laufey's Son:
"Busk yourself, Freya, in a bridal veil.
You must journey with me to Gianthome."

Freya snorted with fierce rage,
The hall shook and shuddered about them,
Broken to bits was the Brising Necklace:
"In the eyes of the gods a whore I should seem,
If I journeyed with you to Gianthome."

The gods hastened to their Hall of Judgment,
Gathered together, goddesses with them,
Sat in council to consider how
To recover the holy Hammer of Thunder.

Heimdal said, sagest of gods,
Who could see the future as his fathers did:
"We must busk Thor in a bridal veil,
Hang about him the Brising Necklace,
Bind to his waist a bunch of keys,

Hide his legs in a long dress,
Broad brooches to his breast pin,
With a neat cap cover his locks."

Thus, then, did Thor speak:
"With coarse laughs you will call me a She
If I busk myself in a bridal veil."

Loki replied, Laufey's Son:
"Be silent, Thunderer, say no more.
Without the Hammer Asgard is lost.
The giants will dwell here, soon drive us out."

They busked Thor then in a bridal veil,
Hung about him the Brising Necklace,
Bound to his waist a bunch of keys,
Hid his legs in a long dress,
Broad brooches to his breast pinned,
With a neat cap covered his locks.

Then said Loki, Laufey's Son:
"I also shall come as your handmaid with you,
We will journey together to Gianthome."

Quickly the goats were gathered from pasture,
Hurried into harness: eagerly they ran.
Fire scorched the earth, the fells cracked,
As Thunderer journeyed to Gianthome.

Thus, then did Thrym speak:
"Stand up giants, lay straw on the benches.
They may well bring me my bride now,
Njord's Daughter, from Noatun.
In my fields there graze gold-horned cattle,
All-black oxen, for my eye's delight.
Much is my treasure, many my gems;
Nothing I lack save lovely Freya."

Evening came: ale and food
Were brought to the benches. The bride quickly
Ate a whole ox and eight salmon,
The sweet dainties reserved for the women,

And more than three measures of mead drank.
Thus, then did Thrym speak:
"Was ever bride with appetite so keen,
Ever a bride who took such big mouthfuls,
When was more mead drunk by one maid alone?"

Loki, the handmaid, leaning forward,
Found the words to befuddle the giant:
"She has not eaten for eight long nights,
So wild her longing for the wedding day."

Thrym lifted her veil, leaned to kiss her,
Back he leaped, the full length of the hall:
"How fierce the look in Freya's eyes!
Dangerous the fire that darts out of them."

Loki, the handmaid, leaning forward,
Found the words to befuddle the giant:
"She has had no sleep for eight long nights,
So wild her longing for the wedding day."

The luckless sister of the luckless giant
Dared to beg for bridal gifts:
"Give me your rings of red gold,
The rings from your fingers, my favour to win,
My good will, my grace and blessing."

Thus, then, did Thrym speak:
"To bless the bride now bring the Hammer,
Lay Mjollnir upon the maiden's lap
And wish us joy with joined hands."

Then in his heart Thunderer laughed,
The savage one, when he saw his Hammer.
First Thrym he felled to the ground,
Then all his kin he killed in turn,
Laid low his luckless sister
Who had dared to beg for bridal gifts:
Instead of gold she got a blow,
Instead of rings a rap on the skull.
Thus Thor came to recover his Hammer.

Dietrich of Bern

In the early days, south of Germany, a king named Dietmar ruled over the Amelungs in the little kingdom of Bern. His elder brother, Ermenrich, was lord of a mighty empire, but Dietmar was content enough with the love and the loyalty of his Amelungs and he acknowledged no man as his master.

His great pride was his son Dietrich, a bold and handsome child, who soon grew tall and strong beyond his years. When he was five years old, his father gave him into the keeping of Hildebrand, the greatest warrior in those parts, that he might train the boy in battle-craft and feats of arms. And so skilled was his teaching and so eager was the boy to learn, that by the time he was twelve, Dietrich was as strong and able as any warrior of twice his years. From the first day that he saw him, Dietrich loved and honoured Hildebrand, and they were firm friends for all their lives.

When Dietrich had grown to be a youth, there came to the king's house one day word of two giants, Grim and his sister, Hilde, who were ravaging the land and killing all who tried to withstand them; King Dietmar immediately set out with his warriors to slay them. but though he searched his kingdom from end to end, the giants had learnt of his coming and had hidden themselves too well, high up in the mountains, and he could not find them. Dietmar returned home, discouraged and angry, and, immediately, the giants came out of hiding and began to plunder farms and villages once more.

Dietrich said to Hildebrand, "Let us go alone, just you and I, and search out these monsters in their lair. Who knows, we might have the luck that was denied my father."

So Hildebrand and young Dietrich set off; but for a long time their search seemed hopeless. And then one day, in the mountains, Dietrich chanced to catch one of the dwarf folk who lived beneath the earth.

"Keep a fast hold of him," said Hildebrand. "He may well be a friend of the giants, and can tell us where they are."

But the dwarf swore that he was no friend to the giants, who had done him and his kind much wrong. "I am Elbegast, the lord of the mountain dwarfs," he said. "If you are foes of Grim and Hilde, then you are friends of mine." And he promised to lead them to where the giants might be found. "But," he said, "you will never slay them without the help of a weapon forged by the dwarfs. For the dwarfs are the finest swordsmiths of all."

So he gave to Dietrich the sword Nagelring, which had no equal in the world. Then, early one morning, he took Dietrich and Hildebrand by a hidden path to where they could see the giants' footprints, huge tracks upon the dewy grass, leading to the hollow mountain where they lived. "Good luck be with you both," said Elbegast. "And may Nagelring prove trusty."

Dietrich and Hildebrand followed the footprints to the great cave where the giants were hidden; but, as they reached the mouth of the cave, Grim heard them and rushed forth like a mountain tempest, brandishing above his hideous head a burning log snatched up from his fire. With this huge cudgel he struck at Dietrich again and again; and had Dietrich not been quick and light upon his feet, he would have been dead in a very little time. But not a chance did Dietrich have to strike a single blow with Nagelring in return, for he needed all his strength and wits to avoid the giant's blows and the sparks which flew from the smouldering log.

Hildebrand would have gone to his aid, had not Hilde, hearing the sounds of the combat, come from an inner cave, and before he could strike at her with his sword, she had caught him up in her two arms and crushed him to her as though she would break all his bones.

Hildebrand struggled in vain in her grip. Closer and closer she clasped him until he thought that death was surely near, and with

his little remaining breath he gasped out, "Dietrich, help me, or I am dead."

Dietrich heard, gave a swift glance round and saw how it was with his friend and, made desperately bold by his fears for Hildebrand, he leapt right over the flaming club as it was swung at him again and brought Nagelring down with all his strength upon the giant's head, splitting his thick skull. Then he turned to Hilde, and before she could fling down Hildebrand to defend herself, he had slain her too.

When he was a little recovered and could speak once more, Hildebrand smiled and said, "I taught you all I know of skill at arms, yet it seems you have surpassed me and could now teach me much."

All the people of Bern rejoiced when they heard that the giants were slain and would trouble them no longer, and King Dietmar was more than ever proud of his son, who had acquitted himself so well on his first adventure.

But soon after, to the great sorrow of the Amelungs, King Dietmar died, and so young Dietrich became king in Bern.

A few years passed and then one day Dietrich learnt of a third giant, Sigenot, more terrible by far than the others, who had entered Bern and was slaying cattle and people alike in vengeance for the death of his kinsfolk Grim and Hilde.

Dietrich called for Nagelring to be brought to him. "I will go to the mountains and slay this Sigenot," he said.

Everyone who heard him, save Hildebrand, cried out, "You must not go. He is too terrible. Not even an army could withstand him."

But Hildebrand said, "You shall not go alone, for I will go with you, my king."

"No," said Dietrich, "for he is only one. One warrior against another, that is the law of fair combat. Two against one is the coward's way. You taught me that yourself."

"Then go alone," said Hildebrand, "and may good fortune go with you. If you have not returned when eight days are passed, I will go after you to free you if you are a prisoner, or to avenge you if you are dead, or to die myself at the giant's hands." They embraced, and Dietrich went.

He tracked Sigenot to a cave in the mountains, and there he came face to face with him; and Sigenot was even taller and broader than Grim had been. With a roar he took up his great club and strode to where Dietrich stood. "You are Dietrich, for no one else would be bold enough to come to me alone," he said. "Now shall my kinsfolk be avenged." And he swung his club above his head.

As he had done with Grim's flaming brand, Dietrich darted here and there to avoid the mighty blows of the club; at the same time giving stroke after stroke with Nagelring, until it seemed as though he might, in spite of the giant's huge bulk, be the victor in their combat. But then, dodging quickly to one side, he came beneath a tree, and as he raised Nagelring high above his head with both his hands to strike at Sigenot once more, the blade caught in the overhanging branches and, before he could free it, Sigenot's club had crashed down upon his helmet and he fell senseless to the ground.

With a great shout of triumph, Sigenot snatched up Dietrich in his arms, flung him over his shoulder, and strode off to his cave; and there, in the darkest corner of the cave, he cast him down into a pit of serpents.

When the eight days were passed and Dietrich had not returned, Hildebrand armed himself, took sword and shield, and rode for the mountains. There he spied the giant's tracks, leading to his cave, and there he found Dietrich's horse wandering alone; and there, too, he saw Nagelring caught fast in the branches of the tree. "So Dietrich is dead," he thought. "Well, I can but avenge him or die too." And he took a firm hold of his sword and went forward to the cave.

Sigenot saw him approaching and came out, swinging his great club. "You are Hildebrand," he shouted. "First I catch the young one and now I catch the old one. Truly, Grim and Hilde will be well avenged." And eagerly he rushed upon Hildebrand.

The combat lasted many hours. In his rage, Sigenot tore up young trees to serve as weapons, and heaved up rocks and stones to hurl at Hildebrand; but with skill Hildebrand evaded all his blows, until he was too spent and the giant's mighty strength proved too much for even his endurance and, like Dietrich, he was felled by Sigenot's club. Sigenot slung him over his shoulder, took his sword as a victor's prize, and strode back to the cave, shouting his triumph till the mountain echoed.

He flung Hildebrand to one side of the cave and the sword to the other and went off to find a chain that he might bind his senseless captive. But the force of the fall brought Hildebrand back to himself and he sat up, dazed and battered, and looked about him. The cave was wide and light enough, though in its farther corners no daylight reached, and Hildebrand saw his sword lying where Sigenot had flung it. He staggered to his feet and took it up and hid himself behind a pillar of rock until the giant should return.

When Sigenot came back, rattling and clanking the chains he had fetched, he gave a roar of anger at seeing Hildebrand gone from where he had left him lying. Then he saw him hidden in the shadow behind the rock and rushed at him, and their combat was begun anew.

But Hildebrand was very weary, and step by step he had to give way to the furious giant, and slowly he was forced deeper and deeper into the cave where the light was bad and he could hardly see to avoid the giant's blows. He felt that his strength was going fast, and he could not fight much longer. "Now Dietrich will never be avenged," he thought, "and in a very little while I, too, shall be dead." And Sigenot, seeing him weaken, laughed till the cave rang. "In a moment now, good Grim and Hilde will be avenged," he cried.

But Dietrich, who had been listening to the shouts of fighting from the cave above him, heard the shout of triumph and called out, "Is it you, Hildebrand, come as you promised? I have been waiting for you."

At the joyful knowledge that Dietrich was not dead, Hildebrand felt himself the equal of ten giants; his strength returned for one last mighty effort and a moment later Sigenot was lying vanquished on the floor of the cave, and Hildebrand struck off his head.

"Where are you, Dietrich?" he called into the shadows.

"I am here, in the pit of serpents at the very end of the cave. I have killed many of them, and eaten some for food; but there are still scores left alive, so help me out with all the speed you can."

With ropes lowered into the pit, Hildebrand drew him out, and as the friends embraced, Dietrich laughed and said, "After all, you are still my master and can teach me much in the matter of fighting skill. For you overcame Sigenot, but I was overcome by him."

For many years after that, Dietrich ruled well and wisely, and he gather about him a little band of skilled warriors from all corners of the world, who had come to him in Bern, drawn by his fame. Yet always his most loved comrade was Hildebrand.

But Dietrich was not destined to rule in peace for all his days. There came a time when his uncle, the Emperor Ermenrich, urged by evil counsellors, cast greedy eyes upon his nephew's little kingdom, and he sent messengers to Dietrich demanding tribute from him and his lords. Now, Dietrich, like his father Dietmar before him, had never paid tribute to any man, and he and his lords were indignant.

"Tell your master," the Amelungs said to the messengers, "that we pay our tribute to our rightful lord, King Dietrich, and to no other."

"And tell my uncle the emperor," said Dietrich, "that if he wants his tribute, he must come and fetch it for himself; and we will pay him with our spearheads and the sharp edges of our swords."

The angry emperor gathered together a great army and marched against Bern. But Dietrich did not wait to be attacked. At the head of his Amelungs he rode out to meet him; and so unprepared for his coming was the emperor that he was taken by surprise; and Dietrich, falling upon his camp before sunrise one morning, won a victory and checked his advance. Though it was no great victory, it cheered the Amelungs and gave them courage for the dark days they knew must lie ahead.

From the emperor's camp Dietrich took much booty, which he sent back to Bern in the charge of Hildebrand and five of his most trusted warriors: old Amelolt, Sigeband, Helmschrott, Lindolt and Dietlieb of Styria; and with them was Hildebrand's young nephew Wolfhart. But on the way to Bern they were ambushed and taken captive, and only Dietlieb escaped to bear the news to Dietrich.

The emperor was planning to attack again; every day more warriors joined him, sure of his eventual victory; and many, even, of Dietrich's own men deserted him, believing that Bern was lost.

But bitterest of all to Dietrich was the knowledge that his trusted friends, and among them Hildebrand, were in the emperor's hands.

Dietrich still had certain of the emperor's lords whom he had taken captive when he had attacked his uncle's camp, and he sent to Ermenrich with an offer to exchange these men for Hildebrand and his five comrades.

But the emperor sent back scornfully, "Do as you will with your captives, I care nothing for them. For my part, I intend to hang your warriors unless I have your word that you will give me Bern, and that you and those who still wish to call you king will go from the land with you, on foot and leaving all they possess."

In his first anger at Ermenrich's reply, Dietrich thought, "I have no hope of victory in battle against his might. Yet he shall at least see how the Amelungs can die. And they would rather die than deign to live dishonoured on her terms." But then he thought how, if he fought and died gloriously with the few men who remained to him, he was condemning to a shameful death, unfitting to any warrior, his good friends: Sigeband, Helmschrott, old Amelolt, Lindolt, rash young Wolfhart, and Hildebrand—above all, Hildebrand. And he knew that he could not do it.

He sent to Ermenrich, agreeing to his demands, and Hildebrand and the others were freed. Together, on foot, leading their horses and taking no possessions with them, Dietrich and Hildebrand and their friends left Bern; and with them went those warriors who chose exile with their king rather than service under the emperor: and out of all the Amelungs, there were only three and forty of them.

They wandered northwards to Bechlaren, beside the Danube, where Rudiger held lands from King Etzel* of the Huns. Rudiger had been a comrade of Dietrich in former days, and he welcomed him kindly and gave him arms and gifts, for he was a good and loyal friend. He gave Dietrich hope, also, for he told him to go to King Etzel and ask his aid. "He is a mighty king and has many warriors to serve him from all the lands of the world. And though he is a heathen, he is no foe to Christian men. He may well give you help

* Etzel is the name given in legend to Attila, King of the Huns, who appears in the next story.

76

in your fight against the emperor. If not today, then at some later time, when he is in a mood to do so."

So Dietrich and his few faithful Amelungs went to Hunland to King Etzel's court, and he received them kindly, for he had heard—as who had not—of the prowess and the sad fate of Dietrich. And in time he gave help to Dietrich, and men to fight for him; and in time, too, Ermenrich died and Dietrich returned to Bern and was welcomed by his people. But of the three and forty Amelungs who had gone into Hunland with him, only one—old Hildebrand— returned home with him, for the others had all by mishap been slain at Etzel's court.

Dietrich became not only king of Bern once more, but his uncle, Ermenrich, having had no other heir, he succeeded to the emperor's lands, and ruled them to the end of his days, honoured by all.

Walter and Hildegund

The dark, trackless forest of Mirkwood spread like a creeping stain on the edges of habitation. It was the boundary between the familiar and the alien: this side the farms and fields of the settled Germanic kingdoms; on the other the endless green plains of Hunmark, land of the nomads.

Great herds of horses had roamed there, the herdsmen following them with their tents in both summer and winter, but now the rolling plains were strangely empty, left to the play of the wind and the crying curlew. And in Hunmark for this state of things there was only one explanation . . .

A rumour came out of Mirkwood that the Huns were mustering for war, and hard on its heels rode men who with their own eyes had seen Attila's war-host. It was numberless, they said, as the stars in the sky or grains of sand on the shore; and it had already crossed the Danube.

The news ran like wildfire, yet it could scarcely outrun the great horde of the Huns, who came sweeping on like a plague, cutting a swathe of death and destruction. Behind them columns of smoke rose up in thin black spirals away to the edge of sight.

There was no defence against them, and now they had crossed the Rhine, and now the earth shook with the tramp of horses, and a forest of iron spears shone through the fields like a bloody sunset. Attila was at the gate.

King Gibich of the Burgundians was in his palace at Worms when the news reached him. He was celebrating the birth of his only son, Gunther, and calling a halt to the feast, he asked his counsellors what to do.

"Resistance is useless," they told him. "All we can do is ask for terms. We must send them a hostage, and gold as tribute. Better that than lose our lives."

Gibich agreed to this. "Now as to the hostage," he went on. "My own son Gunther is too young to be taken from his mother. Whom shall we send in his place?"

The counsellors' choice fell on Hagen, a boy of eleven or twelve who was nobly born and seemed likely to become a great leader when he was older. Envoys took him with the gold to the Hunnish camp, where Attila, being a good judge of money and men, saw fit to accept them.

When they heard what Gibich had done, the other, less powerful kings decided to follow his example. They thought: "We needn't be ashamed of becoming subject-nations if the Burgundians, for all their wealth, have had to do it"; and bought themselves treaties. But they paid a higher price for peace than Gibich, because they had no excuse not to send their own children as hostages.

Hereric rode into the Huns' camp in person, his little daughter Hildegund before him on the saddle, he was so loath to part with her until the last possible moment. And shortly after that, an ambassador from Aquitaine brought the heir of King Albhere, Walter, not much more than ten years old.

Now Hereric and Albhere were allies, and when Hildegund was born they had promised their children to each other in marriage. It was little more than a year since they had solemnized their betrothal, and Walter and Hildegund both took the memory of it into exile.

Attila meant to be kind to his hostages, and gave it out at court that they were to be brought up as his own children. He sent Hildegund to the Queen, to live in the women's quarters, while he trained the boys himself. So the children met seldom, yet whenever they did it was always with affection. They made no other friends.

As if their harsh Tartar features were not frightening enough, the faces of the warriors had been scarred when they were children, so that the hair would grow only in long thin straggling moustaches. They were as devilish as they looked. But the three hostages very soon learnt to hide their disgust, and their terror, and their passionate longing for home, behind a bland mask of contentment, so that Attila if he had been asked would have said that they were happy.

As Hildegund grew older, the Queen taught her how to run Attila's household, as she would her own daughter, and she proved so willing and quick to learn that Queen Helche began to rely on her more and more, and finally left everything to her, even giving the painted chests that were Attila's treasury into her keeping.

All this time, Walter and Hagen were being trained in warfare together. They were never apart, and it was not long before they swore vows of friendship to each other.

Attila's two sons had been killed in battle when they were only boys, and Walter and Hagen had come to fill the gap this had left in his affections. When they reached manhood and proved themselves to be great warriors, he was as proud of them as if they had been his own, and made them his lieutenants.

And so it was a bitter pill for him to swallow when the court woke one morning to find that Hagen was missing. Word had come the day before that Gibich was dead, and that Gunther, the moment he was acclaimed as king, had broken the treaty. Some said that Hagen had run away because he thought he would be killed in reprisal.

"How could he have thought that?" Attila said. "He must have known I'd never kill him. I looked on him as my son."

The Queen, who saw further than most, said: "Hagen wasn't afraid. He simply took his chance to go back to his people."

"After all I've done for him?" raged Attila. "I brought him up as a prince—and then to leave me for a puppy so careless of his life that he broke the treaty with us like a straw!"

"But Gunther is a Burgundian," she said, "and we are aliens. So beware, Attila. The one who had half your heart has fled from you without a backward look: the other may do the same."

"How can I prevent it?" Attila asked.

Helche said: "Let Walter choose himself a wife from among our Hunnish princesses. Then he will not want to leave."

But when Attila made him this offer, the young man turned it down as tactfully as he was able. "Don't make me do it, little father! What sort of leader shall I be with a family to consider? Let me stay as I am!"

This was the sort of argument that Attila understood, and he was only too willing to listen. But Hagen's flight had made Walter chafe at his own long exile, and he too had been making plans.

Not long after this, Walter put down a revolt against the rule of the Huns by one of their subject tribes. When he returned to the citadel, he went straight into the hall to report to Attila, and afterwards made his way to the royal apartments to change his clothes and rest.

There he came on Hildegund, sitting by herself. He asked her to fetch him some wine, and as he gave back the cup he touched her hand lightly and said: "When are we going to be married?"

She did not know what to answer. She had almost come to believe that he only loved her as a sister, for he had said not one word that encouraged her to think otherwise. Now she said: "Why ask such a question? Do you think that I don't know you're going to marry one of the princesses?"

"That isn't so," Walter said. "Surely I don't need to *tell* you that I love you? If I haven't shown it, it's only because we are so seldom alone together. I'm sick of exile, and I might have got away when we were fighting on the borders, if I'd left you behind. Will you come with me, Hildegund?"

Hildegund said in a low voice: "I was only four years old the first time I saw you, and I have loved you ever since more than anything in the world. Where you go, I will go, and endure any hardship. What do you want me to do?"

Making sure that no one was coming, he said quietly: "You must get hold of everything for our journey—the workmen are so used to taking their orders from you that they will not question you. We need four pairs of shoes each, fish-hooks and some line, food for a few days so we can make good speed until we are over the border, and a little wine in case we run into trouble. Last of all, I want you to get two fairly big boxes, and fill them full of gold from Attila's treasury. Can you do all this?"

"I can do it," Hildegund answered. "But why must we steal

their gold? It's dishonourable enough to break the treaty and run away, after all their kindness."

"You must forget their kindness," said Walter. "However fond of us he seems, Attila is a savage who would not scruple to take our lives if it suited his purpose. Your first loyalty, and mine, has to be to our own people. Now that the Burgundians have broken free, they will be looking round for allies, and our fathers can't afford to reject their advances. But they won't act while we are here.

"As for the gold, gold is kingship. The power of a king resides in his treasure. If we take Attila's gold, we diminish him and he will be less able to take revenge.

"And so I will not go home empty-handed, but like the heroes of old will bring a treasure to my people."

About a week later, Walter gave a feast to celebrate his victory. Attila's great hall with the painted beams was shot through with gleams of splendour it did not know by day, as the firelight glinted on war-gear hung around the walls, and on the golden cups on the tables.

When they had finished eating, the women returned to their apartments, and the tables were cleared. Then Walter had the servants bring in huge bowls of wine he had taken as loot, and asked Attila to launch the evening's carousal.

There was nothing Attila liked better. With a laugh, he raised his cup, and swilled the wine down like ale, and called for more; and he and all his men began to vie with each other in drinking.

Only Walter did not drink but plied them with more and more wine until they were sodden, not one left awake, not even a servant.

They lay just as they had fallen late into the next day, Attila sprawled askew in his great carved chair, the other revellers on the floor among the rushes and scattered cups and dogs still foraging for titbits. Not till the burnished light of evening came slanting low through the door did Attila awaken. His men still lay snoring like hogs, but he could not see Walter among them. He stumbled out of the hall to his private quarters, head pounding, calling for Walter as he went to keep him company in his misery. But Walter was not to be found.

Nor, so it shortly appeared, was Hildegund.

The Queen came in, outraged and indignant. "Why didn't you do as I said, and get him safely married? Now he's gone and your gold has gone too. As for Hildegund—oh, what a fool I was to think that I could trust her!"

Attila said nothing. In the whole of his career he had never been so gulled. He could not eat, he could not sleep, but tossed in his bed all night, pulled this way and that by grief and fury. But by next morning the fury was uppermost, and he swore to give his weight in gold to the man who brought him Walter in shackles, yet there was not one of the Huns who would do it for him: they knew Walter too well of old.

As for Walter and Hildegund, as soon as everything was quiet, they got ready to leave the citadel. They loaded Walter's warhorse, Lion, with their bundles and the gold. Then they set out, Walter in front, spear in hand, while Hildegund came behind, leading Lion by the bridle.

All night long they journeyed, but as soon as the sun was up they hid in the woods and waited for darkness; and with darkness they went on. And so they passed like shadows over the land till they were clear of Attila's horse-runs. After that, they travelled by day.

By day or by dark, Walter never slept but only dozed fitfully, leaning on his spear, keeping watch while Hildegund rested.

When they had finished the food they brought with them, they snared birds, fished in streams, or gathered berries, careful to avoid any habitation and keeping always to the woods and the desolate places.

Forty days or so later, when all but their last pairs of shoes were worn into holes, and they felt themselves stretched thin as threads for weariness, they saw against the setting sun the russet hills of the Rhineland. Early next evening they came down to the Rhine, and turned northward along the bank for a little way, to look for some means of crossing over.

King Gunther was sitting at dinner the next night with Hagen at his right hand when two fish dressed with pungent herbs were set on the plate in front of him. "*These* didn't come out of the Rhine!" he exclaimed as soon as he tasted them, and immediately sent for the cook to inquire where he got them.

"I bought them in the market this morning," answered the cook, "from an old ferryman who works down the river, a mile or two below the town. But he didn't say where they came from."

The ferryman was fetched and questioned. He said: "I was on the farther bank yesterday evening, waiting for custom, when along came this tall young man and a girl who was leading a warhorse, and on the horse's back were two big stout wooden boxes, which every now and then gave out a clinking sound—and I said to myself, 'That's gold.' I took them across the river, horse and all, and they gave me the fishes as payment."

Hagen could scarcely wait for the old man to finish before he burst out: "This is welcome news! This must be Walter coming home from Hunmark."

"Not so," said Gunther. "It is the gold my father paid Attila coming home to me."

84

And shoving the table back with his foot, he hurried out of the hall, buckling his armour on as he went, and calling for his horse to be saddled and bridled. He picked a band of twelve men to go with him on his mission, and Hagen was one.

Now Hagen was in a dilemma. "What shall I do?" he thought. "I am bound to Walter by oaths of friendship, but Gunther is the lord to whom I have sworn allegiance. Where does my loyalty lie— Walter or Gunther? It's plain that Gunther intends to take the gold by force if he has to. I must make him change his mind."

He spurred on his horse till he was riding at Gunther's side.

"Gunther, turn back," he pleaded. "It's madness to say that the gold is yours—if gold it is—and it would be shameful for a king to rob a traveller through his kingdom. I beg you to let him go."

But Gunther, the gold-lust upon him, was deaf to all that he said.

Meantime, the two travellers, bearing away from the Rhine, came to the mountainous wooded region known as the Vosges. As they pushed deeper into the wilderness, they came on a lonely ravine that offered them protection, a natural stronghold among the rocks approachable in only one direction, by a narrow way. There was lush green grass at the bottom.

Walter said as soon as he saw it: "Let's rest here for a while. We'll be safe from attack, and there is good grazing for Lion."

Now the need for sleep came suddenly on him. He said to Hildegund: "I have kept watch for you these many nights past—now you must keep watch for me. If you see horsemen, wake me." Too tired for anything more, he took off his armour, stretched himself out on the ground, and fell asleep almost instantly.

Moving quietly so as not to wake him, Hildegund unloaded Lion and turned him loose to graze, then stood guard for many hours, singing softly under her breath to keep herself awake.

Her eyesight was keen, and she saw the cloud of dust that accompanied the Burgundians while they were still some way off. She woke Walter and helped him arm, holding his spear for him while he strapped on his sword, the famous blade Mimming, made by Wayland Smith in ancient times, an heirloom of his clan that had gone with him into exile.

As the troop drew nearer, Hildegund saw their spears and was seized with panic: she thought it was the Huns. She said: "I beg you, Walter, to cut my throat rather than let me fall into their hands again."

But Walter told her to take heart. "For those are not Huns but Burgundians—look, there is Hagen, our friend. They must be after the gold, but there's not one of them I need be afraid of, except Hagen himself, who knows how I fight—and *he* will not come against me. But in any event, no Nibelung is going home to boast to his wife of stealing *our* treasure."

Now Gunther sent Gamelo, the governor of Metz, down the narrow ravine to demand the gold in his name. Walter refused to surrender it, instead offering to pay a tithe for right of way across his country. This was not enough.

Again Gamelo was sent to claim the gold, and again Walter refused to give it up, at the same time raising his offer. Still it was not enough. Gunther wanted the whole, for the gold worked in his mind like some dull poison, deadening every sense.

Hagen said: "Accept his offer. He'll never give up the gold, and we're not men enough to take it. Gunther, make no mistake—if there's a fight, we'll get the worst of it."

"There are twelve of *us*," Gunther said. "But there," he added sourly, "I can see you're turning out to be a coward, like your father."

Hagen slowly went white. "As good as spit in my face," he thought bitterly. "If you want the gold," he said, "why don't you fight for it yourself, man to man in single combat? *I* am unwilling to add disloyalty to dishonour."

He wheeled his horse abruptly and rode it up the side of the ravine, its hooves slithering in the shale and small boulders. He dismounted half way up, and sat down on a rocky outcrop, placed his sword across his knees, and waited to see what would happen.

Gunther sent Gamelo for the third time to claim the gold, and for the third time Walter refused him. "If you want it, take it," he said. "I will never give it up freely."

From where he sat on his horse's back, Gamelo hurled his spear to enforce Gunther's claim: it was the last act of his life. But still

Gunther persisted. Scaramund, Werinhard, Ekivrid—one by one he sent them down into that narrow place, and one by one they fell, like barley before the reaper. Hadaward next—and the Burgundians who were left began to marvel at Walter's tirelessness. Only Hagen was not amazed—Hagen, who had fought so often beside him. But now came the turn of Batavrid, Hagen's sister's-son, and Hagen, who had sat brooding and silent while his companions met their deaths, rose to his feet and cried out in an anguish that was terrible to hear: "Boy, how shall I tell your mother?"

Walter heard his cry from the hillside as it came echoing down the ravine, and waved the boy back. "For your uncle's sake, turn back and don't make me fight you!" he shouted. But the lad came steadily on, too green in judgment, perhaps, to know how to swallow his pride, and so like the rest he perished.

Hagen scarcely cared what followed, though Gunther sent them all down—Gerwit, Randolf, Helmot, Trogus, Tanastus—one by one down to certain destruction. And now here was Gunther climbing up the hill, commanding, exhorting, cajoling, and finally, abject at last, beseeching him to take up the combat, "if only to get your revenge".

"Your gold-lust will be my ruin," Hagen said. "I will not put vengeance for my nephew above the oaths I swore so long ago to Walter, but because you are, God help us, the king, you have first claim on my loyalty. I will do what you want—but not here.

"Let us ride off and hide in the coverts. If Walter thinks we have gone, he'll come out into the open and we can take him from behind. It's the only way we shall kill him."

Gunther flung an arm round his neck and kissed him. Then they rounded up some of the strays that had lost their masters and rode off together to look for a place in which to lay an ambush.

Walter now asked himself what it was best to do, set out at once or remain in his fastness. He thought with foreboding of the kiss given Hagen by the king, and decided to stay where he was until morning.

At sunrise he surveyed his grim harvest. He had killed many men in his time, but none whose deaths gave him less satisfaction. He had to despoil them just the same. But as he stripped them of their armour according to custom, he closed their staring eyes: that much he could do for them.

He had been too restless to sleep and during the night had gathered in six more of the riderless horses. He roped four together in a line, to carry the armour, and saddled the other two to ride. Lion carried the boxes as usual.

Now he woke Hildegund, and they rode cautiously out of the ravine and into the open, Walter taking the lead, his sharp eyes scanning the country all around for signs of danger, listening for the click of hoof on rock or the half-muffled jingle of harness.

As everything seemed quiet, he sent Hildegund ahead with the string of laden horses, while he brought up the rear with Lion. "If they come, they'll come from behind us."

They did not have long to wait. Hildegund kept looking back over her shoulder, and they had scarcely gone a mile when she saw two horsemen riding fast down the hillside behind them. She had no doubt who it was: Gunther and Hagen, come for Walter's life.

"They're here," she said. "Let's leave the gold and escape. They're both fresh and you are tired."

Walter shook his head. "Yesterday's killings would be a senseless waste if we were to run away now. Here, catch hold of Lion's reins and lead him into that knot of trees with the other horses. I'll take my stand on this slope."

Gunther was exultant, certain that very soon now the gold would be his, and already beginning to crow. As he drew near, he shouted: "So you're out of your lair at last! Let's see if you fight so well out in the open."

Walter did not reply, but turned to Hagen. "Hagen, wait!" he said. "You owe me an explanation. I *had* hoped that, if you found out I was in your country, you'd take me back to your King and he'd offer me hospitality. I never expected *this*. In God's name, come to your senses!"

Hagen only looked grim. He answered curtly: "It was you who broke faith with me, by killing my sister's-son. I want vengeance."

Was he speaking the truth? Walter did not think so. But no time to ponder that, for now Hagen was swinging himself off his horse, and Gunther the same. Walter dismounted quickly and slapped his horse on the rump to send it out of the way. Then he took up his stance on the slope, feet apart and lightly balanced, weighing his spear in his hand.

If Gunther and Hagen felt any shame at setting two on one, they did not show it. They came in very fast, with spears and then swords. First one, then the other, attacked him, but he fended them off with his spear so they could not make contact. They changed their tactics then, and began to rush him together, trying to tire him out: the moment he weakened they would have him. But he would not wait for that. He must act while he had the strength, and stake everything on one throw in one powerful, final effort.

Taking Hagen as his target, he hurled his spear with such force that it ran clear through his shield and mailcoat, pinning them into the flesh of his side. Whilst Hagen was busy trying to detach himself, Walter drew his sword and leapt at Gunther, forced his shield aside, and with a great scything stroke swept his right leg clean off at the thigh.

Gunther slowly heeled over, but before Walter could finish him off, Hagen was back in action and interposed his helmeted head between his lord and the blow. The impetus of the stroke was too great for Walter to check it, and Mimming crashed heavily down on Hagen's bronze helm, striking sparks from the ridge-guard, but the rain-patterned blade itself was shattered into pieces.

It was more to him than a weapon. He knew its lineage like his own name. It was his history, his identity, the badge of his kingship, the sign that marked him as Walter, son of Albhere, and in battle it had seemed to channel into him the courage of all those of his line who had wielded it before him. It was his constant friend, on whom his life depended, a living presence, called by name.

And now like Hagen it had failed him.

Only the hilt was left. In a passion of fury, grief, despair, regret, he cast it from him. And while his right hand was still stretched out, in this unguarded moment, Hagen struck it off at the wrist.

One of the lessons Attila had taught them was how to override pain until there was time for it. Walter had learnt it well. No flinching, no hesitation; not a muscle moved in his face. But thrusting the bleeding stump swiftly into the strap of his shield, he freed his left hand to draw a sword he wore on the right, short, one-edged, meant for in-fighting. He had to get inside Hagen's guard in order to use it, had to move quickly. And before Hagen could respond, he had taken a thrust to the head that had gouged out his right eye.

Now the fight was finished. Would they ever fight again? Not Gunther, certainly. And the others were too maimed to go on for the moment. They threw down their weapons and sat down beside him, as he lay there on the ground vainly trying to staunch his gouting blood with a handful of grass.

Walter shouted for Hildegund, and she came running out of the grove with wine to revive them. She was appalled by what she saw. But she had witnessed worse mutilations.

When she had stopped the bleeding, and dressed their wounds with herbs bound with linen torn from her smock, she poured out a cup of wine, and for the first time hesitated. The cup was the only one they had brought with them. Whom should she serve first?

"Give it to Hagen," said Walter. "And next you may give it to me. But serve Gunther last, although he has lost most blood. He has no right to drink before warriors, for he has squandered other men's lives and only risked his own when the odds were in his favour. He's not fit to be called a king."

And Gunther thought about that and said nothing.

Walter and Hagen soon fell to talking of old times as they sat resting, and their bitterness and rage began to ebb away from them. Eventually Walter said: "I don't want to make this a feuding matter. Will you set my killing your sister's-son against your broken oath, your eye against my hand, so that we can be quits?"

"Gladly," Hagen replied. "Gunther is my lord and I'm bound to uphold him, but never in my life shall I have less stomach for it."

He clasped Walter's one good hand, and they renewed their vows of friendship.

And now they lifted Gunther on to his horse, and Hagen led him back to the city. The first thing Gunther did when he got there, before he would let them put him to bed, was to send out an escort for Walter and Hildegund; and they had not long set out on the last stage of their journey before the Burgundians overtook them, and saw them safely home across the border into Aquitaine.

The wedding took place when the forest was in full leaf, and the meadows bright with flowers. Gunther and Hagen came, and the three men were fully reconciled. In the same spirit, Walter sent word of the wedding to Attila, inviting him to attend, but as he expected, got no answer.

The ferocious lord of the Huns had laughed shortly at the message. By now his fury had given way to a bitter amusement at Walter's audacity.

"I bred him," he said to the Queen, "so who am I to complain of his behaviour? I would have done the same. But I will not go to his wedding."

The Curse of Andvari's Ring

While it was still the custom of Odin to wander through Midgard in disguise, he came one day in company with Hoenir and Loki to a beautiful river which ran swiftly through a deep valley.

As they followed it up towards its source they found a big waterfall in a deep and solitary glen; and on a rock beside the fall they saw an otter blinking its eyes happily as it prepared to eat a salmon which it had caught.

Loki at once picked up a stone and flung it at the otter with such good aim that a moment later it lay dead upon the dead salmon.

"Ah-ha!" cried Loki. "Two at a blow! Trust me to get both an otter and a salmon with one stone!"

He picked up his double catch, and the three Æsir went on again until they came to a house set in the midst of rich farm-lands and walled about strongly as if it were the home of some great lord.

The three travellers came up to the gateway, and finding it open, went in to the great hall where sat a dark man with flashing eyes alone on a seat beside the fire.

"Greetings, strangers!" he cried. "Tell me who you are and why you come hither to the hall of Hreidmarr the master of magic?"

"We are poor pilgrims journeying through the world," answered Odin, doffing his broad-brimmed hat politely as he leant on his staff and surveyed Hreidmarr with his one eye, "and seeing your strong house set amidst such fruitful fields of corn, we turned aside to visit you."

"Poor though we may be," added Loki quickly, "we are strong and clever in our own ways. Look here at this otter and salmon which I laid low with the cast of a single stone!"

When he saw what Loki carried in his hands Hreidmarr rose to his feet and shouted:

"Come hither, my sons Fafnir and Reginn! Come and bind these evil men who have slain your brother Otter!"

Then, while he held them powerless by his magic, two strong youths came into the hall and bound them securely with iron chains.

"And now," said Hreidmarr grimly as he sat gloating over his three captives, "it remains only to decide how you shall die."

"For what reason would you kill us?" asked slow Hoenir, hoping to win out of danger by the smooth power of argument.

"You must know," answered Hreidmarr, "that I am a master of black magic such as is known among the trolls and swart elves. And my three sons share my art, but in addition have the power of changing their shapes at will. My eldest son Otter chose to pass his time in the shape of an otter so that he might catch the fish in which he delighted as they sprang down the waterfall not far from here which is called Andvari's Force. The otter which you slew is this very son of mine, and justice demands a life for a life."

"But justice allows also of wergild," Hoenir replied stolidly, "that is a payment for a slaying if it be done by chance. My companion here flung a stone at what seemed but a common beast of the riverside. Come now, decide on the wergild that shall pay for the death of your son."

Then Hreidmarr consulted with Fafnir and Reginn, and at last he said:

"Strangers, we will take wergild, and it shall be this: enough good red gold to fill the skin of the otter which was my son, and to cover it so that not a hair may remain showing. Two of you shall stay here in chains, while the third goes forth to fetch the golden payment."

The three Æsir consulted apart, and the end of it was that cunning Loki was sent out to find the golden ransom. "Go to the black elves and to the dwarfs," Odin instructed him. "Use all your arts, for we are in the hands of wizards who must not know who we are. Therefore I cannot send to Asgard for help."

"Depend upon me," answered Loki with a cunning smile. "I

know where the gold is to be got—though it will indeed require all my arts to win it for our use."

So, while Odin and Hoenir remained in chains, and Fafnir and Reginn skinned the dead otter to measure out the wergild, Loki set forth in search of treasure.

He went straight back to Andvari's Force, from which the otter had taken the shining salmon, and sat himself down beside the rushing waters.

Loki could see through the roaring arch of green and silver, and presently he perceived Andvari the Dwarf in the likeness of a pike hiding in the mouth of his cave which was behind the waterfall; and there was a glimmer of gold in the darkness of the cave behind him.

"How can I catch him?" thought Loki. "I could never take him with my hands, and he is far too wise to be caught by any hook however cunningly I might bait it . . ."

Then Loki thought of Ran, the cruel wife of Ægir, the giant who ruled the Sea, who caught shipwrecked sailors in her net and drew them down to the bottom of the ocean. Ran was not friendly to the Æsir, but she recognised the evil giant blood in Loki, and willingly lent him her net.

"But do not let the Æsir see it," she warned him, "nor yet the men who dwell in Midgard. For a day may come when you will wish to escape, and only a net such as mine could snare you."

Loki took Ran's net and returned to Andvari's Force. There he cast it into the water and drew it up so smartly that the great pike was entangled in its meshes and lay gasping on the bank.

Loki grasped him in his hands and held him until Andvari returned to his own dwarfish shape and asked sulkily what he wanted.

When Loki told him, Andvari to save his life was forced to give up all his treasure. He carried it up out of the cave behind the arch of falling waters and stacked it on the bank—and it was a very great pile indeed, such a treasure of rich gold as had never before been seen in Midgard.

When at last it was all there, Andvari the dwarf turned sulkily away. But as he did so he put out his hand and swept quickly under it one little golden ring.

Watchful Loki saw this, however, and sternly bade him fling it back on to the pile.

"Let me keep just this ring," begged Andvari. "If I have it, I can make more gold: but the charm will not work for any who is not of the dwarf race."

"Not one scrap shall you keep," said Loki viciously, and he snatched back the ring and held it firmly in his own hand.

"Then," answered the dwarf, "take with it my curse. And know that the curse goes with the ring and brings ruin and sorrow upon all who wear it until both ring and gold come back into the deep waters."

So saying Andvari turned himself into a pike once more and dived to the bottom of the river.

But Loki collected the gold and carried it back to Hreidmarr's dwelling where Odin and Hoenir were waiting anxiously for him.

When they saw the gold, Hreidmarr filled the otter skin full of it and set it up on end. Then they piled gold round it until the skin was completely hidden—and the gold was all used up.

As the gold was being stacked, Odin noticed Andvari's Ring and it seemed so fair to him that he took it out of the pile and slipped it on his own finger. When the gold was all heaped up, he exclaimed:

"Now, Hreidmarr, our wergild is paid. See, the skin of the otter is altogether hidden under the gold."

Hreidmarr examined the heap carefully.

"Not so!" he exclaimed. "One hair on the snout is still showing. Cover that also, or the wergild is not paid and your lives are forfeit."

With a sigh Odin took the ring from his finger and covered the last hair with it; and so the wergild was paid and they were set at liberty.

When they were free, and Odin held his spear once more and there was no longer any danger, Loki turned to Hreidmarr and said:

"With the ring of Andvari goes Andvari's Curse: evil and sorrow upon all who wear it!"

Then the three Æsir returned to Asgard. But they left behind them the curse of Andvari's Ring which had already begun to work on Hreidmarr and his two sons.

"You must give us some part of the wergild," Fafnir and Reginn told their father. "Otter was our brother as well as your son."

"Not one gold ring shall either of you have," answered Hreidmarr, and he locked up the treasure in his strongest room.

Then Fafnir and Reginn made a plot together, and the end of it was that Reginn murdered their father Hreidmarr for the sake of Andvari's gold.

"And now," said Reginn when the evil deed was done, "let us share the treasure between us in equal portions."

"Not one gold ring shall you have," answered Fafnir. "Little do you deserve it indeed, seeing that you slew our father for its sake. Now go hence speedily, or I will slay you also! A life for a life is the law: and your life is forfeit for the murder of Hreidmarr."

So Fafnir drove Reginn away, and he himself set Hreidmarr's Helmet of Terror on his head and carried all the treasure which had been Andvari's hoard to Gnita Heath far from the haunts of men and hid it in a cave. Then he took upon himself the form of a terrible dragon and lay down upon the gold and gloated over it after the custom of dragons.

But Reginn, vowing vengeance in his heart, went to the court of Hialprek, King of the Danes, and became his smith. There he received into his charge the young hero Sigurd the Volsung, the son of Sigmund to whom once on a time Odin had given a magic sword. . . .

Sigurd was the greatest of the Germanic heroes. The dwarf-smith Reginn refashioned for him the miraculous sword Gram that had belonged to Sigurd's father, Sigmund, and taunted him into trying his strength against the dragon Fafnir (Reginn's brother). Sigurd killed Fafnir and won the gold hoard, including the cursed ring; but when he tasted a drop of the dragon's blood, he understood the speech of all the birds and was warned that Reginn intended to kill him and so win back the treasure for himself. The story of Sigurd the Volsung is taken up again in the words of William Morris (p. 121).

Beowulf Fights the Dragon

The action of Beowulf, *the only full-length heroic poem that survives from Anglo-Saxon England, takes place in Denmark and Sweden— an indication of the common ancestry of the tribes that settled through-out North-west Europe. Beowulf is a hero who embodies bravery and loyalty and strives for fame. In his youth, he crosses the sea to Denmark and rids King Hrothgar and his court of two appalling monsters, Grendel and his mother. Beowulf becomes King of the Geats (a tribe in South Sweden) and rules in peace for fifty years until his people are attacked by a dragon. Old as he is, Beowulf resolves to fight it alone.*

Then the bold warrior, stern-faced beneath his helmet,
stood up with his shield; sure of his own strength,
he walked in his corslet towards the cliff;
the way of the coward is not thus!
Then that man endowed with noble qualities,
he who had braved countless battles, weathered
the thunder when warrior troops clashed together,
saw a stone arch set in the cliff
through which a stream spurted; steam rose
from the boiling water; he could not stay long
in the hollow near the hoard for fear
of being scorched by the dragon's flames.
Then, such was his fury, the leader of the Geats
threw out his chest and gave a great roar,
the brave man bellowed; his voice, renowned
in battle, hammered the grey rock's anvil.

The guardian of the hoard knew the voice for human;
violent hatred stirred within him. Now no time
remained to entreat for peace. At once
the monster's breath, burning battle vapour,
issued from the barrow; the earth itself snarled.
The lord of the Geats, standing under the cliff,
raised his shield against the fearsome stranger;
then that sinuous creature spoiled
for the fight. The brave and warlike king
had already drawn his keen-edged sword,
(it was an ancient heirloom); a terror of each other
lurked in the hearts of the two antagonists.
While the winged creature coiled himself up,
the friend and lord of men stood unflinching
by his shield; Beowulf waited ready armed.

Then, fiery and twisted, the dragon swiftly
shrithed towards its fate. The shield protected
the life and body of the famous prince
for far less time than he had looked for.
It was the first occasion in all his life
that fate did not decree triumph for him
in battle. The lord of the Geats raised
his arm, and struck the mottled monster
with his vast ancestral sword; but the bright blade's
edge was blunted by the bone, bit
less keenly than the desperate king required.
The defender of the barrow bristled with anger
at the blow, spouted murderous fire, so that flames
leaped through the air. The gold-friend of the Geats
did not boast of famous victories; his proven sword,
the blade bared in battle, had failed him
as it ought not to have done. That great Ecgtheow's
greater son had to journey on from this world
was no pleasant matter; much against his will,
he was obliged to make his dwelling
elsewhere—sooner or later every man must leave
this transitory life. It was not long

before the fearsome ones closed again.
The guardian of the hoard was filled with fresh hope,
his breast was heaving; he who had ruled a nation
suffered agony, surrounded by flame.
And Beowulf's companions, sons of nobles—
so far from protecting him in a troop together,
unflinching in the fight—shrank back into the forest
scared for their own lives. One man alone
obeyed his conscience. The claims of kinship
can never be ignored by a right-minded man.

His name was Wiglaf, a noble warrior,
Weohstan's son, kinsman of Ælfhere,
a leader of the Swedes; he saw that his lord,
helmeted, was tormented by the intense heat.
Then he recalled the honours Beowulf had bestowed
on him—the wealthy citadel of the Wægmundings,
the rights to land his father owned before him.
He could not hold back then; he grasped the round,
yellow shield; he drew his ancient sword,
reputed to be the legacy of Eanmund,
Ohthere's son. . . .
                    This was the first time
the young warrior had weathered the battle storm,
standing at the shoulder of his lord.
His courage did not melt, nor did his kinsman's sword
fail him in the fight. The dragon found that out
when they met in mortal combat.

Wiglaf spoke, constantly reminding
his companions of their duty—he was mournful.
"I think of that evening we emptied the mead-cup
in the feasting-hall, partook and pledged our lord,
who presented us with rings, that we would repay him
for his gifts of armour, helmets and hard swords,
if ever the need, need such as this, arose.
For this very reason he asked us
to join with him in this journey, deemed us
worthy of renown, and gave me these treasures;

he looked on us as loyal warriors,
brave in battle; even so, our lord,
guardian of the Geats, intended to perform
this feat alone, because of all men
he had achieved the greatest exploits,
daring deeds. Now the day has come
when our lord needs support, the might
of strong men; let us hurry forward
and help our leader as long as fire remains,
fearsome, searing flames. God knows
I would rather that fire embraced my body
beside the charred body of my gold-giver;
it seems wrong to me that we should shoulder
our shields, carry them home afterwards,
unless we can first kill the venomous foe,
guard the prince of the Geats. I know
in my heart his feats of old were such
that he should not now be the only Geat to suffer
and fall in combat; in common we shall share
sword, helmet, corslet, the trappings of war."
　　Then that man fought his way through the fumes,
went helmeted to help his lord. He shouted out:
"Brave Beowulf, may success attend you—
for in the days when you were young, you swore
that so long as you lived you would never allow
your fame to decay; now, O resolute king,
renowned for your exploits, you must guard your life
with all your skill. I shall assist you."
　　At this the seething dragon attacked a second time;
shimmering with fire the venomous visitor fell on his foes,
the men he loathed. With waves of flame, he burnt
the shield right up to its boss; Wiglaf's
corslet afforded him no protection whatsoever.
But the young warrior still fought bravely, sheltered
behind his kinsman's shield after his own
was consumed by flames. Still the battle-king
set his mind on deeds of glory; with prodigious strength

he struck a blow so violent that his sword stuck
in the dragon's skull. But Nægling snapped!
Beowulf's old grey-hued sword
failed him in the fight. Fate did not ordain
that the iron edge should assist him
in that struggle; Beowulf's hand was too strong.
Indeed I have been told that he overtaxed
each and every weapon, hardened by blood, that he bore
into battle; his own great strength betrayed him.

    Then the dangerous dragon, scourge of the Geats,
was intent a third time upon attack; he rushed
at the renowned man when he saw an opening:
fiery, battle-grim, he gripped the hero's neck
between his sharp teeth; Beowulf was bathed
in blood; it spurted out in streams.
Then, I have heard, the loyal thane
alongside the Geatish king displayed great courage,
strength and daring, as was his nature.
To assist his kinsman, that man in mail
aimed not for the head but lunged at the belly
of their vile enemy (in so doing his hand
was badly burnt); his sword, gleaming and adorned,
sank in up to the hilt and at once the flames
began to abate. The king still had control then
over his senses; he drew the deadly knife,
keen-edged in battle, that he wore on his corslet;
then the lord of the Geats dispatched the dragon.
Thus they had killed their enemy—their courage
enabled them—the brave kinsmen together
had destroyed him. Such should a man,
a thane, be in time of necessity!

                    That was the last
of all the king's achievements, his last
exploit in the world. Then the wound
the earth-dragon had inflicted with his teeth
began to burn and swell; very soon he
was suffering intolerable pain as the poison

boiled within him. Then the wise leader
tottered forward and slumped on a seat
by the barrow; he gazed at the work of giants,
saw how the ancient earthwork contained
stone arches supported by columns.
Then, with his own hands, the best of thanes
refreshed the renowned prince with water,
washed his friend and lord, blood-stained
and battle-weary, and unfastened his helmet.
      Beowulf began to speak, he defied
his mortal injury; he was well aware
that his life's course, with all its delights,
had come to an end; his days on earth
were exhausted, death drew very close:
"It would have made me happy, at this time,
to pass on war-gear to my son, had I
been granted an heir to succeed me,
sprung of my seed. I have ruled the Geats
for fifty winters; no king of any
neighbouring tribe has dared to attack me
with swords, or sought to cow and subdue me.
But in my own home I have awaited
my destiny, cared well for my dependants,
and I have not sought trouble, or sworn
any oaths unjustly. Because of all these things
I can rejoice, drained now by death-wounds;
for the Ruler of Men will have no cause to blame me
after I have died on the count that I deprived
other kinsmen of their lives. Now hurry,
dear Wiglaf; rummage the hoard
under the grey rock, for the dragon sleeps,
riddled with wounds, robbed of his treasure.
Be as quick as you can so that I may see
the age-old store of gold, and examine
all the priceless, shimmering stones; once I
have set eyes on such a store, it will be
more easy for me to die, to abandon

the life and land that have so long been mine."
   Then, I have been told, as soon as he heard
the words of his lord, wounded in battle,
Wiglaf hastened into the earth-cavern,
still wearing his corslet, his woven coat of mail.
After the fierce warrior, flushed with victory,
had walked past a daïs, he came upon
the hoard—a hillock of precious stones,
and gold treasure glowing on the ground;
he saw wondrous wall-hangings; the lair
of the serpent, the aged twilight-flier;
and the stoups and vessels of a people
long dead, now lacking a polisher,
deprived of adornments. There were many old,
rusty helmets, and many an armlet
cunningly wrought. A treasure hoard,
gold in the ground, will survive its owner
easily, whosoever hides it!
And he saw also hanging high
over the hoard a standard fashioned with gold strands,
a miracle of handiwork; a light shone from it,
by which he was able to distinguish the earth
and look at the adornments. There was no sign
of the serpent, the sword had savaged and slain him.
Then I heard that Wiglaf rifled the hoard
in the barrow, the antique work of giants—
he chose and carried off as many cups and salvers
as he could; and he also took the standard,
the incomparable banner; Beowulf's sword,
iron-edged, had injured
the guardian of the hoard, he who had held it
through the ages and fought to defend it
with flames—terrifying, blistering,
ravening at midnight—until he was slain.
Wiglaf hurried on his errand, eager to return,
spurred on by the treasures; in his heart he was troubled
whether he would find the prince of the Geats,

so grievously wounded, still alive
in the place where he had left him.
Then at last he came, carrying the treasures,
to the renowned king; his lord's life-blood
was ebbing; once more he splashed him
with water, until Beowulf revived a little,
began to frame his thoughts.
                              Gazing at the gold,
the warrior, the sorrowing king, said:
"With these words I thank
the King of Glory, the Eternal Lord,
the Ruler, for all the treasures here before me,
that in my lifetime I have been able
to gain them for the Geats.
And now that I have bartered my old life
for this treasure hoard, you must serve
and inspire our people. I will not long be with you.
Command the battle-warriors, after the funeral fire,
to build a fine barrow overlooking the sea;
let it tower high on Whaleness
as a reminder to my people.
And let it be known as *Beowulf's barrow*
to all seafarers, to men who steer their ships
from far over the swell and the saltspray."

Then the prince, bold of mind, detached
his golden collar and gave it to Wiglaf,
the young spear-warrior, and also his helmet
adorned with gold, his ring and his corslet,
and enjoined him to use them well;
"You are the last survivor of our family,
the Wægmundings; fate has swept
all my kinsmen, those courageous warriors,
to their doom. I must follow them."

Those were the warrior's last words
before he succumbed to the raging flames
on the pyre; his soul migrated from his breast
to meet the judgement of righteous men.

Then the brave warrior, Weohstan's son,
directed that orders be given to many men
(to all who owned houses, elders of the people)
to fetch wood from far to place beneath
their prince on the funeral pyre:
                                   "Now flames,
the blazing fire, must devour the lord of warriors
who often endured the iron-tipped arrow-shower,
when the dark cloud loosed by bow strings
broke above the shield-wall, quivering;
when the eager shaft, with its feather garb,
discharged its duty to the barb."
    I have heard that Weohstan's wise son
summoned from Beowulf's band his seven
best thanes, and went with those warriors
into the evil grotto; the man leading
the way grasped a brand. Then those retainers
were not hesitant about rifling the hoard
as soon as they set eyes on any part of it,
lying unguarded, gradually rusting,
in that rock cavern; no man was conscience-stricken
about carrying out those priceless treasures
as quickly as he could. Also, they pushed the dragon,
the serpent over the precipice; they let the waves take him,
the dark waters embrace the warden of the hoard.
Then the wagon was laden with twisted gold,
with treasures of every kind, and the king,
the old battle-warrior, was borne to Whaleness.
    Then, on the headland, the Geats prepared a mighty pyre
for Beowulf, hung round with helmets and shields
and shining mail, in accordance with his wishes;
and then the mourning warriors laid
their dear lord, the famous prince, upon it.
    And there on Whaleness, the heroes kindled
the most mighty of pyres; the dark wood-smoke
soared over the fire, the roaring flames
mingled with weeping—the winds' tumult subsided—

until the body became ash, consumed even
to its core. The heart's cup overflowed;
they mourned their loss, the death of their lord.
And, likewise, a maiden of the Geats,
with her tresses swept up, intoned
a dirge for Beowulf time after time,
declared she lived in dread of days to come
dark with carnage and keening, terror of the enemy,
humiliation and captivity.
       Heaven swallowed the smoke.
 Then the Geats built a barrow on the headland—
it was high and broad, visible from far
to all seafarers; in ten days they built the beacon
for that courageous man; and they constructed
as noble an enclosure as wise men
could devise, to enshrine the ashes.
They buried rings and brooches in the barrow,
all those adornments that brave men
had brought out from the hoard after Beowulf died.
They bequeathed the gleaming gold, treasure of men,
to the earth, and there it still remains
as useless to men as it was before.
 Then twelve brave warriors, sons of heroes,
rode round the barrow, sorrowing;
they mourned their king, chanted
an elegy, spoke about that great man:
they exalted his heroic life, lauded
his daring deeds; it is fitting for a man,
when his lord and friend must leave this life,
to mouth words in his praise
and to cherish his memory.
Thus the Geats, his hearth-companions,
grieved over the death of their lord;
they said that of all kings on earth
he was the kindest, the most gentle,
the most just to his people, the most eager for fame.

Wayland Smith

Wayland was one of three brothers, alike enough to them in some respects, in others not at all. All three were broad and handsome men, but beside the other two Wayland appeared clumsy, his shoulders almost too broad for the rest of his body, while he moved as clumsily as a bear too, tripping over things, knocking them down; except only when he was at work—and then his clumsiness like a bear's was also elegance; then each of his movements meshed in with the next, each of his muscles co-ordinated, the whole of him was focused to one end, like a sword towards the man it is killing. That end was perfection. For whereas his brothers were mainly warriors and hunters, destroyers of other men and beasts, Wayland was mainly a smith, a maker, the best in his country. There was nothing he could not make; swords and helmets for heroes, shields inlaid and ornamented—brilliant, impenetrable coats of war; but also more peaceable things, drinking cups and plates, arm-rings and collars, even finely-wrought decorations for a woman's breast, over the working of which he bent closely, using the smallest and most delicate of tools, his brown eyes turned green in the light of his furnace.

Now Wayland and his brothers fell in love, but not with ordinary women. They took to wife three swan maidens, hiding their feathered cloaks so that they could not turn back to swans and fly away again. The name of Wayland's wife was Hervor, he loved her utterly, and she in her way loved him—knowing not only how to give him what he wanted, but also how to show him what she wanted and to take it from him gladly—knowing when to talk to him and when to be silent. Wayland even let her come to his smithy

108

while he was working; the furnace glowed equally then on her smooth white skin and on the metal he was working. When he brought his hammer down on the anvil he knew she heard it too, the ring of iron on iron, the even notes of his making. And when he had finished and he held it up to her, whatever it was, the object of war or of peace, she need look at him only without a word and he would know if she liked it.

What she would not do, however, though he wanted it, was wear the jewels that he made. He forged necklaces for her and brooches for her breast and rings for her ears and for her fingers. But she would only ever take one thing from him, perhaps the most beautiful of all, a simple gold arm-ring, engraved with an intricate pattern. And even this she left behind her when she went away from him. For they went away, all three of them, the three swan maidens, one autumn morning early. Hervor had warned the smith often enough. "Always believe I love you," she had said. "No matter what, I love you. Hold me in your heart when I am gone." But he had thought himself safe, all the brothers did, knowing the cloaks safely hidden, knowing they were truly loved. As soon as they discovered their loss, Wayland's two brothers put on their travelling cloaks, took up their hunting bows, buckled on their swords. They swore they would not rest until they had found their wives and set off grimly into the deep green forest. But Wayland remained in his smithy. "I am a maker," he said to himself, "I am not a traveller. I will travel in my making only, Hervor will come to me when she chooses to, when she needs to come to me." And he took up her gold arm-ring and he threaded it on a rope made of flax with seven hundred others and hung it upon the wall where Hervor would see it if she came to find it.

And then he began to work again. The fire in his smithy never died. The ring of hammer on anvil continued day and night. Such things he made, more finely wrought than ever, each one perfect for its purpose, whether of war or peace; whether sword or battle-axe, helmet or battle-shirt, arm-ring or neck-ring, wine-bowl, ale-cup or goblet, ornament for breast or neck or finger. Just as Wayland controlled the might of fire and steel, the huge muscles shifting across his back as he swung the great hammer, so too his eyes and fingers continued to make perfect harmony over work small and cunning, intricate and fine. The fame of his making spread far beyond his hall.

He grew still more bearlike over the years, his back more bent, his shoulders broader. His wiry black hair fell down his back now and had turned just a little grey. Outside his smithy he moved as clumsily as ever, but he did not often leave it or his hall now, with their bright fires burning and the dark shadows stirring in the corners, except to go hunting for his food, pursuing bear and elk through the living forest that surrounded him.

But there was another country quite close by; a cold grey land of rock and ice and darkness where no trees grew or flowers, where no birds sang in the early morning. The king of this land was called King Nidud, and hearing of Wayland's skill he sent armed men over the mountains to find him. Wayland was out hunting at the time, his hall and smithy empty but for all the things he'd made, on which the firelight leapt and glinted. The warriors looked round them in amazement, but in the end took only one thing away with them, the most beautiful thing of all, the ring Wayland had threaded on a thread with seven hundred others, the red-gold ring that was Hervor's, engraved with a pattern like a maze.

When Wayland returned that night he brought branches of pine to throw upon his fires. He brought the carcase of a bear intending to eat all he wanted that night, then smoke the meat that was left for the hungry weeks to come. He skinned the bear and jointed it, he set a leg to roast upon the fire. Then as usual he took from the wall the seven hundred rings, red-gold and white-gold, and lay down beside the fire to count them. He saw immediately that Hervor's ring had gone. Immediately he was overcome with joy. She has been here, he thought. She has taken her ring; soon, she will come back to me.

That night almost for the first time he could not work. He ate such meat he could. He sat by the fire feeding it with pine branches. The next day the same. And at last after darkness had come he heard footsteps outside his door. Then he flung it open widely. But he did not find Hervor standing there, he found a line of warriors, the moonlight glinting on their battle-shirts, on the metal bosses of their round shields, on the chains which they held ready to bind him. They seized him before he had had time to draw his sword. Then they carried him off to their cold grey land, through the forest and over the mountain, until they brought him at last to the hall of King Nidud himself; to where the king sat at meat with his wife and his two small sons whom he was rearing to be warriors, and his beautiful daughter, Bodvild.

King Nidud smiled to see Wayland. He smiled still more to see Wayland's sword still hanging from his belt. He ordered it to be brought to him. He held it in his hand and tested its weight. He ran his fingers along its finely-tempered blade. He gazed at the patterns that were worked upon the hilt, at the inlay of gold set in hardened steel. Then he took it and buckled it at his side. All the time Wayland was watching him, chained between two warriors, quite motionless. Only his eyes moved, his eyes that were brown except sometimes when he was at his forge, but which were green now with fury. They moved from King Nidud's satisfied and smiling face, towards King Nidud's cold, unsmiling queen; from her to the king's sons, the fledgling warriors; and from them at last to his beautiful daughter, Bodvild, the king's most favourite; on whose arm shone the red-gold ring that was Hervor's. Chained as he was then his fury broke; he leapt forward, his movement as concentrated, as precise as it would be if he was working; his strength so huge, two warriors could scarcely hold him, a third and then a fourth had to come to their rescue, and still Wayland struggled, growling like a bear.

"That one," observed King Nidud's queen who had begun to smile at last. "That one is dangerous. If you intend keeping it my lord, you should see it is well-tamed."

"And how should you advise I tame him?" The king was still fingering Wayland's stolen sword.

"It is like a bear, it moves like a bear, clumsy and elegant together. See how its eyes move; see how it shows its teeth. I suggest you lame it like a bear; I would cut the leather sinews of its knees."

Wayland, though panting, stood motionless once more; he was watching her.

"Its eyes are glittering like a serpent's now," observed Nidud's queen. "I tell you this one is dangerous."

But she did not seem afraid of him. King Nidud also smiled, so did his two sons, their eyes shining with excitement to see such things in their father's hall. Only Bodvild looked at Wayland with sorrow and compassion, though touching meanwhile Hervor's golden ring. She gazed at her father beseechingly. King Nidud said,

"So shall it be. He is mine now. Cut the sinews with his own sword, then take him away. He shall work for me now and for no one else. The sun never shines on my land, let me be dazzled instead by the gleam of Wayland's gold."

So they lamed the smith cruelly, as you would clip the pinions of a wild bird and so impede its flight. Afterwards he could only hobble awkwardly. Then they took him to an island off the cold grey land, and made him a smithy there and commanded him to work. But first he had to build King Nidud's treasure house which he made a labyrinth of such intricacy that only he himself and the king would know the secret of it. This the king ordered. "The treasure shall lie at its heart," he said; "no one, except me shall look on it." He sent slaves to work with Wayland Smith by day, small, dark, silent men from the mountains. It took them a year to dig the multiplicity of passages, to build up so many walls, which Wayland then set with designs in metal, showing the battle deeds of King Nidud's forefathers. When it was finished all the slaves were killed to prevent them betraying the secrets of the labyrinth, and Wayland was left quite alone on his island, with no means of escaping it, or so King Nidud thought; who did not know that the maze was not the only thing Wayland had designed and built that year; did not know how each night Wayland had hobbled to the sea-shore and gathered the feathers and bones of dead sea-birds there, how little by little he had worked out the secret of their flight, and so constructed him a pair of wings, setting the sea-birds' feathers on a frame made of their bones. But these wings he had hid in a chest in his smithy. The time for using them had not yet come.

"Hervor, my wife," he said, speaking to her inside his head as he often did these days, "Hervor my white swan. The day will come that I am revenged and you will have a bird too for a husband."

He rarely slept now. The fire in his smithy burned brightly always. His only visitor was King Nidud, Wayland's own sword still hanging at his side. But now he too wore a helmet made by Wayland, and a battle-shirt also of his working. Back in his hall hung a sharp battle-axe and a fine war-collar. On his table stood wine-bowls and ale-cups and chased golden goblets. His sons wore collars made by Wayland. On his wife's breast lay many of his jewels. Only Bodvild would take nothing more, wore nothing but Hervor's ring upon her small white arm and thought of Wayland constantly.

This was the worst time of Wayland's life, who nevertheless, in fear sometimes and in longing always, did not cease to work; though his mind remained with his lost wife, his lost freedom, his lost strength and pride. The flames of his furnace seemed cruel as the fires of hell. And outside his smithy it was dark and bleak and cold and the wind howled and snow fell on snow, all the year long. No trees grew, no flowers; no birds sang in the morning. The only life was Wayland's. The only thing that grew was the gold beneath Wayland's hammer, the beauty that he made with it. There were chests full of the things he had made stacked in the corners of the smithy, waiting to be taken to the treasure chamber in the maze; but only King Nidud ever saw the treasures there. And as for Wayland he could scarcely remember what love and warmth felt like. He could scarcely remember Hervor's face. Despair would have eaten him entirely, if he had not kept it at bay with his thoughts of revenge on King Nidud and his wife and his sons and his daughter, Bodvild.

Now it happened that as the two little boys grew up they became increasingly curious about their father's prisoner. They wanted to see more of the things that Wayland made. They wanted to get closer to the lamed bear themselves, if only to bait him. It is our right, they told themselves. Soon we too will be warriors, soon we too will have the right to wear helmet and battle-shirt, to carry swords and battle-axes. We should be allowed to choose some for ourselves. It is our right, they said.

So they took a boat and they rowed across the sea to Wayland's island. They left the boat hidden behind a rock a little out from the shore and started to walk through the sea towards the beach. Wayland came out of his smithy and saw them coming. "Children," he thought, not recognising them at first. And at first the sight of them, of the bright-faced fair-haired boys, moved him deeply, he had not seen children for many years. One of the boys was so small the water came nearly to his shoulders, and seeing this Wayland thought to himself, I was tall enough once to walk through water nine yards deep, and lame as he was he strode into the sea and took the boy upon his shoulders and carried him dry to shore. The other boy followed them. But he was watching Wayland closely and in a little while began to imitate his awkward walk; the boy on the smith's shoulders began laughing to see it. And Wayland heard the laughter and the cruelty there was in it, and gradually the burden became almost too great for him to bear. He set the boy down thankfully and looked at the brothers, but he was frowning and suspicious now.

"Who are you? What do you want of me?" he asked.

"We are the sons of your master King Nidud. We have seen some of the things you have made. We have heard you make others yet more incredible—swords sharp enough to cut off a dragon's head, steel coats strong enough to withstand a dragon's teeth. We have come to choose the armour we will wear when we are older. We have come to choose some of your weapons for ourselves."

Wayland took them to his smithy and opened a chest or two. But he did not like the way they nudged each other with sly and greedy looks, the way they whispered together and sniggered the moment his back was turned. He began to see his revenge against their father, King Nidud. The two boys were pointing to yet another corner now.

"Show us what you have in there," they said. "Show us jewels, show us gold collars and arm-rings. We are the sons of a king, such things will be for us."

Wayland told them the keys to this chest were lost. "Tonight at at my furnace I will forge some more," he said, "Come back to-morrow. Come secretly. Tell no one where you mean to go, say only you will be hunting in the forest or on the mountain. And we will spend a day together. I will show you all the secrets of my making."

So the two brothers departed, still nudging each other and giggling, still imitating the way that Wayland walked. And the next day having pretended to set out towards the mountains, they came running instead to the sea shore and took their boat and rowed once more towards Wayland's island. The smith waited for them upon the beach, but this time he let the younger boy walk through the water, did not carry him in upon his shoulders.

In his smithy a chest stood ready in a dark corner. Wayland opened it with a bright new key. The light from the furnace barely reached this far, the two boys had to bend closely to see what they would see, their heads close together, their eyes shining at the sight of the riches they had intended plundering. They were too engrossed to hear Wayland come behind them. He felled each of them with an easy blow. They lay without a sound, and at once he took an axe and cut off both their heads.

He buried the bodies in another corner beneath a pile of soot-blackened bellows. And when he had wiped up all the blood he carried the two heads to his workbench beside the fire. There he took out the eyes and extracted all the teeth and laid them carefully aside. Then he scraped the hair from the skulls, and the flesh and skin and he let the brains run out from inside them, until he was left with clean and empty bone; and then, smelting silver, he mounted these skulls most beautifully, engraving the bright metal with pictures of what he had just done, how he had killed the two boys and cut off both their heads.

"These goblets are my gift to King Nidud," he said.

When he had finished he took the two pairs of eyes, one green pair and one brown, the colours of his own, and he polished them to shining jewels and set them too in silver. "A necklace for King Nidud's queen," Wayland told himself and laid them beside the skulls. Then he took all the teeth and polished them also, formed patterns with them and made two brooches, such beautiful brooches that working them he almost forgot they were the result of such destruction. "But to make one thing you must always destroy another," he told himself, angrily. "These brooches are for the breast of King Nidud's daughter."

Now Bodvild had not set eyes on Wayland since that first day he became her father's captive. She had thought of him often with curiosity and pity. She became more and more determined to see him. And at last she broke her golden arm-ring engraved with lines interwoven like a maze, and she too crossed the water to Wayland's island, carrying the pieces with her, and she handed them to him without a word, and looked at him longingly. He stroked them with his fingers, as silent as she was. He thought of Hervor his wife. I have never made anything more beautiful than this, he told himself.

Bodvild said nervously at last, "No one could mend this but you. I love it like myself—will you do it for me?"

Wayland still did not speak to her. He went into his smithy and Bodvild followed him, looking round her curiously to see his tools hung neatly upon the wall, his anvil beside the furnace, the furnace itself not only heat but light, giving each implement a shadow the same size as itself. Bodvild saw her own shadow on the wall, and she saw Wayland's too, his mighty shoulders, his head bent over his work bench. From time to time he looked at her. She was only the second woman who had ever watched him work; on whose face the light of his furnace had glowed, in whose ears had sounded the ring of his hammer on the anvil. And when he had finished he handed the arm-ring to her, and she too did not speak, simply smiled at him, and he knew as he had once known that a woman loved what he did for its own sake and for his, and not simply for the metal from which it had been made.

He could hardly bear to see it. "Your mother," he said, speaking very slowly, "your mother will envy you now still more; that your father should have given you this ring."

"My mother may take everything I have but this. You made it and it is beautiful."

Bodvild sat down on a bearskin beside the fire. Wayland brought her ale in a silver cup. He too sat down and he looked at her, trying not to remember his lost wife, and he too drank ale with Bodvild. But when her cup was empty he filled it up again; and again she emptied it and again he filled it. And the warmth of the fire and the ale entered both of them. His eyes turned green when he looked at her and she was not afraid of him though she thought she ought to be. But she did not want to be afraid of him. And when he looked at her he did not know if it was hate that he felt or love. In the end anyway he did what he had to, what they both wanted, for whatever reason; drowsy and warm Bodvild knew Wayland there on the bearskin beside his furnace, and for the first time in her life she had a husband, and for the second time in his life, so briefly, Wayland himself had a wife.

But he awoke in the cold dawn, angry and mocking her.

"Think of what your father will say to this."

"I do not care what my father says. And how do you think he should ever know?"

"He will know. He will have the bitter knowledge of it and I shall be revenged on both of you." And Bodvild went away weeping because Wayland had forgotten her now, because of his cruelty where there had been some gentleness before. Wayland watching her go felt pity stir in him. But she did not look back; he did not call her.

In King Nidud's hall the queen was weeping for her two lost sons. They had searched for them everywhere, through the forests and across the mountains, but no one had seen them. She thought of Wayland's magic powers, and she too at last sought out the man whose laming she had suggested to the king. She entered his smithy, stood watching as he worked. But he laid his hammer down as soon as he saw that she had come.

"I have lost my two sons, my two warrior boys."

"I can tell you where to find them. You must swear one thing first."

"I will swear anything."

"Then swear on ship and sword and stallion; swear on shield and coat of steel; swear you'll not harm the one who has been my wife; and swear you will not harm our son though she rears him in King Nidud's hall."

King Nidud's wife was still proud, still angry; but worn weak by weeping she did not hesitate, put her hand on the anvil and swore as she was asked.

"*Now* tell me. Where are my sons?"

Wayland took from one of his chests the two skull goblets, mounted in silver; the four eyes, two brown jewels and two green, that he had made into a necklace; the small teeth that were now an ivory brooch for Bodvild, and he laid them down before King Nidud's wife. She looked at them astonished, not knowing what she saw.

"But where are my sons? What have you done with them?"

The smith pointed to a corner, shadowed and dark, to a pile of old bellows and other implements. "Dig there," he said, "under the soot-blackened bellows from my forge. If you look carefully you will see the marks of blood. If you dig further you will find small bones, the bones of boys, your sons. These goblets are their skulls set in silver for your husband; these eyes are theirs made into a necklace for you, these brooches I made from their teeth as breast ornaments for your daughter, Bodvild."

"And that is not all," he said. "Tell your husband this: his gift is death. I have proved now it is also mine. But besides that I have brought to this land what he cannot bring, what he has tried to prevent ever coming here. I have brought life. Life stirs in the belly of your daughter Bodvild, and that too King Nidud cannot now undo."

All the while Wayland had been strapping on to him the wings he had made of bird bones and feathers from the sea-shore. And then, his work done, he rose into the air upon them, leaving behind his smithy, the cold stone of the island, leaving behind all the beautiful things he had made and the maze that was the treasure house for the man who had imprisoned him; whose secret intricacies now lay openly below him. Like the swan maiden Hervor, his wife, he flew high in the air and was free at last, of the gold and silver, the hammer and the anvil, free of his lameness, free of his slavery. Below him the queen was raging and weeping. Below him King Nidud came running to the shore, ordering his tallest horsemen to chase after Wayland on their tallest horses. Rank upon rank of them appeared, but none were tall enough. Wayland had risen far above their heads. King Nidud ordered out his archers, the most far-shooting, far-seeing of his whole war-band. They drew their bows, they released their arrows, higher and higher, they darted, curving as they fell—for Wayland flew far above arrows, above archers, above horsemen, far above King Nidud, his wife and his dead sons; far above Bodvild and the child in her belly.

She wept for him bitterly. She called him in her heart. But when her father reproached her, reviling Wayland too for what he had done to her, she said simply, "I was willing." Nothing more.

How bitter King Nidud was, how furiously angry. But with all his powers he could not put the eyes back in the skull sockets and the skulls back on the bodies and the flesh back on the bones, any more than he could destroy the life that was growing in his daughter's belly.

"I have sworn she shall not be harmed, nor the son that grows inside her," his queen told him coldly; as much death in her voice now as there was death in King Nidud's heart.

Wayland flew far away from that icy, lightless land where no birds sang in the early morning, back to his own smithy, his own hall in the deep green of the forest. He remained lame for ever. He remained a smith for ever; but maybe one day Hervor came to him, maybe one day the light from the furnace fell upon her face and the ring of the anvil sounded in her ears; maybe for a little while again she stayed with him.

How Sigurd Awoke Brynhild upon Hindfell

This episode from the Volsunga Saga *follows immediately after Sigurd has slain the dragon Fafnir on Gnita Heath, called "Glittering Heath" by William Morris. "The Wrath" is another name for Sigurd's sword, Gram; and "Fafnir's bane" is the cursed treasure hoard he has won from the dragon. Until she fell from grace, Brynhild was one of the Valkyries or "Choosers of the Slain" (Morris calls her a "Victory-Wafter"), beautiful young spirit women who gave victory or defeat as Odin dictated and brought the Einheriar or heroes back to Valhalla to await the last great battle at Ragnarok.*

As this triumphant section ends, Sigurd gives Andvari's ring to Brynhild, innocent of the curse upon it. The Volsunga Saga *goes on to record Sigurd's and Brynhild's association with the Niblungs and to chart the tragic course of their lives.*

By long roads rideth Sigurd amidst that world of stone,
And somewhat south he turneth; for he would not be alone,
But longs for the dwellings of man-folk, and the kingly people's speech,
And the days of the glee and the joyance, where men laugh each to each.
But still the desert endureth, and afar must Greyfell fare
From the wrack of the Glittering Heath, and Fafnir's golden lair.
Long Sigurd rideth the waste, when, lo, on a morning of day
From out of the tangled crag-walls, amidst the cloud-land grey
Comes up a mighty mountain, and it is as though there burns
A torch amidst of its cloud-wreath; so thither Sigurd turns,

For he deems indeed from its topmost to look on the best of the
    earth;
And Greyfell neigheth beneath him, and his heart is full of mirth.

So he rideth higher and higher, and the light grows great and
    strange,
And forth from the clouds it flickers, till at noon they gather and
    change,
And settle thick on the mountain, and hide its head from sight;
But the winds in a while are awakened, and day bettereth ere the
    night,
And, lifted a measureless mass o'er the desert crag-walls high,
Cloudless the mountain riseth against the sunset sky,
The sea of the sun grown golden, as it ebbs from the day's desire;
And the light that afar was a torch is grown a river of fire,
And the mountain is black above it, and below is it dark and dun;
And there is the head of Hindfell as an island in the sun.

Night falls, but yet rides Sigurd, and hath no thought of rest,
For he longs to climb that rock-world and behold the earth at its
    best;
But now mid the maze of the foot-hills he seeth the light no more,
And the stars are lovely and gleaming on the lightless heavenly floor.
So up and up he wendeth till the night is wearing thin;
And he rideth a rift of the mountain, and all is dark therein,
Till the stars are dimmed by dawning and the wakening world is
    cold;
Then afar in the upper rock-wall a breach doth he behold,
And a flood of light poured inward the doubtful dawning blinds:
So swift he rideth thither and the mouth of the breach he finds,
And sitteth awhile on Greyfell on the marvellous thing to gaze:
For lo, the side of Hindfell enwrapped by the fervent blaze,
And nought 'twixt earth and heaven save a world of flickering flame,
And a hurrying shifting tangle, where the dark rents went and came.

Great groweth the heart of Sigurd with uttermost desire,
And he crieth kind to Greyfell, and they hasten up, and nigher,
Till he draweth rein in the dawning on the face of Hindfell's steep:

But who shall heed the dawning where the tongues of that wildfire
    leap?
For they weave a wavering wall, that driveth over the heaven
The wind that is born within it; nor ever aside is it driven
By the mightiest wind of the waste, and the rain-flood amidst it is
    nought;
And no wayfarer's door and no window the hand of its builder hath
    wrought.
But thereon is the Volsung smiling as its breath uplifteth his hair,
And his eyes shine bright with its image, and his mail gleams white
    and fair,
And his war-helm pictures the heavens and the waning stars behind:
But his neck is Greyfell stretching to snuff at the flame-wall blind,
And his cloudy flank upheaveth, and tinkleth the knitted mail,
And the gold of the uttermost waters is waxen wan and pale.

Now Sigurd turns in his saddle, and the hilt of the Wrath he shifts,
And draws a girth the tighter; then the gathered reins he lifts,
And crieth aloud to Greyfell, and rides at the wildfire's heart;
But the white wall wavers before him and the flame-flood rusheth
    apart,
And high o'er his head it riseth, and wide and wild is its roar
As it beareth the mighty tidings to the very heavenly floor:
But he rideth through its roaring as the warrior rides the rye,
When it bows with the wind of the summer and the hid spears draw
    anigh;
The white flame licks his raiment and sweeps through Greyfell's
    mane,
And bathes both hands of Sigurd and the hilts of Fafnir's bane,
And winds about his war-helm and mingles with his hair,
But nought his raiment dusketh or dims his glittering gear;
Then it fails and fades and darkens till all seems left behind,
And dawn and the blaze is swallowed in mid-mirk stark and blind.

But forth a little further and a little further on
And all is calm about him, and he sees the scorched earth wan
Beneath a glimmering twilight, and he turns his conquering eyes,
And a ring of pale slaked ashes on the side of Hindfell lies;

And the world of the waste is beyond it; and all is hushed and grey,
And the new-risen moon is a-paleing, and the stars grow faint with
    day.
Then Sigurd looked before him and a Shield-burg there he saw,
A wall of the tiles of Odin wrought clear without a flaw,
The gold by the silver gleaming, and the ruddy by the white;
And the blazonings of their glory were done upon them bright,
As of dear things wrought for the war-lords new come to Odin's hall.
Piled high aloft to the heavens uprose that battle-wall,
And far o'er the topmost shield-rim for a banner of fame there hung
A glorious golden buckler; and against the staff it rung
As the earliest wind of dawning uprose on Hindfell's face
And the light from the yellowing east beamed soft on the shielded
    place.

But the Wrath cried out in answer as Sigurd leapt adown
To the wasted soil of the desert by that rampart of renown;
He looked but little beneath it, and the dwelling of God it seemed,
As against its gleaming silence the eager Sigurd gleamed:
He draweth not sword from scabbard, as the wall he wendeth around,
And it is but the wind and Sigurd that wakeneth any sound:
But, lo, to the gate he cometh, and the doors are open wide,
And no warder the way withstandeth, and no earls by the threshold
    abide;
So he stands awhile and marvels; then the baleful light of the Wrath
Gleams bare in his ready hand as he wendeth the inward path:
For he doubteth some guile of the gods, or perchance some dwarf-
    king's snare,
Or a mock of the giant people that shall fade in the morning air:
But he getteth him in and gazeth; and a wall doth he behold,
And the ruddy set by the white, and the silver by the gold;
But within the garth that it girdeth no work of man is set,
But the utmost head of Hindfell ariseth higher yet;
And below in the very midmost is a giant-fashioned mound,
Piled high as the rims of the Shield-burg above the level ground;
And there, on that mound of the giants, o'er the wilderness forlorn,
A pale grey image lieth, and gleameth in the morn.

So there was Sigurd alone; and he went from the shielded door,
And aloft in the desert of wonder the Light of the Branstock he bore;
And he set his face to the earth-mound, and beheld the image wan,
And the dawn was growing about it; and, lo, the shape of a man
Set forth to the eyeless desert on the tower-top of the world,
High over the cloud-wrought castle whence the windy bolts are
    hurled.

Now he comes to the mound and climbs it, and will see if the man
    be dead;
Some king of the days forgotten laid there with crownèd head,
Or the frame of a god, it may be, that in heaven hath changed his life,
Or some glorious heart belovèd, God-rapt from the earthly strife:
Now over the body he standeth, and seeth it shapen fair,
And clad from head to foot-sole in pale grey-glittering gear,
In a hauberk wrought as straitly as though to the flesh it were grown:
But a great helm hideth the head and is girt with a glittering crown.

So thereby he stoopeth and kneeleth, for he deems it were good
    indeed
If the breath of life abide there and the speech to help at need;
And as sweet as the summer wind from a garden under the sun
Cometh forth on the topmost Hindfell the breath of that sleeping-
    one.
Then he saith he will look on the face, if it bear him love or hate,
Or the bonds for his life's constraining, or the sundering doom of
    fate.
So he draweth the helm from the head, and, lo, the brow snow-white,
And the smooth unfurrowed cheeks, and the wise lips breathing
    light;
And the face of a woman it is, and the fairest that ever was born,
Shown forth to the empty heavens and the desert world forlorn:
But he looketh, and loveth her sore, and he longeth her spirit to
    move,
And awaken her heart to the world, that she may behold him and
    love.
And he toucheth her breast and her hands, and he loveth her passing
    sore;

And he saith: "Awake! I am Sigurd"; but she moveth never the
    more.

Then he looked on his bare bright blade, and he said: "Thou—
    what wilt thou do?
For indeed as I came by the war-garth thy voice of desire I knew."
Bright burnt the pale blue edges for the sunrise drew anear,
And the rims of the Shield-burg glittered, and the east was exceed-
    ing clear:
So the eager edges he setteth to the dwarf-wrought battle-coat
Where the hammered ring-knit collar constraineth the woman's
    throat;
But the sharp Wrath biteth and rendeth, and before it fail the rings,
And, lo, the gleam of the linen, and the light of golden things:
Then he driveth the blue steel onward, and through the skirt, and
    out,
Till nought but the rippling linen is wrapping her about;
Then he deems her breath comes quicker and her breast begins to
    heave,
So he turns about the War-Flame and rends down either sleeve,
Till her arms lie white in her raiment, and a river of sun-bright hair
Flows free o'er bosom and shoulder and floods the desert bare.

Then a flush cometh over her visage and a sigh up-heaveth her
    breast,
And her eyelids quiver and open, and she wakeneth into rest;
Wide-eyed on the dawning she gazeth, too glad to change or smile,
And but little moveth her body, nor speaketh she yet for a while;
And yet kneels Sigurd moveless her wakening speech to heed,
While soft the waves of the daylight o'er the starless heavens speed,
And the gleaming rims of the Shield-burg yet bright and brighter
    grow,
And the thin moon hangeth her horns dead-white in the golden glow.
Then she turned and gazed on Sigurd, and her eyes met the Vol-
    sung's eyes.
And mighty and measureless now did the tide of his love arise,
For their longing had met and mingled, and he knew of her heart
    that she loved,

As she spake unto nothing but him and her lips with the speech-
flood moved:

"O, what is the thing so mighty that my weary sleep hath torn,
And rent the fallow bondage, and the wan woe over-worn?"

He said: "The hand of Sigurd and the Sword of Sigmund's son,
And the heart that the Volsungs fashioned this deed for thee have
done."

But she said: "Where then is Odin that laid me here alow?
Long lasteth the grief of the world, and man-folk's tangled woe!"

"He dwelleth above," said Sigurd, "but I on the earth abide,
And I came from the Glittering Heath the waves of thy fire to ride."

But therewith the sun rose upward and lightened all the earth,
And the light flashed up to the heavens from the rims of the glorious
girth;
But they twain arose together, and with both her palms outspread,
And bathed in the light returning, she cried aloud and said:

"All hail O Day and thy Sons, and thy kin of the coloured things!
Hail, following Night, and thy Daughter that leadeth thy wavering
wings!
Look down with unangry eyes on us today alive,
And give us the hearts victorious, and the gain for which we strive!
All hail, ye Lords of God-home, and ye Queens of the House of
Gold!
Hail thou dear Earth that bearest, and thou Wealth of field and fold!
Give us, your noble children, the glory of wisdom and speech,
And the hearts and the hands of healing, and the mouths and hands
that teach!"
Then they turned and were knit together; and oft and o'er again
They craved, and kissed rejoicing, and their hearts were full and fain.

Then Sigurd looketh upon her, and the words from his heart arise:
"Thou art the fairest of earth, and the wisest of the wise;
O who art thou that lovest? I am Sigurd, e'en as I told;
I have slain the foe of the gods, and gotten the Ancient Gold;

And great were the gain of thy love, and the gift of mine earthly days,
If we twain should never sunder as we wend on the changing ways.
O who art thou that lovest, thou fairest of all things born?
And what meaneth thy sleep and thy slumber in the wilderness
  forlorn?"

She said: "I am she that loveth: I was born of the earthly folk,
But of old Allfather took me from the kings and their wedding yoke:
And he called me the Victory-Wafter, and I went and came as he
  would,
And I chose the slain for his war-host, and the days were glorious
  and good,
Till the thoughts of my heart overcame me, and the pride of my
  wisdom and speech,
And I scorned the earth-folk's Framer and the Lord of the world I
  must teach:
For the death-doomed I caught from the sword, and the fated life I
  slew,
And I deemed that my deeds were goodly, and that long I should do
  and undo.
But Allfather came against me and the god in his wrath arose;
And he cried: 'Thou hast thought in thy folly that the gods have
  friends and foes,
That they wake, and the world wends onward, that they sleep, and
  the world slips back,
That they laugh, and the world's weal waxeth, that they frown and
  fashion the wrack:
Thou hast cast up the curse against me; it shall fall aback on thine
  head;
Go back to the sons of repentance, with the children of sorrow wed!
For the gods are great unholpen, and their grief is seldom seen,
And the wrong that they will and must be is soon as it hath not been.'

"Yet I thought: 'Shall I wed in the world, shall I gather grief on the
  earth?
Then the fearless heart shall I wed, and bring the best to birth,
And fashion such tales for the telling, that Earth shall be holpen at
  least,

If the gods think scorn of its fairness, as they sit at the changeless
   feast.'

"Then somewhat smiled Allfather; and he spake: 'So let it be!
The doom thereof abideth; the doom of me and thee.
Yet long shall the time pass over ere thy waking-day be born:
Fare forth, and forget and be weary 'neath the Sting of the Sleepful
   Thorn!'

"So I came to the head of Hindfell and the ruddy shields and white,
And the wall of the wildfire wavering around the isle of night;
And there the Sleep-thorn pierced me, and the slumber on me fell,
And the night of nameless sorrows that hath no tale to tell.
Now I am she that loveth; and the day is nigh at hand
When I, who have ridden the sea-realm and the regions of the land,
And dwelt in the measureless mountains and the forge of stormy
   days,
Shall dwell in the house of my fathers and the land of the people's
   praise;
And there shall hand meet hand, and heart by heart shall beat,
And the lying-down shall be joyous, and the morn's uprising sweet.
Lo now, I look on thine heart and behold of thine inmost will,
That thou of the days wouldst hearken that our portion shall fulfil;
But O, be wise of man-folk, and the hope of thine heart refrain!
As oft in the battle's beginning ye vex the steed with the rein,
Lest at last in its latter ending, when the sword hath hushed the
   horn,
His limbs should be weary and fail, and his might be over-worn.
O be wise, lest thy love constrain me, and my vision wax o'er-clear,
And thou ask of the thing that thou shouldst not, and the thing that
   thou wouldst not hear.

"Know thou, most mighty of men, that the Norns shall order all,
And yet without thine helping shall no whit of their will befall;
Be wise! 'tis a marvel of words, and a mock for the fool and the
   blind;
But I saw it writ in the heavens, and its fashioning there did I find:
And the night of the Norns and their slumber, and the tide when
   the world runs back,

And the way of the sun is tangled, it is wrought of the dastard's lack.
But the day when the fair earth blossoms, and the sun is bright above,
Of the daring deeds is it fashioned and the eager hearts of love.

"Be wise, and cherish thine hope in the freshness of the days,
And scatter its seed from thine hand in the field of the people's praise;
Then fair shall it fall in the furrow,and some the earth shall speed,
And the sons of men shall marvel at the blossom of the deed:
But some the earth shall speed not; nay rather, the wind of the heaven
Shall waft it away from thy longing—and a gift to the gods hast thou given,
And a tree for the roof and the wall in the house of the hope that shall be,
Thou it seemeth our very sorrow, and the grief of thee and me.

"Strive not with the fools of man-folk: for belike thou shalt overcome;
And what then is the gain of thine hunting when thou bearest the quarry home?
Or else shall the fool overcome thee, and what deed thereof shall grow?
Nay, strive with the wise man rather, and increase thy woe and his woe;
Yet thereof a gain hast thou gotten; and the half of thine heart hast thou won
If thou mayst prevail against him, and his deeds are the deeds thou hast done:
Yea, and if thou fall before him, in him shalt thou live again,
And thy deeds in his hand shall blossom, and his heart of thine heart shall be fain.

"When thou hearest the fool rejoicing, and he saith, 'It is over and past,
And the wrong was better than right, and hate turns into love at the last,
And we strove for nothing at all, and the gods are fallen asleep;

For so good is the world a growing that the evil good shall reap:'
Then loosen thy sword in the scabbard and settle the helm on thine
    head,
For men betrayed are mighty, and great are the wrongfully dead.

"Wilt thou do the deed and repent it? thou hadst better never been
    born:
Wilt thou do the deed and exalt it? then thy fame shall be outworn:
Thou shalt do the deed and abide it, and sit on thy throne on high,
And look on today and tomorrow as those that never die.

"Love thou the gods—and withstand them, lest thy fame should
    fail in the end,
And thou be but their thrall and their bondsman, who wert born
    for their very friend:
For few things from the gods are hidden, and the hearts of men they
    know,
And how that none rejoiceth to quail and crouch alow.

"I have spoken the words, belovèd, to thy matchless glory and
    worth;
But thy heart to my heart hath been speaking, though my tongue
    hath set it forth:
For I am she that loveth, and I know what thou wouldst teach
From the heart of thine unlearned wisdom, and I needs must speak
    thy speech."

Then words were weary and silent, but oft and o'er again
They craved and kissed rejoicing, and their hearts were full and fain.

Then spake the Son of Sigmund: "Fairest, and most of worth,
Hast thou seen the ways of man-folk and the regions of the earth?
Then speak yet more of wisdom; for most meet meseems it is
That my soul to thy soul be shapen, and that I should know thy
    bliss."

So she took his right hand meekly, nor any word would say,
Not e'en of love or praising, his longing to delay;
And they sat on the side of Hindfell, and their fain eyes looked and
    loved,

As she told of the hidden matters whereby the world is moved:
And she told of the framing of all things, and the houses of the
heaven;
And she told of the star-worlds' courses, and how the winds be
driven;
And she told of the Norns and their names, and the fate that abideth
the earth;
And she told of the ways of king-folk in their anger and their mirth;
And she spake of the love of women, and told of the flame that burns,
And the fall of mighty houses, and the friend that falters and turns,
And the lurking blinded vengeance, and the wrong that amendeth
wrong,
And the hand that repenteth its stroke, and the grief that endureth
for long;
And how man shall bear and forbear, and be master of all that is;
And how man shall measure it all, the wrath, and the grief, and the
bliss.

"I saw the body of Wisdom, and of shifting guise was she wrought,
And I stretched out my hands to hold her, and a mote of the dust
they caught;
And I prayed her to come for my teaching, and she came in the
midnight dream—
And I woke and might not remember, nor betwixt her tangle deem:
She spake, and how might I hearken; I heard, and how might I
know;
I knew, and how might I fashion, or her hidden glory show?
All things I have told thee of Wisdom are but fleeting images .
Of her hosts that abide in the Heavens, and her light that Allfather
sees:
Yet wise is the sower that sows, and wise is the reaper that reaps,
And wise is the smith in his smiting, and wise is the warder that
keeps:
And wise shalt thou be to deliver, and I shall be wise to desire;
—And lo, the tale that is told, and the sword and the wakening fire!
Lo now, I am she that loveth, and hark how Greyfell neighs,
And Fafnir's Bed is gleaming, and green go the downward ways,

The road to the children of men and the deeds that thou shalt do
In the joy of thy life-days' morning, when thine hope is fashioned
    anew.
Come now, O Bane of the Serpent, for now is the high-noon come,
And the sun hangeth over Hindfell and looks on the earth-folk's
    home;
But the soul is so great within thee, and so glorious are thine eyes,
And me so love constraineth, and mine heart that was called the
    wise,
That we twain may see men's dwellings and the house where we
    shall dwell,
And the place of our life's beginning, where the tale shall be to tell."

So they climb the burg of Hindfell, and hand in hand they fare,
Till all about and above them is nought but the sunlit air,
And there close they cling together rejoicing in their mirth;
For far away beneath them lie the kingdoms of the earth,
And the garths of men-folk's dwellings and the streams that water
    them,
And the rich and plenteous acres, and the silver ocean's hem,
And the woodland wastes and the mountains, and all that holdeth all;
The house and the ship and the island, the loom and the mine and
    the stall,
The beds of bane and healing, the crafts that slay and save,
The temple of God and the Doom-ring, the cradle and the grave.

Then spake the Victory-Wafter: "O King of the Earthly Age,
As a god thou beholdest the treasure and the joy of thine heritage,
And where on the wings of his hope is the spirit of Sigurd borne?
Yet I bid thee hover awhile as a lark alow on the corn;
Yet I bid thee look on the land 'twixt the wood and the silver sea
In the bight of the swirling river, and the house that cherished me!
There dwelleth mine earthly sister and the king that she hath wed;
There morn by morn aforetime I woke on the golden bed;
There eve by eve I tarried mid the speech and the lays of kings;
There noon by noon I wandered and plucked the blossoming things;
The little land of Lymdale by the swirling river's side,
Where Brynhild once was I called in the days ere my father died;

The little land of Lymdale 'twixt the woodland and the sea,
Where on thee mine eyes shall brighten and thine eyes shall beam
on me."

"I shall seek thee there," said Sigurd, "when the day-spring is
begun,
Ere we wend the world together in the season of the sun."

"I shall bide thee there," said Brynhild, "till the fullness of the days,
And the time for the glory appointed, and the springing-tide of
praise."

From his hand then draweth Sigurd Andvari's ancient Gold;
There is nought but the sky above them as the ring together they
hold,
The shapen ancient token, that hath no change nor end,
No change, and no beginning, no flaw for God to mend:
Then Sigurd cries: "O Brynhild, now hearken while I swear,
That the sun shall die in the heavens and the day no more be fair,
If I seek not love in Lymdale and the house that fostered thee,
And the land where thou awakedst 'twixt the woodland and the sea!"

And she cried: "O Sigurd, Sigurd, now hearken while I swear
That the day shall die for ever and the sun to blackness wear,
Ere I forget thee, Sigurd, as I lie 'twixt wood and sea
In the little land of Lymdale and the house that fostered me!"

Then he set the ring on her finger and once, if ne'er again,
They kissed and clung together, and their hearts were full and fain.

So the day grew old about them and the joy of their desire,
And eve and the sunset came, and faint grew the sunset fire,
And the shadowless death of the day was sweet in the golden tide;
But the stars shone forth on the world, and the twilight changed and
died;
And sure if the first of man-folk had been born to that starry night,
And had heard no tale of the sunrise, he had never longed for the
light:
But Earth longed amidst her slumber, as 'neath the night she lay,
And fresh and all abundant abode the deeds of Day.

ICELANDIC SAGAS

The Burning of Bergthorsknoll

Njal's Saga *was written by an unknown author in about 1280 and is considered the greatest of the Icelandic prose sagas. The action, which takes place about 300 years before the saga was written, spans about fifty years and describes the relationships and blood feuds in which Njal Thorgeirsson and his family become enmeshed. The tragic climax, involving Njal, his family and retainers, is reprinted here. (Before the saga ends, Kari takes full and bloody vengeance for the burning of Bergthorsknoll.)*

Flosi was saying to his men, "We shall now ride to Bergthorsknoll, to reach there by nightfall."

When they arrived, they rode into a hollow in the knoll, where they tethered their horses and waited late into the night.

"Now we shall walk slowly up to the house," said Flosi, "keeping close together, and see what they do."

Njal was standing outside with his sons and Kari and all the servants ranged in front of the house. They were nearly thirty in all.

Flosi halted and said, "We shall note carefully what action they take, for I suspect that we shall never get the better of them if they stay out of doors."

"This would turn out a sorry trip if we did not dare to make an attack on them," said Grani.

"We shall certainly attack them," said Flosi, "even though they remain outside. But we would have to pay a heavy price, and not many would live to tell the tale, whichever side wins."

Njal said to his men, "How many do you think they are?"

"They are a tightly-knit force," said Skarp-Hedin, "and strong in numbers, too; but they suspect that they will have a hard task to overcome us, and that is why they have halted."

"I do not think so," said Njal. "I want everyone to go inside, for they found it hard to overcome Gunnar of Hlidarend, even though he was only one against many. This house is just as strongly built as his was, and they will never be able to overcome us."

"That is the wrong way to look at it," said Skarp-Hedin. "The men who attacked Gunnar were chieftains of such character that they would have preferred to turn back rather than burn him in his house. But these people will not hesitate to use fire if they cannot overcome us in any other way, for they will resort to any means to destroy us. They will assume, and quite rightly, that it will cost them their lives if we escape. And I for one am reluctant to be suffocated like a fox in its den."

Njal said, "Now you are going to override my advice and show me disrespect, my sons—and not for the first time. But when you were younger you did not do so, and things went better for you then."

"Let us do as our father wishes," said Helgi. "That will be best for all of us."

"I am not so sure of that," said Skarp-Hedin, "for he is a doomed man now. But still I do not mind pleasing my father by burning in the house with him, for I am not afraid of dying."

To Kari he said, "Let us all keep close together, brother-in-law, so that we do not get separated."

"That is what I had intended," said Kari, "but if fate wills it otherwise, then it shall be so and nothing can be done about it."

"Then you avenge us," said Skarp-Hedin. "And we shall avenge you if we survive."

Kari agreed. Then they all went inside and stood guard at the doors.

Flosi said, "Now they are doomed, for they have gone indoors. We shall advance on the house at once and form up in strength round the doors to make sure that not one of them escapes, neither Kari nor the Njalssons; for otherwise it will cost us our lives."

Flosi and his men came up to the house and surrounded the whole building, in case there might be a secret door somewhere.

Flosi himself and his own men went up to the front of the house. Hroald Ozurarson rushed at Skarp-Hedin and lunged at him with a spear; Skarp-Hedin hacked the spear-shaft in two and sprang at him, swinging his axe. The axe fell on Hroald's shield and dashed it against him; the upper horn of the axe caught him full in the face, and he fell back dead at once.

Kari said, "There is no escaping you, Skarp-Hedin; you are the bravest of us all."

"I don't know about that," said Skarp-Hedin, and he was seen to draw back his lips in a grin.

Kari and Grim and Helgi lunged often with their spears and wounded many men, and Flosi and the attackers were kept at bay.

Flosi said, "We have suffered heavy losses amongst our men, several wounded and one dead, the one we would least have wanted to lose. It is obvious that we cannot defeat them with weapons; and there are many here who are showing less fight than they said they would. Now we must resort to another plan. There are only two courses open to us, neither of them good: we must either abandon the attack, which would cost us our own lives, or we must set fire to the house and burn them to death, which is a grave responsibility before God, since we are Christian men ourselves. But that is what we must do."

Then they kindled a fire and made a great blaze in front of the doors.

Skarp-Hedin said, "So you're making a fire now, lads! Are you thinking of doing some cooking?"

"Yes," said Grani, "and you won't need it any hotter for roasting."

"So this is your way," said Skarp-Hedin, "of repaying me for avenging your father, the only way you know; you value more highly the obligation that has less claim on you."

The women threw whey on the flames and doused the fire.

Kol Thorsteinsson said to Flosi, "I have an idea. I have noticed that there is a loft above the cross-beams of the main room. That is where we should start a fire, and we can use the heap of chickweed behind the house as kindling."

They brought the chickweed up and set fire to it, and before those inside knew what was happening, the ceiling of the room was ablaze from end to end. Flosi's men also lit huge fires in front of all the doors. At this, the womenfolk began to panic.

Njal said to them, "Be of good heart and speak no words of fear, for this is just a passing storm and it will be long before another like it comes. Put your faith in the mercy of God, for He will not let us burn both in this world and the next."

Such were the words of comfort he brought them, and others more rousing than these.

Now the whole house began to blaze. Njal went to the door and said, "Is Flosi near enough to hear my words?"

Flosi said that he could hear him.

Njal said, "Would you consider making an agreement with my sons, or letting anyone leave the house?"

"I will make no terms with your sons," replied Flosi. "We shall settle matters now, once and for all, and we are not leaving until every one of them is dead. But I shall allow the women and children and servants to come out."

Njal went back inside the house and said to his household, "All those with permission to go out must do so now. Leave the house now, Thorhalla Asgrim's-daughter, and take with you all those who are allowed to go."

Thorhalla said, "This is not the parting from Helgi I had ever expected; but I shall urge my father and my brothers to avenge the killings that are committed here."

"You will do well," said Njal, "for you are a good woman."

She went out, taking many people with her.

Astrid of Djupriverbank said to Helgi, "Come out with me. I will drape you in a woman's cloak and put a head-scarf over you."

Helgi protested at first, but finally yielded to their entreaties. Astrid wrapped a scarf round his head, and Thorhild laid the cloak over his shoulders. Then he walked out between them, along with his sisters Thorgerd and Helga and several other people.

When Helgi came outside, Flosi said, "That's a very tall and broad-shouldered woman—seize her." When Helgi heard this, he threw off the cloak; he was carrying a sword under his arm, and now he struck out at one of the men, slicing off the bottom of the shield and severing his leg. Then Flosi came up and struck at Helgi's neck, cutting off his head with one blow.

Flosi went up to the door and called Njal and Bergthora over to speak to him; when they came, he said, "I want to offer you leave to come out, for you do not deserve to burn."

"I have no wish to go outside," said Njal, "for I am an old man now and ill-equipped to avenge my sons; and I do not want to live in shame."

Flosi said to Bergthora, "You come out, Bergthora, for under no circumstances do I want you to burn."

Bergthora replied, "I was given to Njal in marriage when young, and I have promised him that we would share the same fate."

Then they both went back inside.

"What shall we do now?" asked Bergthora.

"Let us go to our bed," said Njal, "and lie down."

Then Bergthora said to little Thord, Kari's son, "You are to be taken out. You are not to burn."

The boy replied, "But that's not what you promised, grandmother. You said that we would never be parted; and so it shall be, for I would much prefer to die beside you both."

She carried the boy to the bed. Njal said to his steward, "Take note where we lay ourselves down and how we dispose ourselves, for I shall not move from here however much the smoke or flames distress me. Then you can know where to look for our remains."

The steward said he would.

An ox had recently been slaughtered, and the hide was lying nearby. Njal told the steward to spread the hide over them, and he promised to do so.

Njal and Bergthora lay down on the bed and put the boy between them. Then they crossed themselves and the boy, and commended their souls to God. These were the last words they were heard to speak. The steward took the hide and spread it over them, and then left the house. Ketil of Mork seized his arm and dragged him clear, and questioned him closely about his father-in-law Njal; the steward told him everything that had happened.

Ketil said, "Great sorrow has been allotted us, that we should all share such terrible ill luck."

Skarp-Hedin had seen his father go to lie down and the preparations he had made.

"Father is going early to bed," he said. "And that is only natural, for he is an old man."

Skarp-Hedin and Kari and Grim snatched up the blazing brands as soon as they fell and hurled them at those outside. After a while the attackers threw spears at them, which they caught in flight and hurled back. Flosi told his men to stop—"for we shall always come off worse in every exchange of blows with them. You would be wiser to wait until the fire conquers them."

They did as he said.

Now the main beams fell down from the roof.

Skarp-Hedin said, "My father must be dead now, and not a groan or a cough has been heard from him."

They went over to the far end of the room. One end of the cross-beam had fallen there, and it was almost burned through in the middle. Kari said to Skarp-Hedin, "Use that beam to jump out, and I shall give you a hand and come right behind you. That way we can both escape, for the smoke is all drifting in this direction."

"You go first," said Skarp-Hedin, "and I shall follow you at once."

"That is not wise," said Kari, "for I can go out some other way if this does not succeed."

"No," said Skarp-Hedin, "you go out first, and I shall be right on your heels."

Kari said, "It is every man's instinct to try to save his own life, and I shall do so now. But this parting will mean that we shall never see each other again. Once I jump out of the flames, I shall not feel inclined to run back into the fire to you; and then each of us must go his own way."

"I shall laugh, brother-in-law, if you escape," said Skarp-Hedin, "for you will avenge us all."

Kari took hold of a blazing brand and ran up the sloping cross-beam; he hurled the brand down from the wall at those who were in his way outside, and they scattered. Kari's clothes and hair were on fire by now, as he threw himself down off the wall and dodged away in the thick of the smoke.

Someone said, "Was that a man jumping down from the roof?"

"Far from it," said someone else. "It was Skarp-Hedin throwing another brand at us."

After that, no one suspected anything.

Kari ran until he reached a small stream; he threw himself into it and extinguished his blazing clothes. From there he ran under cover of the smoke until he reached a hollow, where he rested. It has ever since been called Kari's Hollow.

Meanwhile, Skarp-Hedin had jumped on to the cross-beam directly behind Kari, but when he reached that part of the beam which was most severely burned, it broke beneath him. Skarp-Hedin managed to land on his feet and made a second attempt at once, by taking a run at the wall. But the roof-beam came down on him and he toppled back once more.

"It is clear now what is to be," said Skarp-Hedin, and made his way along the side wall.

Gunnar Lambason jumped up on to the wall and saw Skarp-Hedin. "Are you crying now, Skarp-Hedin?" he asked.

"No," said Skarp-Hedin, "but it is true that my eyes are smarting. Am I right in thinking that you are laughing?"

"I certainly am," said Gunnar, "and for the first time since you killed Thrain."

"Then here is something to remind you of it," said Skarp-Hedin.

He took from his purse the jaw-tooth he had hacked out of Thrain, and hurled it straight at Gunnar's eye; the eye was gouged from its socket on to the cheek and Gunnar toppled off the wall.

Skarp-Hedin went over to his brother Grim. They joined hands and stamped on the fire. But when they reached the middle of the room, Grim fell dead. Skarp-Hedin went to the gable-end of the house; then, with a great crash, the whole roof fell in. Skarp-Hedin was pinned between roof and gable, and could not move an inch.

Flosi and his men stayed by the blaze until broad daylight. Then a man came riding towards them. Flosi asked him his name, and he replied that he was Geirmund, a kinsman of the Sigfussons.

"You have taken drastic action here," said Geirmund.

"People will call it a drastic action, and an evil one too," said Flosi. "But nothing can be done about it now."

143

Geirmund asked, "How many people of note have perished here?"

Flosi said, "Among the dead here are Njal and Bergthora, their sons Helgi, Grim, and Skarp-Hedin, Kari Solmundarson and his son Thord, and Thord Freedman. We are not sure about those others who are less well known to us."

"You have listed amongst the dead a man who to my certain knowledge has escaped," said Geirmund, "for I talked to him only this morning."

"Who is that?" asked Flosi.

"Kari Solmundarson," said Geirmund. "My neighbour Bard and I met him with his hair burnt off and his clothes badly charred, and Bard lent him a horse."

"Had he any weapons with him?" asked Flosi.

"He was carrying the sword 'Life-Taker'," said Geirmund, "and one of its edges was blue and discoloured. We said that the metal must have softened, but Kari replied that he would soon harden it again in the blood of the Sigfussons and the other Burners."

"What did he tell you of Skarp-Hedin and Grim?" asked Flosi.

"He said that they were both alive when he left them," replied Geirmund, "but that they must be dead by now."

144

The Burning of Bergthorsknoll

"What you have told us," said Flosi, "gives us little hope of being left in peace; for the man who has escaped is the one who comes nearest to being the equal of Gunnar of Hlidarend in everything. You had better realise, you Sigfussons and all the rest of our men, that this Burning will have such consequences that many of us will lie lifeless and others will forfeit all their wealth.

"I suspect that none of you Sigfussons will now dare to stay on at your farms, and I certainly cannot blame you for that. So I invite you all to stay with me in the east, and let us all stand or fall together." They thanked him.

Then Modolf Ketilsson said:

> One pillar of Njal's house
> Was not destroyed in the fire
> That devoured all the others,
> The fire the bold Sigfussons lit.
> Now at last, Njal,
> Brave Hoskuld's death is avenged;
> Fire swept through the building,
> Bright flames blossomed in the house.

"We must find other things to boast about than burning Njal to death," said Flosi, "for there is no achievement in that."

Flosi climbed on to the gable wall with Glum Hildisson and several others.

"Is Skarp-Hedin dead yet, do you think?" asked Glum.

The others said that he must have been dead for some time.

The fire still burned fitfully, flaring up and sinking again. Then they heard this verse being uttered somewhere down amongst the flames:

> The woman will find it hard
> To stop the cloudburst of her tears
> At this outcome
> Of the warrior's last battle....

Grani Gunnarsson said, "Was Skarp-Hedin alive or dead when he spoke that verse?"

"I shall not make any guesses about that," replied Flosi.

Gestumblindi's Riddles

There was a great man in Reithgotaland called Gestumblindi, who was not on good terms with King Heithrek.

In the King's retinue there were seven men whose duty it was to decide all the disputes that arose in that country.

King Heithrek worshipped Frey, and he used to give Frey the biggest boar he could find. They regarded it as so sacred that in all important cases they used to take the oath on its bristles. It was the custom to sacrifice this boar at the "sacrifice of the herd". On Yule Eve the "boar of the herd" was led into the hall before the King. Then men laid their hands on his bristles and made solemn vows. King Heithrek himself made a vow that however deeply a man should have wronged him, if he came into his power he should not be deprived of the chance of receiving a trial by the King's judges; but he should get off scot free if he could propound riddles which the King could not answer. But when people tried to ask the King riddles, not one was put to him which he could not solve.

The King sent a message to Gestumblindi bidding him come to him on an appointed day; otherwise the King said that he would send to fetch him. Neither alternative pleased Gestumblindi, because he knew himself to be no match for the King in a contest of words; neither did he think he had much to hope from a trial before the judges, for his offences were many. On the other hand, he knew that if the King had to send men to bring him it would cost him his life. Then he proceeded to sacrifice to Odin and to ask his help, promising him great offerings.

One evening a stranger visited Gestumblindi, and said that he also was called Gestumblindi. They were so much alike that neither could be distinguished from the other. They exchanged clothes, and the landowner went into hiding, and everyone thought the stranger was the landowner himself.

This man went to vist the King and greeted him. The King looked at him and was silent.

Gestumblindi said: "I am come, Sire, to make my peace with you."

"Will you stand trial by the judges?" asked the King.

"Are there no other means of escape?" asked Gestumblindi.

"If," replied the King, "you can ask me riddles which I cannot answer, you shall go free."

"I am not likely to be able to do that," replied Gestumblindi; "yet the alternative is severe."

"Do you prefer the trial?" asked the King.

"Nay," said he, "I would rather ask riddles."

"That is quite in order," said the King, "and much depends on the issue. If you can get the better of me you shall marry my daughter and none shall gainsay you. Yet I don't imagine you are very clever, and it has never yet happened that I have been unable to solve the riddles that have been put to me."

Then a chair was placed for Gestumblindi, and the people began to listen eagerly to the words of wisdom.

Gestumblindi began as follows:

I would that I had that which I had yesterday. Guess O King, what that was:—Exhauster of men, retarder of words, yet originator of speech. King Heithrek, read me this riddle!

Heithrek replied:

Your riddle is a good one, Gestumblindi. I have guessed it.— Give him some ale. That is what confounds many people's reason. Some are made garrulous by it, but some become confused in their speech.

Gestumblindi said:

I went from home, I made my way from home, I looked upon a road of roads. A road was beneath me, a road above and a road on every side. King Heithrek, read me this riddle!

Heithrek replied:

Your riddle is a good one, Gestumblindi. I have guessed it. You went over a bridge, and the course of the river was beneath it, and birds were flying over your head and on either side of you; that was their road; you saw a salmon in the river, and that was his road.

Gestumblindi said:

What was the drink that I had yesterday? It was neither wine nor water, mead nor ale, nor any kind of food; and yet I went away with my thirst quenched. King Heithrek, read me this riddle!

Heithrek replied:

Your riddle is a good one, Gestumblindi. I have guessed it. You lay in the shade and cooled your lips in dew. But if you are the Gestumblindi I took you for, you are a more intelligent man than I expected; for I had heard that your conversation showed no brains, yet now you are setting to work cleverly.

Gestumblindi said:

I expect that I shall soon come to grief; yet I should like you to listen a while longer.

Then he continued:

Who is that clanging one who traverses hard paths which he has trod before? He kisses very rapidly, has two mouths and walks on gold alone. King Heithrek, read me this riddle!

Heithrek replied:

Your riddle is a good one, Gestumblindi. I have guessed it. That is the goldsmith's hammer, with which gold is forged.

Gestumblindi said:

What is that huge one that passes over the earth, swallowing lakes and pools? He fears the wind, but he fears not man, and carries on hostilities against the sun. King Heithrek, read me this riddle!

Heithrek replied:

Your riddle is a good one, Gestumblindi. I have guessed it. That

148

is fog. One cannot see the sea because of it. Yet as soon as the wind blows, the fog lifts; but men can do nothing to it. Fog kills the sunshine. You have a cunning way of asking riddles and conundrums, whoever you are.

Gestumblindi said:

What is that huge one that controls many things and of which half faces towards Hell? It saves people's lives and grapples with the earth, if it has a trusty friend. King Heithrek, read me this riddle!

Heithrek replied:

Your riddle is a good one, Gestumblindi. I have guessed it. That is an anchor with its thick strong cable. It controls many a ship, and grips the earth with one of its flukes which is pointing towards Hell. It is a means of safety to many people. Greatly do I marvel at your readiness of speech and wisdom.

Gestumblindi said:

What is the marvel which I have seen outside Delling's doorway? —White fliers smiting the rock, and black fliers burying themselves in sand! King Heithrek, read me this riddle!

Heithrek replied:

Your riddle is a good one, Gestumblindi. I have guessed it. But now your riddles are growing trivial. That is hail and rain; for hail beats upon the street; whereas rain-drops fall into the sand and sink into the earth.

Gestumblindi said:

What is the marvel which I have seen outside Delling's doorway? I saw a black hog wallowing in mud, yet no bristles were standing up on his back. King Heithrek, read me this riddle!

Heithrek replied:

Your riddle is a good one, Gestumblindi. I have guessed it. That is a dung-beetle. But we have talked too long when dung-beetles come to exercise the wits of great men.

Gestumblindi said:

"It is best to put off misfortune"; and though there are some who overlook this truth, many will want to go on trying. I myself too

149

see now that I shall have to look out for every possible way of escape. What is the marvel that I have seen outside Delling's doorway? This creature has ten tongues, twenty eyes, forty feet, and walks with difficulty. King Heithrek, read me this riddle!

Heithrek replied:

Your riddle is a good one, Gestumblindi. I have guessed it. That was a sow with nine little pigs.

Then the King had the sow killed and they found they had killed with her nine little pigs, as Gestumblindi had said.
Then the King said:

I am beginning to suspect that I have to deal with a cleverer man than myself in this business; but I don't know who you can be.

Gestumblindi said:

I am such as you can see; and I am very anxious to save my life and be quit of this task.
    You must go on asking riddles, replied the King, till you have exhausted your stock, or else till I fail to solve them.

Gestumblindi said:

What is the marvel which I have seen outside Delling's doorway? It flies high, with a whistling sound like the whirring of an eagle. Hard it is to clutch, O King. King Heithrek, read me this riddle!

Heithrek replied:

Your riddle is a good one, Gestumblindi. I have guessed it. That is an arrow, said the King.

Gestumblindi said:

What is the marvel which I have seen outside Delling's doorway? It has eight feet and four eyes, and carries its knees higher than its body. King Heithrek, read me this riddle!

Heithrek replied:

I notice firstly that you have a long hood; and secondly that you look downwards more than most people, since you observe every creature of the earth.—That is a spider.

Gestumblindi said:

What is the marvel which I have seen outside Delling's doorway?

It shines upon men in every land; and yet wolves are always struggling for it. King Heithrek, read me this riddle!

Heithrek replied:

Your riddle is a good one, Gestumblindi. I have guessed it. It is the sun. It gives light to every land and shines down on all men. But the wolves are called Skoll and Hati. Those are the wolves who accompany the sun, one in front and one behind.

Gestumblindi said:

Who are the girls who fight without weapons around their lord? The dark red ones always protect him, and the fair ones seek to destroy him. King Heithrek, read me this riddle!

Heithrek replied:

Your riddle is a good one, Gestumblindi. I have guessed it. That is a game of chess. The pieces smite one another without weapons around the king, and the red assist him.

Gestumblindi said:

Who are the merry-maids who glide over the land for the father's pleasure? They bear a white shield in winter and a black one in summer. King Heithrek, read me this riddle!

Heithrek replied:

Your riddle is a good one, Gestumblindi. I have guessed it. Those are ptarmigan.

Gestumblindi said:

Who are the damsels who go sorrowing for their father's pleasure? These white-hooded ladies have shining hair, and are very wide awake in a gale. King Heithrek, read me this riddle!

Heithrek replied:

Your riddle is a good one, Gestumblindi. I have guessed it. Those are the billows, which are called Ægir's maidens.

Gestumblindi said:

Who are the brides who go about the reefs and trail along the firths? These white-hooded ladies have a hard bed and do not play much when the weather is calm. King Heithrek, read me this riddle.

Heithrek replied:

Your riddle is a good one, Gestumblindi. I have guessed it. Those again are Ægir's maidens; but your pleading has now become so weak that you will have to stand trial by the judges.

Gestumblindi said:

I am loath to do so; and yet I fear that it will very soon come to that. I saw a barrow-dweller pass by, a corpse sitting on a corpse, the blind riding on the blind towards the ocean-path. Lifeless was the steed. King Heithrek, read me this riddle!

Heithrek replied:

Your riddle is a good one, Gestumblindi. I have guessed it. It is that you came to a river; and an ice-floe was floating along the stream, and on it a dead horse way lying, and on the horse was a dead snake; and thus the blind was carrying the blind when they were all three together.

Gestumblindi said:

What is that beast which protects the Danes? Its back is bloody but it shields men, encounters spears and saves men's lives. Man fits his hand to its body. King Heithrek, read me this riddle!

Heithrek replied:

Your riddle is a good one, Gestumblindi. I have guessed it. That is a shield. It protects many people and often has a bloody back.

Gestumblindi said:

Four walking, four hanging, two pointing the way, two warding off the dogs, one, generally dirty, dangling behind! King Heithrek, read me this riddle!

Heithrek replied:

Your riddle is a good one, Gestumblindi. I have guessed it. That is a cow. She has four feet and four udders, two horns and two eyes, and the tail dangles behind.

Gestumblindi said:

Who is that solitary one who sleeps in the grey ash, and is made from stone only? This greedy one has neither father nor mother. There will he spend his life. King Heithrek, read me this riddle.

Heithrek replied:

Your riddle is a good one, Gestumblindi. I have guessed it. That is a spark struck by a flint and hidden in the hearth.

Gestumblindi said:

In summer time at sunset I saw the King's body-guard awake and very joyful. The nobles were drinking their ale in silence, but the ale-butts stood screaming. King Heithrek, read me this riddle!

Heithrek replied:

Your riddle is a good one, Gestumblindi. I have guessed it. That is a sow with her litter. When the little pigs are feeding, she squeals and they are silent.—But I can't imagine who you are who can compose such things so deftly out of such unpromising materials!

The King then silently made a sign that the door of the hall was to be closed.

Gestumblindi said:

I saw maidens like dust. Rocks were their beds. They were black and swarthy in the sunshine, but the darker it grew, the fairer they appeared. King Heithrek, read me this riddle!

Heithrek replied:

Your riddle is a good one, Gestumblindi. I have guessed it. They are pale embers on the hearth.

Gestumblindi said:

Who are those two who have ten feet, three eyes and one tail? King Heithrek, read me this riddle!

Heithrek replied:

You are hard up when you have to turn back to things of long ago to bring forward against me. That is Odin riding his horse Sleipnir. It had eight feet and Odin two, and they had three eyes —Sleipnir two and Odin one.

Gestumblindi said:

Tell me lastly, Heithrek, if you are wiser than any other prince,

what did Odin whisper in Balder's ear, before he was placed upon
the pyre?

The King replied:

I am sure it was something scandalous and cowardly and
thoroughly contemptible. You are the only person who knows
the words which you spoke, you evil and wretched creature.

Then the King drew Tyrfing, and struck at Gestumblindi; but
he changed himself into a falcon and flew out through the window
of the hall. And the sword struck the tail of the falcon; and that is
why it has had a short tail ever since, according to heathen superstition. But Odin had now become wroth with the King for striking
at him; and that night he was slain.

Thorstein Staff-Struck

There was a man living in Sunnudal by the name of Thorarin, an old man of ailing sight. He had been a stark red viking in his youth, and was no easy person to deal with now that he was old. He had an only son, whose name was Thorstein, a big man, strong and calm tempered, who worked so hard on his father's farm that the labour of three other men would not have stood them in better stead. Thorarin was on the poor side rather, yet he owned a fine assortment of weapons. They owned stud-horses too, this father and son, and selling horses was their main source of wealth, for never a one of them fell short in heart or performance.

There was a man called Thord, a housecarle of Bjarni of Hof, who had charge of Bjarni's riding-horses, for he had the name of one who really knew horses. Thord was a very overbearing sort of person; he also made many aware that he was a great man's servant, yet he was none the better man for that, and became no better liked. There were other men too staying at Bjarni's, one named Thorhall and the other Thorvald, great mouthers-over of everything they heard in the district. Thorstein and Thord arranged a horse-fight for the young stallions, and when they drove them at one another Thord's horse showed the less heart for biting. Once he saw his horse getting the worst of it, Thord struck Thorstein's horse a great blow over the nose, but Thorstein saw this and struck Thord's horse a far greater blow in return, whereupon Thord's horse took to its heels, and everyone raised a loud hullabaloo of derision. With that Thord struck at Thorstein with his horse-staff and caught him on the eyebrow, so that the skin hung down over the eye. Thorstein tore a strip from his shirt and tied up his forehead,

155

acting as though nothing in particular had happened. He asked them to keep this from his father, and there the matter ended for the time being. But Thorvald and Thorhall made it a subject of ill-natured jest and nicknamed him Thorstein Staff-struck.

That winter, a short while before Yule, the women rose for their work at Sunnudal. At the same time Thorstein rose; he carried in hay, and afterwards lay down on a bench. The next thing, in came old Thorarin his father, and asked who was lying there. Thorstein said it was he.

"Why are you afoot so early, son?" asked old Thorarin.

"There are few, I fancy, to leave any of the work to that I am responsible for here," replied Thorstein.

"There is nothing wrong with your head-bones, son?" asked old Thorarin.

"Not that I know of," said Thorstein.

"Have you nothing to tell me, son, of the horse-fighting that was held last summer? Were you not knocked dizzy as a dog there, kinsman?"

"I saw no gain in honour," Thorstein told him, "by reckoning it a blow rather than an accident."

"I would never have thought," said Thorarin, "that I could have a coward for a son."

"Speak only those words now, father," Thorstein advised him, "which you will not consider overmuch in the days to come."

"I will not speak about it as much as my heart would have me," Thorarin agreed.

At these words Thorstein rose to his feet, took his weapons, and left the house. He walked on till he came to the stables where Thord looked after Bjarni's horses, and where he happened then to be. He met Thord face to face and had this to say to him: "I want to know, friend Thord, whether it was by accident that I got a blow from you last summer at the horse-fight, or did it come about intentionally—in which case are you willing to pay reparation for it?"

"If you have two cheeks," retorted Thord, "then stick your tongue into each in turn, and, if you like, call it accident in one and intention in the other. And that is all the reparation you are going to get from me."

"Then rest assured," said Thorstein, "it may well be I shall not come claiming payment a second time."

Then Thorstein ran at Thord and dealt him his death-blow, after which he walked to the house at Hof and met a woman outside and said to her, "Tell Bjarni that an ox has gored his groom Thord, and that he will be waiting for him there till he comes, alongside the stables."

"Get off home, man," said she. "I will report this when I think fit."

So now Thorstein went off home and the woman went about her work. Bjarni rose during the morning, and when he was seated to his food he asked where was Thord, and men answered that he must have gone off to the horses. "All the same," said Bjarni, "I think he would have come home by now if he was all right." Then the woman whom Thorstein had met started on her piece. "True it is what they often say of us women, how there is little sense to draw on where we she-creatures are concerned. Thorstein Staff-struck came here only this morning to report that an ox had so gored Thord that he was past helping himself; but I lacked the heart to wake you at the time, and it has slipped my mind ever since."

Bjarni got up from table. He went to the stables where he found Thord dead, and later he was buried. Bjarni now set on foot a lawsuit and had Thorstein outlawed for the killing. But Thorstein went on living at home in Sunnudal and working for his father, and Bjarni let things lie just the same.

That autumn there were men sitting by the singeing-fires at Hof, while Bjarni lay out of doors by the kitchen wall and listened from there to their conversation. And now the brothers Thorhall and Thorvald began to hold forth. "We did not expect when first we came to live with Killer-Bjarni that we would be singeing lambs' heads here, while Thorstein, his forest outlaw, should singe the heads of wethers. It would be no bad thing to have been more sparing of his kinsmen in Bodvarsdal,* and his outlaw not sit as high

---

* There had been a bitter feud between the kinsmen Bjarni and Thorkel, who was supported by Thorstein's father, Thorarin. Although it was inconclusive, four men were killed on either side; the result of this was that Thorstein—filling the gap—became a man of greater influence at Sunnudal than would otherwise have been the case. The story of this feud comprises part of the saga of *The Vapnfjord Men*.

as he now in Sunnudal. But, 'E'en doers are done for once wounds befall them', and we have no idea when he proposes to wipe this stain from his honour."

Some man or other answered: "Such words are better swallowed than spoken, and it sounds as though trolls must have plucked at your tongues. For our part, we believe that he has no mind to take the food out of the mouth of Thorstein's blind father or those other poor creatures who live at Sunnudal. And I shall be very surprised if you are singeing lambs' heads here much oftener, or gloating over what happened in Bodvarsdal."

Men now went to their meal and afterwards to sleep, and Bjarni gave no indication of knowing what had been talked about. In the morning he routed out Thorhall and Thorvald, bidding them ride to Sunnudal and bring him Thorstein's head, divorced from his trunk, by breakfast-time, "For you appear to me the likeliest to remove this stain from my honour, considering I have not the courage for it myself." They now felt they had opened their mouths too wide for sure, but made off even so until they came to Sunnudal. Thorstein was standing in the doorway, whetting a short-sword, and when they came up he asked them what they were up to.

They said they had the job of looking for stray horses.

Then they had only a short way to look, Thorstein told them— "Here they are, by the home-fence."

"It is not certain," they said, "that we shall find them, unless you show us the way more clearly."

So Thorstein came outside, and when they had come down into the home-field Thorvald hoisted up his axe and ran at him, but Thorstein gave him such a shove with his arm that he fell headlong forward, and Thorstein drove the short-sword through him. Then Thorhall would have attacked him, but he too went the same road as Thorvald. Thorstein then bound them both on horseback, fixed the reins on the horses' necks, got the whole outfit headed in the right direction, and the horses made their way home to Hof.

There were housecarles out of doors at Hof, and they went inside and told Bjarni that Thorvald and his brother had returned home, adding that they had not run their errand to no purpose. Bjarni went outside and saw how things had turned out. In the main he had no comment to make, but had them buried, and everything now stayed quiet till Yule was past.

Then one evening when she and Bjarni had gone to bed, his wife Rannveig began to hold forth. "What do you imagine is now the most talked-about thing in the district?" she asked.

"I have no idea," said Bjarni. "There are plenty whose chatter strikes me as not worth bothering about."

"Well, the most frequent subject of gossip is this," she told him. "Men just cannot imagine what Thorstein Staff-struck must do for you to decide you need take vengeance on him. He has now killed three of your housecarles, and it seems to your followers that there is no hope of support where you are concerned if this is left unavenged. You do all the wrong things and leave the right undone."

"It comes to this, here again," replied Bjarni, "just as the proverb has it: 'None takes warning from his fellow's warming.' So I will see that you get what you are asking for. And yet Thorstein has killed few without good reason."

They gave over talking and slept the night through. In the morning Rannveig woke up as Bjarni was taking down his shield. She asked him what he was proposing to do.

"Thorstein and I," he replied, "must now settle a point of honour in Sunnudal."

"How many men are you taking with you?" she asked.

"I shall not lead an army against him," said Bjarni. "I am going alone."

"Don't do it," she begged. "Don't expose yourself all alone to the weapons of that fiend!"

"Aye," said Bjarni, "and are you now not carrying on like a true woman, crying one minute over the very thing you provoked the minute before? For a long while now I have suffered only too often the jeers both of you and of others, and it is useless to try and stop me now that I am settled to go."

Bjarni now made his way to Sunnudal, where Thorstein was standing in the doorway. They exchanged a few words.

"You must come and fight with me today, Thorstein," said Bjarni, "in single combat on this same mound which stands here in the home-field."

"It is quite hopeless for me to fight with you," maintained Thorstein, "but I will get abroad by the first ship that sails, for I know the manliness of your nature, how you will get all the work I see to done for my father, if I must be off and leave him."

"It is useless to cry off," warned Bjarni.

"Then let me go in and see my father first," said Thorstein.

"Do that," said Bjarni.

Thorstein went into the house and told his father that Bjarni had come there and challenged him to single combat. Old Thorarin answered him thus: "Any one, if he contends with a man higher in rank than himself, and lives in the same district with him, and does him some dishonour too, can expect to find that he will not wear out many shirts. Nor can I make outcry for you, for you seem to me richly to have deserved it. Now take your weapons and defend yourself like a man, for I have known the day when I would not have bowed my back to such as Bjarni, great champion though he is. And I would rather lose you than have a coward for a son."

Out again went Thorstein, and he and Bjarni went off to the mound, where they began fighting in deadly earnest, and cut away most of each other's shield. And when they had been fighting for a very long time, Bjarni said to Thorstein, "Now I grow thirsty, for I am less used to the work than you."

"Then go to the brook," said Thorstein, "and drink."

Bjarni did so, laying his sword down beside him. Thorstein picked it up, looked at it, and said: "You will not have had this sword in Bodvarsdal."

Bjarni made no reply. They went back up on to the mound and fought for a while again, and Bjarni found his opponent skilled with his weapons and altogether tougher than he had expected. "A lot goes wrong for me today," he complained. "Now my shoe-string is loose."

"Tie it up then," said Thorstein.

Bjarni bent down, but Thorstein went indoors to fetch out two shields and a sword; he went back to Bjarni on the mound, saying to him, "Here is a shield and sword which my father sends you. The sword will not prove blunter in the stroke than the one you have owned so far. Besides, I have no heart to stand defenceless under your blows any longer. Indeed, I would gladly give over this game, for I fear that your good fortune will show better results than my ill luck. And if I could have the say here—well, in the last resort, every man loves his life."

"It is useless to beg off," said Bjarni. "We must fight on."

"I'll not be the one to strike first," said Thorstein.

Then Bjarni cut away Thorstein's entire shield, whereupon Thorstein cut away Bjarni's too.

"A great stroke that!" cried Bjarni.

"You struck one no less," replied Thorstein.

"That same weapon you have had all day so far is biting better for you now," said Bjarni.

"I would spare myself disaster, if I might," Thorstein told him. "For I fight with you in fear and trembling. I should like to commit the whole thing to your verdict."

It was now Bjarni's turn to strike, and they were both quite defenceless. Said Bjarni: "It would be a bad bargain to choose a foul deed in place of good hap. I shall count myself fully repaid for my three housecarles by you alone, if only you will be true to me."

"I have had opportunity enough today to betray you, if my weak fortune was to prove stronger than your good luck. No, I will not betray you."

"I see," said Bjarni, "that you are past question a man. Will you now give me leave to go inside to your father, to tell him just what I like?"

"Go how you will, for all I care," warned Thorstein. "But watch your step!"

Bjarni then went inside to the bed-closet where old Thorarin was lying. Thorarin asked who came there, and Bjarni told him it was he.

"What news have you to tell me, Bjarni mine?"

"The slaying of Thorstein your son."

"Did he show fight?" asked Thorarin.

"In my opinion, no man was ever brisker in battle than your son Thorstein."

"It is not surprising then," said the old man, "that you were hard to handle in Bodvarsdal, if you have now got the better of my son."

"I want to invite you to Hof," said Bjarni, "where you shall sit in the second high-seat for as long as you live, and I will be to you in place of a son."

"My state," said the old man, "is like any other man's whose say goes for nothing—and a fool dotes on a promise. And such are the promises of you chieftains, when you wish to comfort a man after any such mishap, that nothing is too good for us for a month, but then our worth is fixed at that of other paupers, and with that our sorrows drop but slowly out of mind. And yet anyone who shakes hands on a deal with a man like you can rest well satisfied with his lot, whatever the verdict given. So I will take your offer after all. Now come over here to where I am in bed—you will have to come close, for the old fellow is all a-tremble in his legs for age and sickness, and never believe that my son's death has not pierced my old heart!"

Bjarni now went up to the bed and took old Thorarin by the hand, and found him fumbling for a big knife which he wanted to stick into Bjarni. "Why, you old stinkard!" cried Bjarni. "Any settlement between us now must be hitched to your deserts. Your son Thorstein is alive and shall come home with me to Hof, but you shall be provided with thralls to do your work, and shall lack for nothing for the rest of your days."

Thorstein went home with Bjarni to Hof and followed him till his death-day, and was reckoned pretty well any man's match for valour and prowess. Bjarni fully maintained his reputation, and was the more beloved and magnanimous the older he grew. He was the most undaunted of men, and became a firm believer in Christ in the last years of his life. He went abroad and made a pilgrimage south, and on that journey he died. He rests in a town called Sutri, a short way this side of Rome. Bjarni was a man blest in his offspring. His son was Skegg-Broddi, a man widely known to story and in his day unrivalled.

And that is the end of what there is to tell about Thorstein Staff-struck.

The Hauntings at Frodriver

In the year 1000, the Christian religion was introduced into Iceland by her apostles Gizur the White, and Hialto. The same year is assigned as the date of a very curious legend. A ship from Iceland chanced to winter in a haven near Helgafels. Among the passengers was a woman named Thorgunna, a native of the Hebrides, who was reported by the sailors to possess garments and household furniture of a fashion far surpassing those used in Iceland. Thurida, sister of the pontiff Snorro, and wife of Thorodd, a woman of a vain and covetous disposition, attracted by these reports, made a visit to the stranger, but could not prevail upon her to display her treasures. Persisting, however, in her enquiries, she pressed Thorgunna to take up her abode at the house of Thorodd. The Hebridean reluctantly assented, but added, that as she could labour at every usual kind of domestic industry, she trusted in that manner to discharge the obligation she might lie under to the family, without giving any part of her property, in recompense of her lodging. As Thurida continued to urge her request, Thorgunna accompanied her to Froda, the house of Thorodd, where the seamen deposited a huge chest and cabinet, containing the property of her new guest, which Thurida viewed with curious and covetous eyes. So soon as they had pointed out to Thorgunna the place assigned for her bed, she opened the chest, and took forth such an embroidered bed coverlid, and such a splendid and complete set of tapestry hangings, and bed furniture of English linen, interwoven with silk, as had never been seen in Iceland. "Sell to me," said the covetous matron, "this fair bed furniture."—"Believe me," answered Thorgunna, "I will not lie upon straw in order to feed thy pomp and vanity;" an

answer which so greatly displeased Thurida, that she never again repeated her request. Thorgunna, to whose character subsequent events added something of a mystical solemnity, is described as being a woman of a tall and stately appearance, of a dark complexion, and having a profusion of black hair. She was advanced in age; assiduous in the labours of the field and of the loom; a faithful attendant upon divine worship; grave, silent, and solemn in domestic society. She had little intercourse with the household of Thorodd, and shewed particular dislike to two of its inmates. These were Thorer, who, having lost a leg in the skirmish between Thorbiorn and Thorarin the Black, was called Thorer-Widlegr (woodenleg), from the substitute he had adopted; and his wife, Thorgrima, called Galldrakinna (wicked sorceress) from her supposed skill in enchantments. Kiartan, the son of Thurida, a boy of excellent promise, was the only person of the household to whom Thorgunna shewed much affection; and she was much vexed at times when the childish petulance of the boy made an indifferent return to her kindness.

After this mysterious stranger had dwelt at Froda for some time, and while she was labouring in the hay-field with other members of the family, a sudden cloud from the northern mountain led Thorodd to anticipate a heavy shower. He instantly commanded the hay-workers to pile up in ricks the quantity which each had been engaged in turning to the wind. It was afterwards remembered that Thorgunna did not pile up her portion, but left it spread on the field. The cloud approached with great celerity, and sunk so heavily around the farm, that it was scarce possible to see beyond the limits of the field. A heavy shower next descended, and so soon as the clouds broke away, and the sun shone forth, it was observed that it had rained blood. That which fell upon the ricks of the other labourers soon dried up, but what Thorgunna had wrought upon remained wet with gore. The unfortunate Hebridean, appalled at the omen, betook herself to her bed, and was seized with a mortal illness. On the approach of death she summoned Thorodd, her landlord, and entrusted to him the disposition of her property and effects. "Let my body," said she, "be transported to Skalholt, for my mind presages that in that place shall be founded the most distinguished church in this island. Let my golden ring be given to the priests who shall celebrate my obsequies, and do thou indemnify thyself for the funeral charges out of my remaining effects. To thy wife I bequeath my purple mantle, in order that, by this sacrifice to her avarice, I may secure the right of disposing of the rest of my effects at my own pleasure. But for my bed, with its covering, hangings, and furniture, I entreat they may be all consigned to the flames. I do not desire this, because I envy any one the possession of these things after my death, but because I wish those evils to be avoided which I plainly foresee will happen if my will be altered in the slightest particular." Thorodd promised faithfully to execute this extraordinary testament in the most pointed manner. Accordingly, so soon as Thorgunna was dead, her faithful executor prepared a pile for burning her splendid bed. Thurida entered, and learned with anger and astonishment the purpose of these preparations. To the remonstrances of her husband she answered, that the menaces of future danger were only caused by Thorgunna's selfish envy, who did not wish any one should enjoy her treasures after the decease. Then, finding Thorodd inaccessible to argument, she had recourse to caresses and blandishments, and at length extorted permission to separate, from the rest of the bed-furniture, the tapestried curtains and coverlid; the rest was consigned to the flames, in obedience to the will of the testator. The body of Thorgunna being wrapt in new linen, and placed in a coffin, was next to be transported through the precipices and morasses of Iceland to the distant district she had assigned for her place of sepulture. A remarkable incident occurred on the way. The transporters of the body arrived at evening late, weary, and drenched with rain, in a house called Nether-Ness, where the niggard hospitality of the proprietor only afforded them house-room, without any supply of food or fuel. But so soon as they entered, an unwonted noise was heard in the kitchen of the mansion, and the figure of a woman, soon recognised to be the deceased Thorgunna, was seen busily employed in preparing victuals. Their inhospitable landlord being made acquainted with this frightful circumstance, readily agreed to supply every refreshment which was necessary, on which the vision instantly disappeared. The apparition having become public, they

167

had no reason to ask twice for hospitality, as they proceeded on their journey, and arrived safely at Skalholt, where Thorgunna, with all due ceremonies of religion, was deposited quietly in the grave. But the consequences of the breach of her testament were felt severely at Froda.

The author, for the better understanding of the prodigies which happened, describes the manner of living at Froda; a simple and patriarchal structure, built according to the fashion used by the wealthy among the Icelanders. The apartment was very large, and a part boarded off contained the beds of the family. On either side was a sort of store-room, one of which contained meal, the other dried fish. Every evening large fires were lighted in this apartment, for dressing the victuals; and the domestics of the family usually sat around them for a considerable time, until supper was prepared. On the night when the conductors of Thorgunna's funeral returned to Froda, there appeared, visible to all who were present, a meteor, or spectral appearance, resembling a half-moon, which glided around the boarded walls of the mansion in an opposite direction to the course of the sun, and continued to perform its revolutions until the domestics retired to rest. This apparition was renewed every night during a whole week, and was pronounced by Thorer with the wooden leg, to presage pestilence or mortality. Shortly after a herdsman shewed signs of mental alienation, and gave various indications of having sustained the persecution of evil demons. This man was found dead in his bed one morning, and then commenced a scene of ghost-seeing unheard of in the annals of superstition. The first victim was Thorer, who had presaged the calamity. Going out of doors one evening, he was grappled by the spectre of the deceased shepherd as he attempted to re-enter the house. His wooden leg stood him in poor stead in such an encounter; he was hurled to the earth, and so fearfully beaten, that he died in consequence of the bruises. Thorer was no sooner dead, than his ghost associated itself to that of the herdsman and joined him in pursuing and assaulting the inhabitants of Froda. Meantime an infectious disorder spread fast among them, and several of the bondsmen died one after the other. Strange portents were seen within doors, the meal was displaced and mingled, and the dried fish flung about in a most alarming manner, without any visible agent. At length, while the servants were forming their evening circle round the fire, a spectre, resembling the head of a seal-fish, was seen to emerge out of the pavement of the room, bending its round black eyes full on the tapestried bed-curtains of Thorgunna. Some of the domestics ventured to strike at this figure, but, far from giving way, it rather erected itself further from the floor, until Kiartan, who seemed to have a natural predominance over these supernatural prodigies, seizing a huge forge-hammer, struck the seal repeatedly on the head, and compelled it to disappear, forcing it down into the floor, as if he had driven a stake into the earth. This prodigy was found to intimate a new calamity. Thorodd, the master of the family, had some time before set forth on a voyage to bring home a cargo of dried fish; but, in crossing the river Enna, the skiff was lost, and he perished with the servants who attended him. A solemn funeral feast was held at Froda, in memory of the deceased, when, to the astonishment of the guests, the apparition of Thorodd and his followers seemed to enter the apartment dropping with water. Yet this vision excited less horror than might have been expected; for the Icelanders, though nominally Christians, retained, among other pagan superstitions, a belief that the spectres of such drowned persons as had been favourably received by the goddess Ran, were wont to shew themselves at their funeral feast. They saw, therefore, with some composure, Thorodd, and his dripping attendants, plant themselves by the fire, from which all mortal guests retreated to make room for them. It was supposed this apparition would not be renewed after the conclusion of the festival. But so far were their hopes disappointed, that, so soon as the mourning guests had departed, the fires being lighted, Thorodd and his comrades marched in on one side, drenched as before with water; on the other entered Thorer, heading all those who had died in the pestilence, and who appeared covered with dust. Both parties seized the seats by the fire, while the half-frozen and terrified domestics spent the night without either light or warmth. The same phenomenon took place the next night, though the fires had been lighted in a separate house, and at length Kiartan was obliged to compound matters with the spectres by kindling a large fire for them in the principal apartment, and one for the family and domestics in a separate hut. This prodigy continued during the whole feast of Jol; other portents also happened to appal this devoted family, the contagious disease again broke forth, and when any one fell a sacrifice to it, his spectre was sure to join the troop of persecutors, who had now almost full possession of the mansion of Froda. Thorgrima Galldrakinna, wife of Thorer, was one of these victims, and, in short, of thirty servants belonging to the household, eighteen died, and five fled for fear of the apparitions, so that only seven remained in the service of Kiartan.

Kiartan had now recourse to the advice of his maternal uncle Snorro, in consequence of whose counsel, what will perhaps appear surprising to the reader, judicial measures were instituted against the spectres. A Christian priest was, however, associated with Thordo Kausa, son of Snorro, and with Kiartan, to superintend and sanctify the proceedings. The inhabitants were regularly summoned to attend upon the inquest, as in a cause between man and man, and the assembly was constituted before the gate of the mansion, just as the spectres had assumed their wonted station by the fire. Kiartan boldly ventured to approach them, and snatching a brand from the fire, he commanded the tapestry belonging to Thorgunna to be carried out of doors, set fire to it, and reduced it to ashes with all the other ornaments of her bed, which had been so inconsiderately preserved at the request of Thurida. A tribunal being then constituted with the usual legal solemnities, a charge was preferred by Kiartan against Thorer with the wooden leg, by Thordo Kausa against Thorodd, and by others chosen as accusers against the individual spectres present, accusing them of molesting the mansion, and introducing death and disease among its inhabitants. All the solemn rites of judicial procedure were observed on this singular occasion; evidence was adduced, charges given, and the cause formally decided. It does not appear that the ghosts put themselves on their defence, so that sentence of ejectment was pronounced against them individually in due and legal form. When Thorer heard the judgment, he arose, and saying, "I have sate while it was lawful for me to do so," left the apartment by the door opposite to that at which the judicial assembly were constituted.

Each of the spectres, as they heard their individual sentence, left the place, saying something which indicated their unwillingness to depart, until Thorodd himself was solemnly appointed to depart. "We have here no longer," said he, "a peaceful dwelling, therefore will we remove." Kiartan then entered the hall with his followers, and the priest with holy water, and celebration of a solemn mass, completed the conquest over the goblins, which had been commenced by the power and authority of the Icelandic law.

The Expedition of Thorfin Karlsefni

Late in the tenth century, the Norwegian Eric the Red, banished first from Norway and then from Iceland for lawless killings, discovered Greenland and founded a colony at Brattahlid. He had in his care there a woman called Gudrid whom Eric's son, Leif, had rescued from shipwreck and who had been twice widowed. Leif sailed on west from Greenland and set foot on land (first sighted fifteen years before by Bjarni Herjolfsson) that he called Vinland or "Wineland" because of the grapes growing there. This discovery quickly led to further explorations. Thorfin Karlsefni, hero of this extract from the thirteenth-century Eric the Red's Saga *was Leif Ericsson's brother-in-law; he was the first man to try to colonise Vinland—an ambition reluctantly called off when it became clear that the "savages" (in fact, American Indians) would give them no peace.*

The location of the places mentioned in the saga has been much argued: Helluland is probably south Baffin Island and Markland south-eastern Labrador; Vinland itself probably extended from north Newfoundland, perhaps as far south as New England. A Norse settlement dating from c. 1000 has been unearthed in Newfoundland.

Ireland, mentioned at the end of the extract, was part of the kingdom of Norway at this time; and a 'teredo' is a ship-worm, a mollusc that bores into and destroys submerged timbers.

Thord Horsehead had a son called Thorfin Karlsefni, who lived in the north at Reynisness in Skagafjord, as it now is called. Besides being of a good stock Karlsefni was a wealthy man. His mother's name was Thorunn. He was in the cruising trade, and had a good reputation as a sailor.

One summer Karlsefni made ready his ship for a voyage to Greenland. Snorri Thorbrandson from Alptafjord joined him, and they had forty men with them. A man named Bjarni Grimolfson from Breidafjord, and another called Thorhall Gamlison from Eastfjord both made ready their ship the same summer as Karlsefni to go to Greenland; they had forty men on board. They put to sea with these two ships, when they were ready. We are not told how long they were at sea; suffice it to say that both these ships arrived at Ericsfjord in the autumn. Eric and other settlers rode to the ships, where they began to trade freely: the skippers told Gudrid to help herself from their wares, but Eric was not behindhand in generosity, for he invited the crews of both ships to his home at Brattahlid for the winter. The traders accepted this offer and went with Eric. Thereupon their stuff was removed to the house at Brattahlid, where there was no lack of good large out-buildings in which to store their goods, and the merchants had a good time with Eric during the winter.

But as it drew towards Christmas Eric began to be less cheerful than usual. One day Karlsefni came to speak to Eric, and said: "Is anything the matter, Eric? It seems to me that you are rather more silent than you used to be; you are treating us with the greatest generosity, and we owe it to you to repay you so far as lies in our power, so tell us what is troubling you." "You have been good and courteous guests," replied Eric, "my mind is not troubled by any lack of response on your part, it is rather that I am afraid it will be said when you go elsewhere that you never passed a worse Christmas than when you stayed with Eric the Red at Brattahlid in Greenland." "That shall not be so," replied Karlsefni, "we have on our ships malt and meal and corn, and you are welcome to take of it what you will, and make as fine a feast as your ideas of hospitality suggest." Eric accepted this offer, and a Christmas feast was prepared, which was so splendid that people thought they had hardly ever seen so magnificent a feast in a poor country.

And after Christmas Karlsefni asked Eric for Gudrid's hand, since it appeared to him to be a matter under Eric's control, and moreover he thought her a beautiful and accomplished woman. Eric answered, saying that he would certainly entertain his suit, but that she was a good match; that it was likely that she would be fulfilling her destiny if she was married to him, and that he had heard good of Karlsefni. So then the proposal was conveyed to her, and she left it to Eric to decide for her. And now it was not long before this proposal was accepted, and the festivities began again, and their wedding was celebrated. There was a very merry time at Brattahlid in the winter with much playing at draughts and story-telling, and a great deal to make their stay pleasant.

At this time there was much discussion at Brattahlid during the winter about a search for Wineland the Good, and it was said that it would be a profitable country to visit; Karlsefni and Snorri resolved to search for Wineland, and the project was much talked about, so it came about that Karlsefni and Snorri made ready their ship to go and look for the country in the summer. The man named Bjarni, and Thorhall, who have already been mentioned, joined the expedition with their ship, and the crew which had accompanied them. There was a man named Thorvard, who was connected by marriage with Eric the Red. He also went with them, and Thorhall who was called the Hunter, he had been long engaged with Eric as hunter in the summer, and had many things in his charge. Thorhall was big and strong and dark, and like a giant: he was rather old, of a temper hard to manage, taciturn and of few words as a rule, cunning but abusive, and he was always urging Eric to the worse course. He had had little dealings with the faith since it came to Greenland. Thorhall was rather unpopular, yet for a long time Eric had been in the habit of consulting him. He was on the ship with Thorvard's men, for he had a wide experience of wild countries. They had the ship which Thorbjörn had brought out there, and they joined themselves to Karlsefni's party for the expedition, and the majority of the men were Greenlanders. The total force on board their ships was 160 men. After this they sailed away to the Western Settlement and the Bear Isles. They sailed away from the Bear Isles with a northerly wind. They were at sea two days. Then they found land, and rowing ashore in boats they examined the country, and found there a quantity of flat stones, which were so

large that two men could easily have lain sole to sole on them: there were many arctic foxes there. They gave the place a name, calling it Helluland. Then they sailed for two days with north wind, and changed their course from south to south-east, and then there was a land before them on which was much wood and many beasts. An island lay there off shore to the south-east, on which they found a bear, and they called it Bjarney (Bear Island), but the land where the wood was they called Markland (woodland).

Then when two days were passed they sighted land, up to which they sailed. There was a cape where they arrived. They beat along the coast, and left the land to starboard: it was a desolate place, and there were long beaches and sands there. They rowed ashore, and found there on the cape the keel of a ship, so they called the place Keelness: they gave the beaches also a name, calling them Furdu-strands (the Wonder Beaches) because the sail past them was long. Next the country became indented with bays, into one of which they steered the ships.

Now when Leif was with king Olaf Tryggvason and he commissioned him to preach Christianity in Greenland, the king gave him two Scots, a man called Hake and a woman Hekja. The king told Leif to make use of these people if he had need of speed, for they were swifter than deer: these people Leif and Eric provided to accompany Karlsefni. Now when they had coasted past Furdu-strands they set the Scots ashore, telling them to run southward along the land to explore the resources of the country and come back before three days were past. They were dressed in what they called a "kjafal", which was made with a hood above, and open at the sides without sleeves: it was fastened between the legs, where a button and a loop held it together: otherwise they were naked. They cast anchor and lay there in the meanwhile. And when three days were past they came running down from the land, and one of them had in his hand a grape-cluster while the other had a wild ear of wheat. They told Karlsefni that they thought that they had found that the resources of the country were good. They received them into their ship, and went their ways, till the country was indented by a fjord. They took the ships into the fjord. There was an island outside, about which there were strong currents, so they called it

Straumsey (Tide or Current Island). There were so many birds on the island that a man's feet could hardly come down between the eggs. They held along the fjord, and called the place Straumsfjord, and there they carried up their goods from the ships and prepared to stay: they had with them all sorts of cattle, and they explored the resources of the country there. There were mountains there, and the view was beautiful. They did nothing but explore the country. There was plenty of grass there. They were there for the winter, and the winter was severe, but they had done nothing to provide for it, and victuals grew scarce, and hunting and fishing deteriorated. Then they went out to the island, in the hope that this place might yield something in the way of fishing or jetsam. But there was little food to be obtained on it, though their cattle throve there well. After this they cried to God to send them something to eat, and their prayer was not answered as soon as they desired. Thorhall disappeared and men went in search of him: that lasted three successive days. On the fourth day Karlsefni and Bjarni found Thorhall on a crag; he was gazing into the air with staring eyes, open mouth, and dilated nostrils, and scratching and pinching himself and reciting something. They asked him why he had come there. He said it was no business of theirs, told them not to be surprised at it, and said that he had lived long enough to make it unnecessary for them to trouble about him. They told him to come home with them, and he did so. Soon afterwards there came a whale, and they went to it and cut it up, but no one knew what sort of whale it was. Karlsefni had a great knowledge of whales, but still he did not recognise this one. The cooks boiled this whale, and they ate it, but were all ill from it: then Thorhall came up and said: "Was not the Red-Beard more useful than your Christ? This is my reward for chanting of Thor my patron; seldom has he failed me." But when they heard this none of them would avail themselves of the food, and they threw it down off the rocks and committed their cause to God's mercy: the state of the weather then improved and permitted them to row out, and from that time there was no lack of provision during the spring. They went into Straumsfjord, and got supplies from both places, hunting on the mainland, and eggs and fishing from the sea.

Now they consulted about their expedition, and were divided.
Thorhall the Hunter wished to go north by Furdustrands and past
Keelness, and so look for Wineland, but Karlsefni wished to coast
south and off the east coast, considering that the region which lay
more to the south was the larger, and it seemed to him the best plan
to explore both ways. So then Thorhall made ready out by the
islands, and there were no more than nine men for his venture, the
rest of the party going with Karlsefni. And one day as Thorhall
was carrying water to his ship he drank it, and recited this verse:

> *They flattered my confiding ear*
> *With tales of drink abounding here:*
> *My tale upon the thirsty land!*
> *A warrior, trained to bear a brand,*
> *A pail instead I have to bring,*
> *And bow my back beside the spring:*
> *For ne'er a single draught of wine*
> *Has passed these parching lips of mine.*

After this they set out, and Karlsefni accompanied them by the
islands.

Before they hoisted their sail Thorhall recited a verse:

> *Now let the vessel plough the main*
> *To Greenland and our friends again:*
> *Away, and leave this strenuous host*
> *Who praise this God-forsaken coast*
> *To linger in a desert land,*
> *And boil their whales in Furdustrand.*

Afterwards they parted, and they sailed north past Furdustrands
and Keelness, and wished to bear westward; but they were met by a
storm and cast ashore in Ireland, where they were much ill-treated
and enslaved. There Thorhall died, according to the reports of
traders.

Karlsefni coasted south with Snorri and Bjarni and the rest of
their party. They sailed a long time, till they came to a river which
flowed down from the land and through a lake into the sea: there
were great shoals of gravel there in front of the estuary and they

could not enter the river except at high tide. Karlsefni and his party sailed into the estuary, and called the place Hop.

They found there wild fields of wheat wherever the ground was low, but vines wherever they explored the hills. Every brook was full of fish. They made pits where the land met high-water mark, and when the tide ebbed there were halibut in the pits. There was a great quantity of animals of all sorts in the woods. They were there a fortnight, enjoying themselves, without noticing anything further: they had their cattle with them.

And one morning early, as they looked about them, they saw nine skin canoes, on which staves were waved with a noise just like threshing, and they were waved with the sun. Then Karlsefni said, "What is the meaning of this?" Snorri answered him, "Perhaps this is a sign of peace, so let us take a white shield and lift it in answer," and they did so. Then these men rowed to meet them, and, astonished at what they saw, they landed. They were swarthy men and ugly, with unkempt hair on their heads. They had large eyes and broad cheeks. They stayed there some time, showing surprise. Then they rowed away south past the cape.

Karlsefni and his men had made their camp above the lake, and some of the huts were near the mainland while others were near the lake. So they remained there that winter; no snow fell, and their cattle remained in the open, finding their own pasture. But at the beginning of spring they saw one morning early a fleet of skin canoes rowing from the south past the cape, so many that the sea was black with them, and on each boat there were staves waved. Karlsefni and his men raised their shields, and they began to trade: the people wanted particularly to buy red cloth, in exchange for which they offered skins and grey furs. They wished also to buy swords and spears, but Karlsefni and Snorri forbade this. The savages got for a dark skin a span's length of red cloth, which they bound round their heads. Thus things continued for awhile, but when the cloth began to give out they cut it into pieces so small that they were not more than a finger's breadth. The savages gave as much for it as before, or more.

It happened that a bull belonging to Karlsefni's party ran out of the wood, and bellowed loudly: this terrified the savages, and they ran out to their canoes, and rowed south along the coast, and there was nothing more seen of them for three consecutive weeks. But when that time had elapsed they saw a great number of the boats of the savages coming from the south like a rushing torrent, and this time all the staves were waved widdershins, and all the savages yelled loudly. Upon this Karlsefni's men took a red shield and raised it in answer. The savages ran from their boats and thereupon they met and fought; there was a heavy rain of missiles; the savages had war-slings too. Karlsefni and Snorri observed that the savages raised up on a pole a very large globe, closely resembling a sheep's paunch and dark in colour, and it flew from the pole up on land over the party, and made a terrible noise where it came down. Upon this a great fear came on Karlsefni and his party, so that they wished for nothing but to get away up stream, for they thought that the savages were setting upon them from all sides, nor did they halt till they came to some rocks where they made a determined resistance.

Freydis came out, and seeing Karlsefni's men retreating she cried out, "Why are such fine fellows as you running away from these unworthy men, whom I thought you could have butchered like cattle? Now if I had a weapon it seems to me that I should fight better than any of you." They paid no attention to what she said. Freydis wished to follow them, but was rather slow because she was not well; yet she went after them into the wood, pursued by the savages. She found before her a dead man, Thorbrand Snorreson, with a flat stone standing in his head: his sword lay beside him. This she took up, and prepared to defend herself with it. Then the savages set upon her, but she drew out her breast from beneath her clothes and beat the sword upon it: with that the savages were afraid, and running back to their ships they withdrew. Karlsefni's men came up to her and praised her courage. Two men of Karlsefni's force fell, but four of the savages, although the former were outnumbered. So then they went back to their huts, and bound their wounds, and considered what that force could have been which set upon them from the land side; it now appeared to them that the attacking party consisted solely of those who came from the ships, and that the others must have been a delusion.

Moreover the savages found a dead man with an axe lying beside him. One of them took up the axe and cut at a tree, and then each of the others did so, and they thought it a treasure and that it cut well. Afterwards one of them cut at a stone, and the axe broke, whereupon he thought that it was useless, since it did not stand against the stone, and threw it down.

It now appeared to Karlsefni's party that though this country had good resources yet they would live in a perpetual state of warfare and alarm on account of the aborigines. So they prepared to depart, intending to return to their own country. They coasted northward, and found five savages in skins sleeping by the sea; these had with them receptacles in which was beast's marrow mixed with blood. They concluded that these men must have been sent from the country: they killed them. Later on they discovered a promontory and a quantity of beasts: the promontory had the appearance of a cake of dung, because the beasts lay there in the winter. Now they came to Straumsfjord, where there was plenty of every kind.

Some men say that Bjarni and Freydis stayed there with a hundred men and went no further, while Karlsefni and Snorri went south with forty men, staying no longer at Hop than a scant two months, and returning the same summer.

Karlsefni went with one ship to look for Thorhall the Hunter, while the main body remained behind, and they travelled north past Keelness, and then bore along to the west of it, leaving the land on their port side. Then there was nothing but desolate woods, with hardly any open places. And when they had sailed a long time, a river came down from the land from the east to the west: they entered the mouth of the river and lay by its southern bank. It happened one morning that Karlsefni and his men saw before them on an open place a speck, which glittered before them, and they shouted at it; it moved, and it was a uniped, which darted down to the bank of the river by which they lay. Thorvald, son of Eric the Red, was sitting by the rudder, and the uniped shot an arrow into his entrails. Thorvald drew out the arrow, crying, "There is fat about my belly, we have reached a good country, though we are hardly allowed to enjoy it." Thorvald died of this wound soon afterwards. Then the uniped rushed away, and back northward. Karlsefni and his men pursued him, and saw him from time to time.

The last they saw of him was that he ran towards a certain creek. Then Karlsefni and his men turned back. Thereupon a man sang this little ditty:

> *Hear, Karlsefni, while I sing*
> *Of a true but wondrous thing,*
> *How thy crew all vainly sped,*
> *Following a uniped:*
> *Strange it was to see him bound*
> *Swiftly o'er the broken ground.*

Then they went away, and back north, and imagined that they saw Uniped Land. They would not then risk their people further.

They considered that those mountains which were at Hop and those which they now found were all one, and were therefore close opposite one another, and that the distance from Straumsfjord was the same in both directions. They were at Straumsfjord the third winter.

At this time the men were much divided into parties, which happened because of the women, the unmarried men claiming the wives of those who were married, which gave rise to the greatest disorder. There Karlsefni's son, Snorri, was born the first autumn, and he was three winters old when they left.

On sailing from Wineland they got a south wind, and came to Markland, where they found five savages, one of whom was bearded. There were two women and two children: Karlsefni's men caught the boys, but the others escaped, disappearing into the ground. But they kept the two boys with them and taught them speech, and they were christened. They called their mother Vætilldi and their father Uvægi. They said that the savages' country was governed by kings, one of whom was called Avalldamon and the other Valldidida. They said that there were no houses there: people lived in dens or caves. They reported that another country lay on the other side, opposite to their own, where people lived who wore white clothes, and uttered loud cries, and carried poles, and went with flags. It is thought that this was Hvitramannaland, or Ireland the Great. So then they came to Greenland, and stayed with Eric the Red for the winter.

Then Bjarni Grimolfson was carried into the sea of Ireland, and came into a sea infested by the teredo, and the first thing they noticed was that the ship beneath them was worm-eaten. So they discussed what plan should be adopted. They had a boat which was coated with seal-tar. It is said that the teredo does not eat wood which is coated with seal-tar. The majority declared in favour of the proposal to man the boat with such men as she would accommodate. But when this was tested the boat would not accommodate more than half the crew. Bjarni then said that the manning of the boat should be by lot, and not by rank. But every man who was there wished to go in the boat, and she could not take them all. For this reason they agreed to the course of drawing lots for the manning of the boat from the ship. So the result of the drawing was that Bjarni drew a seat in the boat, and about half the crew with him. So those who had been chosen by the lots went from the ship into the boat. When they had got into the boat, a young Icelander, who had been one of Bjarni's companions, said, "Do you mean, Bjarni, to desert me here?" Bjarni replied, "So it has turned out." "This is not what you promised me", said he, "when I left my father's house in Iceland to go with you." "But still", said Bjarni, "I do not see any other course in this predicament: but answer me, what course do you advise?" "The course I see," said he, "is that we change places, and you come here while I go there." Bjarni answered, "Be it so. For I see that you cling greedily to life, and think it a hard thing to die." Thereupon they changed places. This man went down into the boat, while Bjarni got on board the ship, and men say that Bjarni was lost there in the teredo sea, with those men who were on board with him. But the boat and those on board of her went their ways, till they came to land, at Dublin in Ireland, where they afterwards told this story.

Authun and the Bear

There was a man by the name of Authun, a Westfirther by origin, and rather poorly off. He went abroad from the Westfirths with the help of a good farmer, Thorstein, and of skipper Thorir, who had received hospitality from Thorstein over the winter. Authun had been staying there too, and working for Thorir, and received this for his reward, a passage abroad with the skipper to look after him. Before going on board ship Authun set aside the bulk of his money for his mother, and it was reckoned enough to keep her for three years. They now sailed out and away. They had an easy passage and Authun spent the winter with skipper Thorir, who owned a farm in Mœr, in Norway. The following summer they sailed for Greenland, and spent the winter there.

The story tells how Authun bought a bear there, an absolute treasure, and gave every penny he had for it. The following summer they returned to Norway and had an excellent passage. Authun took his bear with him, and was proposing to go south to Denmark, find king Svein, and make him a present of the beast. So when he reached the south of Norway, where the Norwegian king was then in residence, he left the ship, taking his bear with him, and rented himself a lodging.

King Harald was soon told how a bear, an absolute treasure, had come ashore, and that his owner was an Icelander. The king sent for him immediately, and when Authun came into the king's presence he greeted him with due courtesy. The king received his greeting affably, and then: "You have a bear," he said, "an absolute treasure?"

Well, yes, he agreed, he had a beast of a kind.

"Are you willing to sell him to us," asked the king, "for the same price you gave for him?"

"I don't want to, sire," he replied.

"Then would you like me to give you twice the price?" asked the king. "And indeed that would be fairer, since you paid out all you had for him."

"I don't want to, sire."

"You want to give him to me then?" said the king.

"No, sire," he replied.

"Then what do you want to do with him?"

"Go to Denmark," replied Authun, "and give him to king Svein."

"Is it possible," asked king Harald, "that you are such a silly man that you have not heard how a state of war exists between our two countries? Or do you think yourself so blest with luck that you can make your way there with this precious thing when others, for all that they have compelling business there, cannot manage it unscathed?"

"Sire," said Authun, "it is for you to command, yet I cannot willingly agree to anything except what I have already decided."

"Then why should you not go your road," said the king to that, "even as you wish? But come and see me when you return, and tell me how king Svein rewards you for the bear. It may be that you are a man of happy fortune."

"I promise to do so," said Authun.

He now proceeded south along the coast, and east to Vik, and from there to Denmark, and by this time had spent his last penny and was forced to beg food, both for himself and for the bear. He went to see king Svein's steward, a man named Aki, and asked him for some victuals, both for himself and for the bear. "For I am proposing," he said, "to make a present of him to king Svein." Aki said he would sell him food if that was what he was after, but Authun confessed that he had no money to pay for it. "And yet," he said, "I should like my business to be so forwarded that I can produce my bear before the king." "I will give you food and lodging then, whatever you need, until you see the king, but in return I require a half share in this creature. You might look at it this way: the bear will only die on your hands, for you need considerable

provisioning and your money is all gone, and in that case you get no profit of your bear."

When he looked at it that way, it seemed to him that what the steward said went pretty close to the mark, so that was what they settled on, that he should make over half the beast to Aki, and it was for the king to set a value on the whole.

And now they were to go together to see the king, and so they did, and stood before his table. The king was puzzled who this man, whom he did not know, could be, and, "Who are you?" he asked Authun.

"I am an Icelander, sire," he replied, "and have just come from Greenland, and more recently still from Norway. I had been meaning to present you with this bear, which I purchased with every penny I had, but I am now in something of a quandary, for I own only half of him." And he went on to tell the king what had taken place between him and his steward Aki.

"Is this true, Aki, what he says?" asked the king.

"Yes," he said, "it is."

"And did you think it seemly, when I had raised you up to be a great man, to obstruct and hinder his path when a man was trying to bring me this fine beast, for which he had given his all, when even king Harald, who is our enemy, saw fit to let him go in peace? Think then how honourable this was on your part! It would be only right to have you put to death—and though I will not do that, you shall leave this land without a moment's delay, and never come into my sight again. As for you, Authun, I owe you the same thanks as if you were giving me the whole animal. So stay here with me." He agreed to this, and remained with king Svein for a while.

But after some time had gone by Authun said to the king, "I should like to go away now, sire." The king answered, rather coldly, "What do you want, if you don't want to stay with us?" "I want to go south on a pilgrimage." "If you did not wish to follow so good a course," the king admitted, "I should be displeased by your eagerness to be off." The king now gave him a large amount of silver, and he travelled southwards with the pilgrims to Rome. The king made the arrangements for his journey, and told him to come and see him when he returned.

Now he went his ways until he came south to Rome, and when he had spent as much time there as he wished, he set out on his way back. He fell sick, very sick, and grew woefully thin. All the money the king had given him for his journey was now spent, he took the style of a beggar and begged for his food. He had become bald and quite pitiful to see.

He came back to Denmark at Easter, to the very place where the king was in residence. He did not dare let himself be seen but remained in the church transept, hoping to encounter the king when he went to church that evening. But when he saw the king with his handsomely attired courtiers, again he dare not let himself be seen. And when the king went to the drinking in hall, Authun ate his food outside, as is the custom of pilgrims to Rome before they lay aside their staff and scrip.

And now in the evening, as the king went to evensong, Authun reckoned on meeting him; but however daunting a prospect this had looked before, it had by now grown far worse, for the courtiers were in drink. And yet, as they were going back in, the king noticed a man who he felt sure lacked the confidence to come forward and speak to him, and as the courtiers were entering the king turned back, saying, "Let anyone now come forward who craves audience of me, for I believe there is such a man here present." Then Authun came forward and fell at the king's feet, and the king could hardly recognise him. But as soon as he knew who he was, he took Authun by the hand and welcomed him. "How greatly you are changed," he said, "since last we met," and he led him inside behind him. When the courtiers saw him they laughed at him, but, "You need not laugh at him," said the king, "he has provided for his soul better than you." Then the king had a bath prepared for him and gave him clothes to wear, and Authun remained with him.

One day in spring, so the story goes, the king invited Authun to stay with him for the rest of his days, promising that he would make him his cup-bearer and heap him with honours.

"God reward you, sire," said Authun, "for all the honour you would do me, but what I really have in mind is to return to Iceland."

"That strikes me as a curious choice," said the king.

"I cannot bear, sire," said Authun, "that I should enjoy such honours here with you, and my mother tramp the beggar's path out in Iceland, for by now the provision I made for her before I left home will be at an end."

"That is well spoken, and like a man," replied the king, "and you will prove a man of happy fortune. This is the only reason for your departure which would not displease me. But stay with me now till the ships make ready." And so he did.

One day, towards the end of spring, king Svein walked down to the jetties, where ships were being overhauled in readiness for voyages to many lands, to the Baltic and Germany, Sweden, and Norway. He and Authun came to a very fine ship which men were making ready, and "What do you think of this for a ship, Authun?" asked the king. "Very fine, sire," was his answer. "I am going to give you this ship," said the king, "in return for the bear." Authun thanked him for his gift as well as he knew how.

When time had passed and the ship was quite ready, king Svein had this to say to Authun: "Since you want to be away it is not for me to stop you. But I have heard that your country is ill supplied with havens, the coasts often wide open and dangerous to shipping. Now should you be wrecked and lose both ship and lading, there will be little to show that you have met king Svein and given him a princely gift." With that the king gave him a leather purse full of silver. "You will not be entirely penniless, even if you are ship-wrecked, so long as you hold on to this. And yet," said the king, "it may happen that you lose this money too, and you will then reap little benefit from having found king Svein and given him a princely gift." With that the king drew a ring from his arm and gave it to Authun, saying, "Even if you are so unlucky as to suffer ship-wreck and lose your money, you will not be penniless should you manage to get ashore, for many carry gold on them in case of ship-wreck, and it will be clear that you have met king Svein if you save the ring. But I would urge upon you," said the king, "not to give away the ring unless you consider yourself under a great enough obligation to some great man—but give him the ring, for it well becomes men of rank to accept such. And now, good luck go with you."

Then he put to sea and sailed to Norway, where he had his goods carried ashore—and he needed more help for this than when he was in Norway last. He then went to visit king Harald, to make good the promise he had made him before going to Denmark. He had a courteous greeting for the king, and the king took it affably. "Sit down," he said, "and take a drink with us." And so he did.

"And how did king Svein reward you for the bear?" king Harald asked him.

"By accepting it from me, sire," replied Authun.

"So too would I have rewarded you," said the king. "How else did he reward you?"

"He gave me silver for my pilgrimage," replied Authun.

"King Svein gives many men silver for pilgrimages, and for other things too," said the king, "and they don't have to bring him a grand present for it. What else was there?"

"He offered to make me his cup-bearer," said Authun, "and heap me with honours."

"In that he spoke well," said the king. "Still, he would give you more of a reward than that."

"He gave me a merchant ship and such wares as sell best here in Norway."

"That was handsome of him," said the king, "but so too would I have rewarded you. Did he reward you with anything further?"

"He gave me a leather purse full of silver, saying I should not then be penniless if I held on to it, even though my ship was wrecked off Iceland."

"That was nobly done," said the king, "and something I would not have done. I should have held us quits had I given you the ship. Did he reward you any further?"

"To be sure he rewarded me, sire," said Authun. "He gave me this ring I have on my arm, arguing it might so turn out that I should lose all that money and yet, said he, not be penniless if I held on to the ring. And he charged me never to part with it unless I should consider myself under so great an obligation to some great man that I wanted to give it him. And now I have found him, for you had the opportunity to deprive me of both these things, the bear and my life too; yet you let me go in peace where others might not."

The king accepted his gift graciously, and gave Authun fine gifts in return before they parted. Authun used his money for a passage to Iceland, promptly left for home that summer, and was thought to be a man of the happiest good fortune.

The Battle of Stamford Bridge

The Battle of Stamford Bridge, near York, was fought on September 25th, 1066, nineteen days before the Battle of Hastings. The defeat and death of Harald Hardradi (called Sigurdsson in this translation), claimant to the English throne together with Harold Godwinson and Duke William of Normandy, put an end to the Viking domination of Europe. This extract from King Harald's Saga, *written by the Icelandic historian and saga writer Snorri Sturluson (1179– 1241), is a rousing mixture of fact and legend. The battle is described from the point of view of the Norwegians, who are thought to have numbered about 9000 men and 300 ships. Harald was joined by Harold Godwinson's own brother, Tostig, who had been deposed as Earl of Northumbria in the previous year for treachery. Tostig was killed in the battle and twenty-four ships were sufficient to carry the Norwegian survivors home.*

On Monday, when King Harald Sigurdsson had taken breakfast, he ordered the trumpets to sound for going on shore. The army accordingly got ready, and he divided the men into the parties who should go and who should stay behind. In every division he allowed two men to land and one to remain behind. Earl Tostig and his retinue prepared to land with King Harald; and, for watching the ships, remained behind the king's son Olaf, the Earls of Orkney, Paul, and Erlend, and also Eystein Orre, a son of Thorberg Arneson, who was the most able and best beloved by the king of all his liegemen, and to whom the king had promised his daughter Maria. The weather was uncommonly fine, and it was hot sunshine. The men therefore laid aside their armour, and went on the land only with their shields, helmets, and spears, and girt with swords; and many had also arrows and bows, and all were very merry. Now as they came near the castle a great army seemed coming against them, and they saw a cloud of dust as from horses' feet, and under it shining shields and bright armour. The king halted his people, and called to him Earl Tostig, and asked him what army this could be. The earl replied that he thought it most likely to be a hostile army; but possibly it might be some of his relations who were seeking for mercy and friendship in order to obtain certain peace and safety from the king. Then the king said: "We must all halt to discover what kind of a force this is." They did so; and the nearer this force came the greater it appeared, and their shining arms were to the sight like glittering ice.

Then said King Harald: "Let us now fall upon some good, sensible counsel; for it is not to be concealed that this is an hostile army, and the king himself without doubt is here."

Then said the earl: "The first counsel is to turn about as fast as we can to our ships to get our men and our weapons, and then we will make a defence according to our ability; or otherwise let our ships defend us, for there these horsemen have no power over us."

Then King Harald said: "I have another counsel. Put three of our best horses under three of our briskest lads, and let them ride with all speed to tell our people to come quickly to our relief. The Englishmen shall have a hard fray of it before we give ourselves up for lost."

The earl said the king must order in this, as in all things, as he thought best; adding, at the same time, it was by no means his wish to fly. Then King Harald ordered his banner Land-ravager to be set up; and Frirek was the name of him who bore the banner.

Then King Harald arranged his army, and made the line of battle long, but not deep. He bent both wings of it back, so that they met together, and formed a wide ring equally thick all round, shield to shield, both in the front and rear ranks. The king himself and his retinue were within the circle; and there was the banner, and a body of chosen men. Earl Tostig, with his retinue, was at another place, and had a different banner. The army was arranged in this way because the king knew that horsemen were accustomed to ride forwards with great vigour, but to turn back immediately. Now the king ordered that his own and the earl's attendants should ride forwards where it was most required. "And our bowmen," said he, "shall be near to us; and they who stand in the first rank shall set the spear-shaft on the ground, and the spear-point against the horseman's breast if he rides at them; and those who stand in the second rank shall set the spear-point against the horse's breast."

King Harold Godwinson had come with an immense army, both of cavalry and infantry. Now King Harald Sigurdsson rode around his array to see how every part was drawn up. He was upon a black horse, and the horse stumbled under him, so that the king fell off. He got up in haste, and said: "A fall is lucky for a traveller."

The English king Harold said to the Northmen who were with him: "Do ye know the stout man who fell from his horse, with the blue kirtle and the beautiful helmet?"

"That is the king himself," said they.

The English king said: "A great man, and of stately appearance is he; but I think his luck has left him."

Twenty horsemen rode forward from the Thingmen's troops against the Northmen's array; and all of them, and likewise their horses, were clothed in armour.

One of the horsemen said: "Is Earl Tostig in this army?"

The earl answered: "It is not to be denied that ye will find him here."

The horseman says, "Thy brother King Harold sends thee salutation, with the message that thou shalt have the whole of Northumberland; and, rather than thou shouldst not submit to him, he will give thee the third part of his kingdom to rule over along with himself."

The earl replies: "This is something different from the enmity and scorn he offered last winter; and if this had been offered then it would have saved many a man's life who now is dead, and it would have been better for the kingdom of England. But if I accept of this offer, what will he give King Harald Sigurdsson for his trouble?"

The horseman replied: "He has also spoken of this, and will give him seven feet of English ground, or as much more as he may be taller than other men."

"Then," said the earl, "go now and tell King Harold to get ready for battle; for never shall the Northmen say with truth that Earl Tostig left King Harald Sigurdsson to join his enemy's troops when he came to fight west here in England. We shall rather all take the resolution to die with honour, or to gain England by a victory."

Then the horsemen rode back.

King Harald Sigurdsson said to the earl: "Who was the man who spoke so well?"

The earl replied: "That was King Harold Godwinson."

Then said King Harald Sigurdsson: "That was by far too long concealed from me; for they had come so near to our army that this Harold should never have carried back the tidings of our men's slaughter."

Then said the earl: "It was certainly imprudent for such chiefs, and it may be as you say; but I saw he was going to offer me peace and a great dominion, and that, on the other hand, I would be his murderer if I betrayed him; and I would rather he should be my murderer than I his, if one of two be to die."

King Harald Sigurdsson observed to his men, "That was but a little man, yet he sat firmly in his stirrups."

It is said that Harald made these verses at this time:—

> *Advance! advance!*
> *No helmets glance,*
> *But blue swords play*
> *In our array.*

> *Advance! advance!*
> *No mail-coats glance,*
> *But hearts are here*
> *That ne'er knew fear.*

His coat of mail was called Emma; and it was so long that it reached almost to the middle of his leg and so strong that no weapon ever pierced it. Then said King Harald Sigurdsson: "These verses are but ill composed; I must try to make better;" and he composed the following:—

The Battle of Stamford Bridge

In battle-storm we seek no lee,
With skulking head, and bending knee,
Behind the hollow shield.
With eye and hand we fend the head;
Courage and skill stand in the stead
Of panzer,* helm, and shield,
In Hilda's† deadly field.

Now the battle began. The Englishmen made a hot assault upon the Northmen, who sustained it bravely. It was no easy matter for the English to ride against the Northmen on account of their spears, therefore they rode in a circle around them. And the fight at first was but loose and light as long as the Northmen kept their order of battle; for although the English rode hard against the Northmen, they gave way again immediately, as they could do nothing against them. Now when the Northmen thought they perceived that the enemy were making but weak assaults, they set after them, and would drive them into flight; but when they had broken their shield-rampart, the Englishmen rode up from all sides and threw arrows and spears on them. Now when King Harald Sigurdsson saw this, he went into the fray where the greatest crash of weapons was; and there was a sharp conflict, in which many people fell on both sides. King Harald then was in a rage, and ran out in front of the array and hewed down with both hands; so that neither helmet nor armour could withstand him, and all who were nearest gave way before him. It was then very near with the English that they had taken to flight. So says Arnor, the earl's scald:—

Where battle-storm was ringing,
Where arrow-cloud was singing,
Harald stood there
Of armour bare,
His deadly sword still swinging.
The foemen feel its bite;
His Norsemen rush to fight,

---

* and † Samuel Laing explains that *panzer* is a coat of mail and that *Hilda* was the goddess of war. Maybe he was thinking of Hild, one of the Valkyries.

The Battle of Stamford Bridge

Danger to share
With Harald there,
Where steel on steel was ringing.

King Harald Sigurdsson was hit by an arrow in the windpipe, and that was his death-wound. He fell, and all who had advanced with him, except those who retired with the banner. There was afterwards the warmest conflict, and Earl Tostig had taken charge of the king's banner. They began on both sides to form their array again, and for a long time there was a pause in fighting.

But before the battle began again Harold Godwinson offered his brother Earl Tostig peace, and also quarter to the Northmen who were still alive; but the Northmen called out, all of them together, that they would rather fall, one across the other, than accept of quarter from the Englishmen. Then each side set up a war-shout, and the battle began again.

Eystein Orre came up at this moment from the ships with the men who followed him, and all were clad in armour. Then Eystein got King Harald's banner Land-ravager; and now was, for the third time, one of the sharpest of conflicts, in which many Englishmen fell, and they were near to taking flight. This conflict is called Orre's storm. Eystein and his men had hastened so fast from the ships that they were quite exhausted, and scarcely fit to fight before they came into the battle; but afterwards they became so furious that they did not guard themselves with their shields as long as they could stand upright. At last they threw off their coats of ring-mail, and then the Englishmen could easily lay their blows at them; and many fell from weariness, and died without a wound. Thus almost all the chief men fell among the Norway people. This happened towards evening; and then it went, as one might expect, that all had not the same fate, for many fled, and were lucky enough to escape in various ways; and darkness fell before the slaughter was altogether ended.

Styrkar, King Harald Sigurdsson's marshal, a gallant man, escaped upon a horse, on which he rode away in the evening. It was blowing a cold wind, and Styrkar had not much other clothing upon him but his shirt, and had a helmet on his head and a drawn sword in his hand. As soon as his weariness was over, he began to feel cold. A waggoner met him in a lined skin-coat. Styrkar asks him: "Wilt thou sell thy coat, friend?"

"Not to thee," says the peasant. "Thou art a Northman; that I can hear by thy tongue."

Styrkar replies: "If I were a Northman, what wouldst thou do?"

"I would kill thee," replied the peasant; "but, as ill luck would have it, I have no weapon just now by me that would do it."

Then Styrkar says: "As you can't kill me, friend, I shall try if I can't kill you." And with that he swung his sword and struck him on the neck, so that his head came off. He then took the skin-coat, sprang on his horse, and rode down to the strand.

Olaf Haraldsson had not gone on land with the others, and when he heard of his father's fall he made ready to sail away with the men who remained.

NORSE MYTHS

THE TWILIGHT OF THE GODS

How Thor Went to Jotunheim

Once on a time, then, Asa Thor and Loki set out on a journey from Asgard to Jotunheim. They travelled in Thor's chariot, drawn by two milk-white goats. It was a somewhat cumbrous iron chariot, and the wheels made a rumbling noise as it moved, which sometimes startled the Æsir of Asgard, and made them tremble; but Thor liked it, thought the noise sweeter than any music, and was never so happy as when he was journeying in it from one place to another.

They travelled all day, and in the evening they came to a countryman's house. It was a poor, lonely place; but Thor descended from his chariot, and determined to pass the night there. The countryman, however, had no food in his house to give these travellers; and Thor, who liked to feast himself and make every one feast with him, was obliged to kill his own two goats and serve them up for supper. He invited the countryman and his wife and children to sup with him; but before they began to eat he made one request of them.

"Do not, on any account," he said, "break or throw away any of the bones of the goats you are going to eat for supper."

"I wonder why," said the peasant's son, Thialfi, to his sister Roskra. Roskra could not think of any reason, and by-and-by Thialfi happened to have a very nice little bone given him with some marrow in it. "Certainly there can be no harm in my breaking just this one," he said to himself; "it would be such a pity to lose the marrow;" and as Asa Thor's head was turned another way, he slyly broke the bone in two, sucked the marrow, and then threw the pieces into the goats' skins, where Thor had desired that all the bones might be placed. I do not know whether Thialfi was uneasy during the night about what he had done; but in the morning he found out the reason of Asa Thor's command, and received a lesson on "wondering why", which he never forgot all his life after.

As soon as Asa Thor rose in the morning he took his hammer, Mjollnir, in his hand, and held it over the goat-skins as they lay on the floor, whispering runes the while. They were dead skins with dry bones on them when he began to speak; but as he said the last word, Thialfi, who was looking curiously on, saw two live goats spring up and walk towards the chariot, as fresh and well as when they brought the chariot up to the door, Thialfi hoped. But no; one of the goats limped a little with his hind leg, and Asa Thor saw it. His brow grew dark as he looked, and for a minute Thialfi thought he would run far, far into the forest, and never come back again; but one look more at Asa Thor's face, angry as it was, made him change his mind. He thought of a better thing to do than running away. He came forward, threw himself at the Asa's feet, and, confessing what he had done, begged pardon for his disobedience. Thor listened, and the displeased look passed away from his face.

"You have done wrong, Thialfi," he said, raising him up; "but as you have confessed your fault so bravely, instead of punishing you, I will take you with me on my journey, and teach you myself the lesson of obedience to the Æsir which is, I see, wanted."

Roskra chose to go with her brother, and from that day Thor had two faithful servants, who followed him wherever he went.

The chariot and goats were now left behind; but, with Loki and his two new followers, Thor journeyed on to the end of Manheim, over the sea, and then on, on, on in the strange, barren, misty land of Jotunheim. Sometimes they crossed great mountains; sometimes they had to make their way among torn and rugged rocks, which often, through the mist, appeared to them to wear the forms of men, and once for a whole day they traversed a thick and tangled forest. In the evening of that day, being very much tired, they saw with pleasure that they had come upon a spacious hall, of which the door, as broad as the house itself, stood wide open.

"Here we may very comfortably lodge for the night," said Thor; and they went in and looked about them.

The house appeared to be perfectly empty; there was a wide hall, and five smaller rooms opening into it. They were, however, too tired to examine it carefully, and as no inhabitants made their appearance, they ate their supper in the hall, and lay down to sleep. But they had not rested long before they were disturbed by strange noises, groanings, mutterings, and snortings, louder than any animal that they had ever seen in their lives could make. By-and-by the house began to shake from side to side, and it seemed as if the very earth trembled. Thor sprang up in haste, and ran to the open door; but, though he looked earnestly into the starlit forest, there was no enemy to be seen anywhere. Loki and Thialfi, after groping about for a time, found a sheltered chamber to the right, where they thought they could finish their night's rest in safety; but Thor, with Mjollnir in his hand, watched at the door of the house all night. As soon as the day dawned he went out into the forest, and there, stretched on the ground close by the house, he saw a strange, un-couth, gigantic shape of a man, out of whose nostrils came a breath which swayed the trees to their very tops. There was no need to wonder any longer what the disturbing noises had been. Thor fear-lessly walked up to this strange monster to have a better look at him; but at the sound of his footsteps the giant-shape rose slowly, stood up an immense height, and looked down upon Thor with two great misty eyes, like blue mountain-lakes.

"Who are you?" said Thor, standing on tiptoe, and stretching his neck to look up; "and why do you make such a noise as to prevent your neighbours from sleeping?"

"My name is Skrymir," said the giant sternly; "I need not ask yours. You are the little Asa Thor of Asgard; but pray, now, what have you done with my glove?"

As he spoke he stooped down, and picked up the hall where Thor and his companions had passed the night, and which, in truth, was nothing more than his glove, the room where Loki and Thialfi had slept being the thumb.

Thor rubbed his eyes, and felt as if he must be dreaming. Rous-ing himself, however, he raised Mjollnir in his hand, and, trying to keep his eyes fixed on the giant's face, which seemed to be always changing, he said, "It is time that you should know, Skrymir, that

I am come to Jotunheim to fight and conquer such evil giants as you are, and, little as you think me, I am ready to try my strength against yours."

"Try it, then," said the giant.

And Thor, without another word, threw Mjollnir at his head.

"Ah! Ah!" said the giant; "did a leaf touch me?"

Again Thor seized Mjollnir, which always returned to his hand, however far he cast it from him, and threw it with all his force.

The giant put up his hand to his forehead. "I think," he said, "that an acorn must have fallen on my head."

A third time Thor struck a blow, the heaviest that ever fell from the hand of an Asa; but this time the giant laughed out loud.

"There is surely a bird on that tree," he said, "who has let a feather fall on my face."

Then, without taking any further notice of Thor, he swung an immense wallet over his shoulder, and, turning his back upon him, struck into a path that led from the forest. When he had gone a little way he looked round, his immense face appearing less like a human countenance than some strange, uncouthly-shaped stone toppling on a mountain precipice.

"Winged-Thor," he said, "let me give you a piece of good advice before I go. When you get to Utgard don't make much of yourself. You think me a tall man, but you have taller still to see; and you yourself are a very little mannikin. Turn back home whence you came, and be satisfied to have learned something of yourself by your journey to Jotunheim."

"Mannikin or not, *that* will I never do," shouted Asa Thor after the giant. "We will meet again, and something more will we learn, or teach each other."

The giant, however, did not turn back to answer, and Thor and his companions, after looking for some time after him, resumed their journey. Before the sun was quite high in the heavens they came out of the forest, and at noon they found themselves on a vast barren plain, where stood a great city, whose walls of dark, rough stone were so high, that Thor had to bend his head quite far back to see the top of them. When they approached the entrance of this city they found that the gates were closed and barred; but the space between the bars was so large that Thor passed through easily, and his companions followed him. The streets of the city were gloomy and still. They walked on for some time without meeting any one; but at length they came to a very high building, of which the gates stood open.

"Let us go in and see what is going on here," said Thor; and they went.

After crossing the threshold they found themselves in an immense banqueting-hall. A table stretched from one end to the other of it; stone thrones stood round the table, and on every throne sat a giant, each one, as Thor glanced round, appearing more grim, and cold, and stony than the rest. One among them sat on a raised seat, and appeared to be the chief; so to him Thor approached, and paid his greetings.

The giant chief, Utgard-Loki, just glanced at him, and, without rising, said, in a somewhat careless manner, "It is, I think, a foolish custom to tease tired travellers with questions about their journey. I know without asking that you, little fellow, are Asa Thor. Perhaps, however, you may be in reality taller than you appear; and as it is a rule here that no one shall sit down to table till they have performed some wonderful feat, let us hear what you and your followers are famed for, and in what way you choose to prove yourselves worthy to sit down in the company of giants."

At this speech, Loki, who had entered the hall cautiously behind Thor, pushed himself forward.

"The feat for which I am most famed," he said, "is eating, and it is one which I am just now inclined to perform with right good will. Put food before me, and let me see if any of your followers can despatch it as quickly as I can."

"The feat you speak of is one by no means to be despised," said the King Utgard-Loki, "and there is one here who would be glad to try his powers against yours. Let Logi," he said to one of his followers, "be summoned to the hall."

At this, a tall, thin, yellow-faced man approached, and a large trough of meat having been placed in the middle of the hall, Loki sat to work at one end, and Logi at the other, and they began to eat.

I hope *I* shall never see any one eat as they ate; but the giants all turned their slow-moving eyes to watch them, and in a few minutes they met in the middle of the trough. It seemed, at first, as if they had both eaten exactly the same quantity; but, when the thing came to be examined into, it was found that Loki had, indeed, eaten up all the meat, but that Logi had also eaten the bones and the trough. Then the giants nodded their huge heads, and determined that Loki was conquered. The King now turned to Thialfi, and asked what he could do.

"I was thought swift of foot among the youth of my own country," answered Thialfi; "and I will, if you please, try to run a race with any one here."

"You have chosen a noble sport, indeed," said the King; "but you must be a good runner if you could beat him with whom I shall match you."

Then he called a slender lad, Hugi by name, and the whole company left the hall, and, going out by an opposite gate to that by which Thor had entered, they came out on to an open space, which made a noble race-ground. There the goal was fixed, and Thialfi and Hugi started off together.

Thialfi ran fast—fast as the reindeer which hears the wolves howling behind; but Hugi ran so much faster that, passing the goal, he turned round, and met Thialfi half-way in the course.

"Try again, Thialfi," cried the King; and Thialfi, once more taking his place, flew along the course with feet scarcely touching the ground—swiftly as an eagle when, from his mountain-crag, he swoops on his prey in the valley; but with all his running he was still a good bow-shot from the goal when Hugi reached it.

"You are certainly a good runner," said the King; "but if you mean to win you must do a little better still than this; but perhaps you wish to surprise us all the more this third time."

The third time, however, Thialfi was wearied, and though he did his best, Hugi, having reached the goal, turned and met him not far from the starting-point.

The giants again looked at each other, and declared that there was no need of further trial, for that Thialfi was conquered.

It was now Asa Thor's turn, and all the company looked eagerly at him, while Utgard-Loki asked by what wonderful feat he chose to distinguish himself.

"I will try a drinking-match with any of you," Thor said, shortly; for, to tell the truth, he cared not to perform anything very worthy in the company in which he found himself.

Utgard-Loki appeared pleased with this choice, and when the giants had resumed their seats in the hall, he ordered one of his servants to bring in his drinking-cup, called the "cup of penance", which it was his custom to make his guests drain at a draught, if they had broken any of the ancient rules of the society.

"There!" he said, handing it to Thor, "we call it well drunk if a person empties it at a single draught. Some, indeed, take two to it; but the very puniest can manage it in three."

Thor looked into the cup; it appeared to him long, but not so very large after all, and being thirsty he put it to his lips, and thought to make short work of it, and empty it at one good, hearty pull. He drank, and put the cup down again; but, instead of being empty, it was now just so full that it could be moved without danger of spilling.

"Ha! ha! You are keeping all your strength for the second pull I see," said Utgard-Loki, looking in. Without answering, Thor lifted the cup again, and drank with all his might till his breath failed; but, when he put down the cup, the liquor had only sunk down a little from the brim.

"If you mean to take three draughts to it," said Utgard-Loki, "you are really leaving yourself a very unfair share for the last time. Look to yourself, Winged-Thor; for, if you do not acquit yourself better in other feats, we shall not think so much of you here as they say the Æsir do in Asgard."

At this speech Thor felt angry, and, seizing the cup again, he drank a third time, deeper and longer than he had yet done; but, when he looked into the cup, he saw that a very small part only of its contents had disappeared. Wearied and disappointed he put the cup down, and said he would try no more to empty it.

"It is pretty plain," said the King, looking round on the company, "that Asa Thor is by no means the kind of man we always supposed him to be."

"Nay," said Thor, "I am willing to try another feat, and you yourselves shall choose what it shall be."

"Well," said the King, "there is a game at which our children are used to play. A short time ago I dare not have named it to Asa Thor; but now I am curious to see how he will acquit himself in it. It is merely to lift my cat from the ground—a childish amusement truly."

As he spoke a large, grey cat sprang into the hall, and Thor, stooping forward, put his hand under it to lift it up. He tried gently at first; but by degrees he put forth all his strength, tugging and straining as he had never done before; but the utmost he could do was to raise one of the cat's paws a little way from the ground.

"It is just as I thought," said Utgard-Loki, looking round with a smile; "but we all are willing to allow that the cat *is* large, and Thor but a little fellow."

"Little as you think me," cried Thor, "who is there who will dare to wrestle with me in my anger?"

"In truth," said the King, "I don't think there is any one here who would choose to wrestle with you; but, if wrestle you must, I will call in that old crone Elli. She has, in her time, laid low many a better man than Asa Thor has shown himself to be."

The crone came. She was old, withered, and toothless, and Thor shrank from the thought of wrestling with her; but he had no choice. She threw her arms round him, and drew him towards the ground, and the harder he tried to free himself, the tighter grew her grasp. They struggled long. Thor strove bravely, but a strange feeling of weakness and weariness came over him, and at length he tottered and fell down on one knee before her. At this sight all the giants laughed aloud, and Utgard-Loki coming up, desired the old woman to leave the hall, and proclaimed that the trials were over. No one of his followers would *now* contend with Asa Thor, he said, and night was approaching. He then invited Thor and his companions to sit down at the table, and spend the night with him as his guests. Thor, though feeling somewhat perplexed and mortified, accepted his invitation courteously, and showed, by his agreeable behaviour during the evening, that he knew how to bear being conquered with a good grace.

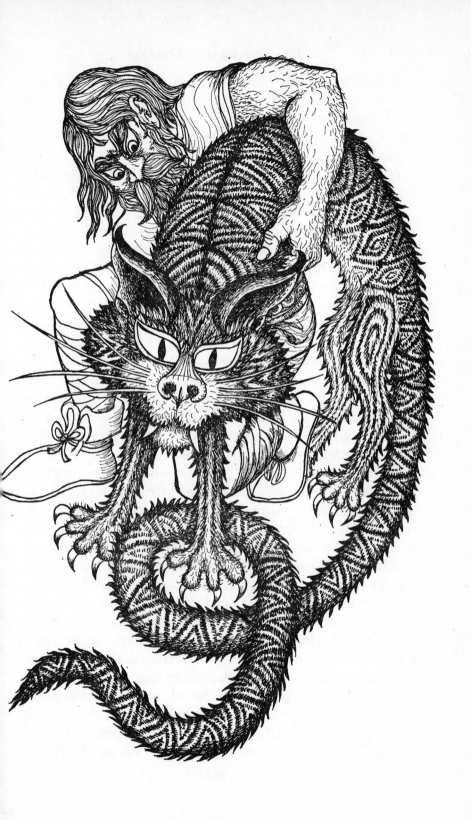

In the morning, when Thor and his companions were leaving the city, the King himself accompanied them without the gates; and Thor, looking steadily at him when he turned to bid him farewell, perceived, for the first time, that he was the very same Giant Skrymir with whom he had met in the forest.

"Come, now, Asa Thor," said the giant, with a strange sort of smile on his face, "tell me truly, before you go, how you think your journey has turned out, and whether or not I was right in saying that you would meet with better men than yourself in Jotunheim."

"I confess freely," answered Asa Thor, looking up without any false shame on his face, "that I have acquitted myself but humbly, and it grieves me; for I know that in Jotunheim henceforward it will be said that I am a man of little worth."

"By my troth! no," cried the giant, heartily. "Never should you have come into my city if I had known what a mighty man of valour you really are; and, now that you are safely out of it, I will, for once, tell the truth to you, Thor. All this time I have been deceiving you by my enchantments. When you met me in the forest, and hurled Mjollnir at my head, I should have been crushed by the weight of your blows had I not skilfully placed a mountain between myself and you, on which the strokes of your hammer fell, and where you cleft three deep ravines, which shall henceforth become verdant valleys. In the same manner I deceived you about the contests in which you engaged last night. When Loki and Logi sat down before the trough, Loki, indeed, ate like hunger itself; but Logi is fire, who, with eager, consuming tongue, licked up both bones and trough. Thialfi is the swiftest of mortal runners; but the slender lad, Hugi, was my thought; and what speed can ever equal his? So it was in your own trials. When you took such deep draughts from the horn, you little knew what a wonderful feat you were performing. The other end of that horn reached the ocean, and when you come to the shore you will see how far its waters have fallen away, and how much the deep sea itself has been diminished by your draught. Hereafter, men watching the going out of the tide will call it the ebb, or draught of Thor. Scarcely less wonderful was the prowess you displayed in the second trial. What appeared to you to be a cat, was, in reality, the Midgard serpent, which encircles the world. When we saw you succeed in moving it we trembled lest the very foundations of earth and sea should be shaken by your strength. Nor need you be ashamed of having been overthrown by the old woman Elli, for she is old age; and there never has, and never will be, one whom she has not the power to lay low. We must now part, and you had better not come here again, or attempt anything further against my city; for I shall always defend it by fresh enchantments, and you will never be able to do anything against me."

At these words Thor raised Mjollnir, and was about to challenge the giant to a fresh trial of strength; but, before he could speak, Utgard-Loki vanished from his sight; and, turning round to look for the city, he found that it, too, had disappeared, and that he was standing alone on a smooth, green, empty plain.

"What a fool I have been," said Asa Thor, aloud, "to allow myself to be deceived by a mountain giant!"

"Ah," answered a voice from above, "I told you, you would learn to know yourself better by your journey to Jotunheim. It is the great use of travelling."

Thor turned quickly round again, thinking to see Skrymir behind him; but, after looking on every side, he could perceive nothing, but that a high, cloud-capped mountain, which he had noticed on the horizon, appeared to have advanced to the edge of the plain.

Thor Goes Fishing with Hymir

Thor left the shores of Midgard disguised as a young blade and on a certain evening arrived at a giant's called Hymir. Thor stayed the night with him as a lodger. At daybreak, Hymir got out of bed, dressed and fettled his row boat to put to sea fishing. Thor too sprang up and quickly got ready, asking Hymir to let him row the boat in the sea with him. Hymir said he couldn't see his being much help, so small and youthful as he was, "and you'll freeze if I stay as long and as far out as I am in the habit of doing". Thor replied if that was so Hymir should be sure to row as far as he pleased from the shore for Thor didn't think he would be the first to ask to row back. In fact, Thor was so consumed with rage at the giant that he was ready at any moment to let his hammer crash down on him: but he held himself in since he firmly intended to try his strength in another quarter.

He asked Hymir what to use for bait and Hymir grunted he must see to himself for bait. Thor turned at once to where he saw a herd of oxen belonging to Hymir. He grabbed the biggest ox called Himinhriod Heaven-springer, cut off its head and went with it to the shore; by which time Hymir was launching the boat. Thor leapt aboard, made himself comfortable in the bottom, picked up a pair of oars and started to row. In spite of his efforts at pulling, they seemed to Hymir to be crawling along. Hymir rowed forrard in the prow and did his best to speed up the strokes. At last he said they were come to the fishing banks where he usually angled for flat-fish, but Thor protested he wanted to row much farther out: so they pulled on smartly for a bit. Again Hymir spoke: they had come so far out it was dangerous to hang about there on account of the

212

World Serpent; and again Thor answered they ought to keep rowing for a spell. He got his way and Hymir took it good-humouredly. Thor at last dropped his oars and busied himself with a fishing rod, rather a huge one, nor was the hook either small or weak. Thor fastened the ox's head on to his hook and cast it over the side, when the hook sank to the bottom of the sea.

Now I'll let you into a secret: in their previous encounter, the World Serpent's belly hadn't really fooled Thor when he tried to lift it in the guise of a cat from the ground. But Utgard-Loki had indeed made him into a laughing-stock. Well, now it was the turn of the World Serpent to swallow the bait in the shape of the ox's head; but the fish-hook stuck in his gullet and when the serpent realised it he threshed about so monstrously that Thor's wrists were skinned along the gunwale. This made the god fizz with rage and he called up all his divine power and dug in with his heels, bracing both feet so hard against the boat bottom that he hauled the serpent up to the side!

I can tell you this for a fact: nobody ever saw a more blood-freezing sight than Thor did, as his eyes goggled down at the serpent and the Great Worm from below glared up and blew a cloud of poison. At that, they say the giant Hymir blenched, then turned yellow in his terror, what with the sea swashing into the boat and out of the boat! But Thor grabbed his hammer and flung it above his head just as Hymir fumbled for the knife he used for chopping bait and hacked Thor's fishing rod overboard!

The serpent sank down into the depths of the sea.

But Thor cast his hammer after it, and some people think he would have liked its head and horns. I myself believe it is true to say that the World Serpent still lives and lies weltering at the bottom of the Ocean. Still, Thor raised his fist in a mad mortification and made a dead set at Hymir so that he up-ended him into the sea and the last Thor saw of him was the soles of his feet. Then Thor waded ashore.

Balder's Doom

In Asgard there were two places that meant strength and joy to the Æsir: one was the garden where grew the apples that Iduna gathered, and the other was the Peace Stead, where, in a palace called Breidablik, Balder the Well-beloved dwelt.

In the Peace Stead no crime had ever been committed, no blood had ever been shed, no falseness had ever been spoken. Contentment came into the minds of all in Asgard when they thought upon this place. Ah! Were it not that the Peace Stead was there, happy with Balder's presence, the minds of the Æsir might have become gloomy and stern from thinking on the direful things that were arrayed against them.

Balder was beautiful. So beautiful was he that all the white blossoms on the earth were called by his name. Balder was happy. So happy was he that all the birds on the earth sang his name. So just and so wise was Balder that the judgement he pronounced might never be altered. Nothing foul or unclean had ever come near where he had his dwelling:

> *'Tis Breidablik called,*
> *Where Balder the Fair*
> *Hath built him a bower,*
> *In the land where I know*
> *Least loathliness lies.*

Healing things were done in Balder's Stead. Tyr's wrist was healed of the wounds that Fenrir's fangs had made.

Now after Fenrir had been bound to the rock in the far-away island the Æsir knew a while of contentment. They passed bright days in Balder's Stead, listening to the birds that made music there. And it was there that Bragi the Poet wove into his never-ending story the tale of Thor's adventures amongst the giants.

But even into Balder's Stead foreboding came. One day little Hnossa, the child of Freya, was brought there in such sorrow that no one outside could comfort her. Nanna, Balder's gentle wife, took the child upon her lap and found ways of soothing her. Then Hnossa told of a dream that had filled her with fright.

She had dreamt of Hel, the Queen that is half living woman and half corpse. In her dream Hel had come into Asgard saying, "A lord of the Æsir I must have to dwell with me in my realm beneath the earth." Hnossa had such fear from this dream that she had fallen into a deep sorrow.

A silence fell upon all when the dream of Hnossa was told. Nanna looked wistfully at Odin All-Father. And Odin, looking at Frigg, saw that a fear had entered her breast.

He left the Peace Stead and went to his watch-tower Hlidskjalf. He waited there till Huginn and Muninn should come to him. Every day his two ravens flew through the world, and coming back to him told him of all that was happening. And now they might tell him of happenings that would let him guess if Hel had indeed turned her thoughts towards Asgard, or if she had the power to draw one down to her dismal abode.

The ravens flew to him, and lighting one on each of his shoulders, told him of things that were being said up and down Yggdrasill, the World Tree. Ratatosk the Squirrel was saying them. And Ratatosk had heard them from the brood of serpents that with Nidhogg, the great dragon, gnawed ever at the root of Yggdrasill. He told it to the Eagle that sat ever on the topmost bough, that in Hel's habitation a bed was spread and a chair was left empty for some lordly comer.

And hearing this, Odin thought that it were better that Fenrir the Wolf should range ravenously through Asgard than that Hel should win one from amongst them to fill that chair and lie in that bed.

He mounted Sleipnir, his eight-legged steed, and rode down towards the abodes of the Dead. For three days and three nights of

silence and darkness he journeyed on. Once one of the hounds of
Helheim broke loose and bayed upon Sleipnir's tracks. For a day
and a night Garm, the hound, pursued them, and Odin smelled the
blood that dripped from his monstrous jaws.

At last he came to where, wrapped in their shrouds, a field of the
Dead lay. He dismounted from Sleipnir and called upon one to rise
and speak with him. It was on Volva, a dead prophetess, he called.
And when he pronounced her name he uttered a rune that had the
power to break the sleep of the Dead.

There was a groaning in the middle of where the shrouded ones
lay. Then Odin cried out, "Arise, Volva, prophetess." There was a
stir in the middle of where the shrouded ones lay, and a head and
shoulders were thrust up from amongst the Dead.

"Who calls on Volva the Prophetess? The rains have drenched
my flesh and the storms have shaken my bones for more seasons
than the living know. No living voice has a right to call me from my
sleep with the Dead."

"It is Vegtam the Wanderer who calls. For whom is the bed prepared and the seat left empty in Hel's habitation?"

"For Balder, Odin's son, is the bed prepared and the seat left
empty. Now let me go back to my sleep with the Dead."

But now Odin saw beyond Volva's prophecy. "Who is it," he
cried out, "that stands with unbowed head and that will not lament
for Balder? Answer, Volva, prophetess!"

"Thou seest far, but thou canst not see clearly. Thou art Odin.
I can see clearly but I cannot see far. Now let me go back to my
sleep with the Dead."

"Volva, prophetess!" Odin cried out again.

But the voice from amongst the shrouded ones said, "Thou canst
not wake me any more until the fires of Muspellheim blaze above
my head."

Then there was silence in the field of the Dead, and Odin turned
Sleipnir, his steed, and for four days, through the gloom and silence,
he journeyed back to Asgard.

Frigg had felt the fear that Odin had felt. She looked towards
Balder, and the shade of Hel came between her and her son. But

then she heard the birds sing in the Peace Stead and she knew that none of all the things in the world would injure Balder.

And to make it sure she went to all the things that could hurt him and from each of them she took an oath that it would not injure Balder, the Well-beloved. She took an oath from fire and from water, from iron and from all metals, from earths and stones and great trees, from birds and beasts and creeping things, from poisons and diseases. Very readily they all gave the oath that they would work no injury on Balder.

Then when Frigg went back and told what she had accomplished the gloom that had lain on Asgard lifted. Balder would be spared to them. Hel might have a place prepared in her dark habitation, but neither fire nor water, nor iron nor any metal, nor earths nor stones nor great woods, nor birds nor beasts nor creeping things, nor poisons nor diseases, would help her to bring him down. "Hel has no arms to draw you to her," the Æsir cried to Balder.

Hope was renewed for them and they made games to honour Balder. They had him stand in the Peace Stead and they brought against him all the things that had sworn to leave him hurtless. And neither the battle-axe flung full at him, nor the stone out of the sling, nor the burning brand, nor the deluge of water would injure the beloved of Asgard. The Æsir laughed joyously to see these things fall harmlessly from him while a throng came to join them in the games: dwarfs and friendly giants.

But Loki the Hater came in with that throng. He watched the games from afar. He saw the missiles and the weapons being flung and he saw Balder stand smiling and happy under the strokes of metal and stones and great woods. He wondered at the sight, but he knew that he might not ask the meaning of it from the ones who knew him.

He changed his shape into that of an old woman and he went amongst those who were making sport for Balder. He spoke to dwarfs and friendly giants. "Go to Frigg and ask. Go to Frigg and ask," was all the answer Loki got from any of them.

Then to Fensalir, Frigg's mansion, Loki went. He told those in the mansion that he was Groa, the old Enchantress who was drawing out of Thor's head the fragments of a grindstone that a giant's throw had embedded in it. Frigg knew about Groa and she praised the Enchantress for what she had done.

"Many fragments of the great grindstone have I taken out of Thor's head by the charms I know," said the pretended Groa. "Thor was so grateful that he brought back to me the husband that he once had carried off to the end of the earth. So overjoyed was I to find my husband restored that I forgot the rest of the charms. And I left some fragments of the stone in Thor's head."

So Loki said, repeating a story that was true. "Now I remember the rest of the charm," he said, "and I can draw out the fragments of the stone that are left. But will you not tell me, O Queen, what is the meaning of the extraordinary things I saw the Æsir doing?"

"I will tell you," said Frigg, looking kindly and happily at the pretended old woman. "They are hurling all manner of heavy and dangerous things at Balder, my beloved son. And all Asgard cheers to see that neither metal nor stone nor great wood will hurt him."

"But why will they not hurt him?" said the pretended Enchantress.

"Because I have drawn an oath from all dangerous and threatening things to leave Balder hurtless," said Frigg.

"From all things, lady? Is there no thing in all the world that has not taken an oath to leave Balder hurtless?"

"Well, indeed, there is one thing that has not taken the oath. But that thing is so small and weak that I passed it by without taking thought of it."

"What can it be, lady?"

"The Mistletoe that is without root or strength. It grows on the eastern side of Valhalla. I passed it by without drawing an oath from it."

"Surely you were not wrong to pass it by. What could the Mistletoe—the rootless Mistletoe—do against Balder?"

Saying this the pretended Enchantress hobbled off.

But not far did the pretender go hobbling. He changed his gait and hurried to the eastern side of Valhalla. There a great oak tree flourished and out of a branch of it a little bush of Mistletoe grew. Loki broke off a spray and with it in his hand he went to where the Æsir were still playing games to honour Balder.

All were laughing as Loki drew near, for the giants and the dwarfs were casting missiles; the giants threw too far and the dwarfs could not throw far enough. In the midst of all that glee and gamesomeness it was strange to see one standing joyless. But one stood so, and he was of the Æsir—Hoder, Balder's blind brother.

"Why do you not enter the game?" said Loki to him in his changed voice.

"I have no missile to throw at Balder," Hoder said.

"Take this and throw it," said Loki. "It is a twig of the Mistletoe."

"I cannot see to throw it," said Hoder.

"I will guide your hand," said Loki. He put the twig of Mistletoe in Hoder's hand and he guided the hand for the throw. The twig flew towards Balder. It struck him on the breast and it pierced him. Then Balder fell down with a deep groan.

The Æsir, the dwarfs and the friendly giants, stood still in doubt and fear and amazement. Loki slipped away. And blind Hoder, from whose hand the twig of Mistletoe had gone, stood quiet, not knowing that his throw had bereft Balder of life.

Then a wailing rose around the Peace Stead. Balder was dead, and they began to lament him. And while they were lamenting him, the beloved of Asgard, Odin came amongst them.

"Hel has won our Balder from us," Odin said to Frigg as they both bent over the body of their beloved son.

"Nay, I will not say it," Frigg said.

When the Æsir had won their senses back the mother of Balder went amongst them. "Who amongst you would win my love and good-will?" she said. "Whoever would let him ride down to Hel's dark realm and ask the Queen to take ransom for Balder. It may be she will take it and let Balder come back to us. Who amongst you will go? Odin's steed is ready for the journey."

Then forth stepped Hermod the Nimble, the brother of Balder. He mounted Sleipnir and turned the eight-legged steed down towards Hel's dark realm.

For nine days and nine nights Hermod rode on. His way was through rugged glens, one deeper and darker than the other. He came to the river that is called Gjoll and to the bridge across it that is all glittering with gold. The pale maid who guards the bridge spoke to him.

"The hue of life is still on thee," said Modgud, the pale maid. "Why dost thou journey down to Hel's deathly realm?"

"I am Hermod," he said, "and I go to see if Hel will take ransom for Balder."

"Fearful is Hel's habitation for one to come to," said Modgud, the pale maid. "All round it is a steep wall that even thy steed might hardly leap. Its threshold is Precipice. The bed therein is Care, the table is Hunger, the hanging of the chamber is Burning Anguish."

"It may be that Hel will take ransom for Balder."

"If all things in the world still lament for Balder, Hel will have to take ransom and let him go from her," said Modgud, the pale maid that guards the glittering bridge.

"It is well, then, for all things lament Balder. I will go to her and make her take ransom."

"Thou mayst not pass until it is of a surety that all things still lament him. Go back to the world and make sure. If thou dost come to this glittering bridge and tell me that all things still lament Balder, I will let thee pass and Hel will have to hearken to thee."

"I will come back to thee, and thou, Modgud, pale maid, wilt have to let me pass.'"

"Then I will let thee pass," said Modgud.

Joyously Hermod turned Sleipnir and rode back through the rugged glens, each one less gloomy than the other. He reached the upper world, and he saw that all things were still lamenting for Balder. Joyously Hermod rode onward, went through the world seeking out each thing and finding that each thing still wept for Balder. But one day Hermod came upon a crow that was sitting on the dead branch of a tree. The crow made no lament as he came near. She rose up and flew away and Hermod followed her to make sure that she lamented for Balder.

He lost sight of her near a cave. And then before the cave he saw a hag with blackened teeth who raised no voice of lament. "If thou art the crow that came flying here, make lament for Balder," Hermod said.

"I, Thokk, will make no lament for Balder," the hag said, "let Hel keep what she holds."

"All things weep tears for Balder," Hermod said.

"I will weep dry tears for him," said the hag.

She hobbled into her cave, and as Hermod followed a crow fluttered out. He knew that this was Thokk, the evil hag, transformed. He followed her, and she went through the world croaking, "Let Hel keep what she holds. Let Hel keep what she holds."

Then Hermod knew that he might not ride to Hel's habitation. All things knew that there was one thing in the world that would not lament for Balder. With head bowed over Sleipnir's mane, Hermod rode into Asgard.

Now the Æsir, knowing that no ransom would be taken for Balder and that the joy and content of Asgard were gone indeed, made ready his body for the burning. First they covered Balder's body with a rich robe, and each left beside it his most precious possession. Then they all took leave of him, kissing him upon the brow. But Nanna, his gentle wife, flung herself on his dead breast and her heart broke and she died of her grief. Then did the Æsir weep afresh. And they took the body of Nanna and they placed it side by side with Balder's.

On his own great ship, Ringhorn, would Balder be placed with Nanna beside him. Then the ship would be launched on the water and all would be burned with fire.

But it was found that none of the Æsir were able to launch Balder's great ship. Hyrrokkin, a giantess, was sent for. She came mounted on a great wolf with twisted serpents for a bridle. Four giants held fast the wolf when she alighted. She came to the ship and with a single push she sent it into the sea. The rollers struck out fire as the ship dashed across them.

Then when it rode the water fires mounted on the ship. And in the blaze of the fires one was seen bending over the body of Balder and whispering into his ear. It was Odin All-Father. Then he went down off the ship and all the fires rose into a mighty burning. Speechlessly the Æsir watched with tears streaming down their faces while all things lamented, crying, "Balder the Beautiful is dead, is dead."

And what was it that Odin All-Father whispered to Balder as he bent above him with the flames of the burning ship around? He whispered of a heaven above Asgard that Surt's flames might not reach, and of a life that would come to beauty again after the world of men and the world of the gods had been searched through and through with fire.

After the death of Balder, Loki sneered openly at the helplessness of the gods. They resolved to punish him and, although Loki changed himself into a salmon, he was finally unable to escape them. The gods bound him to stone slabs in an underground cavern. There, poison dripped on to his face; and there Loki remained, waiting for his bonds to break at Ragnarok.

Ragnarok

Even from the morning of time Odin had known, the Æsir soon knew, and even the dwellers in Midgard learnt to know also, that the whole world would perish on a day—the Day of Ragnarok, the Twilight of the Gods—the Day of the Last Great Battle.

Balder was dead and Hoder was dead also. Loki was bound, and Valhalla was growing full of the Einheriar. There were shadows over Asgard, and in Jotunheim the Giants stirred and muttered threateningly. In Midgard men turned towards the evil Loki had taught them, treachery grew and greed and pride also.

Odin knew much of what was to happen when Ragnarok came: but there was much he did not know, for even he could not see the future. If the Norns knew, they would not speak: their task was to weave the web of each man's life, but not the life of the whole world.

But here and there a strange woman was born or died who could see into the future, some a little way and concerning little things; but one or two with powers of sight beyond that of any other creature. Such a one was the dead Volva whom Odin had raised from her grave to tell him of the death of Balder. Such another was born and lived her life in Midgard. Her name was Haid and she was famed among men for her prophecies.

Seated in Lidskialf, whence he could see all that happened in the Nine Worlds, Odin saw Haid, the wise sibyl, passing from house to house among men. And suddenly he knew that here was one wiser even than Volva, one who could answer what he desired most to know.

So he went down to Midgard wearing his usual disguise of wide-brimmed hat, blue cloak, and tall staff. Before he went in search of

224

Haid, the Valkyries had visited her, bringing such gifts as the high ones of Asgard could give: cunning treasure-spells, rune sticks, and rods of divination.

Odin came to her as she sat alone before a cave overlooking the broad land of the Danes and the blue waters of the Sound. He came as a man, bringing her presents of rings and necklaces, and begging her to read the future for him. But she knew him at once and spoke to him in the deep, thrilling tones of a prophetess:

"What ask you of me? Why would you tempt me? I know all, Odin: yes, I know where you have hidden your eye in the holy well of Mimir. I can see all things: both the world's beginning and the world's ending. I can see Ginnungagap as it was before the Sons of Bor raised the earth out of it: the giant Ymir I know, and the Cow Audumla. . . . I can see the shaft of death, the mistletoe that Loki cut from the oak; the dart that flew into Balder's heart, and Frigg weeping in Fensalir."

"You know of the past, and that I know also," said Odin. "But, since the gift is yours and yours alone, look into the future, wise Haid—you whom we in Asgard call Vola, the Sibyl—look and tell me of the World's Ending: tell me of Ragnarok and the Great Battle on the Plain of Vigrid."

Then he took his stand behind Haid the Vola, placing his hands above her head and murmuring the runes of wisdom so that his knowledge should be mingled with hers.

And now her eyes grew wide and vacant as she gazed out across the land and over the water, seeing neither: seeing things unseen.

"There shall come the Fimbul Winter," she cried, "after man's evil has reached its height. For brother shall slay brother, and son shall not spare father, and honour shall be dead among men.

"In that awful Winter snow shall drive from all quarters, frost shall not break, the winds shall be keen, and the sun give no heat. And for three years shall that Fimbul Winter last.

"Eastward in Iron Wood an aged witch is sitting, breeding the brood of Fenris and the wolf that shall swallow the Sun. He shall feed on the lives of death-doomed mortals, spattering the heavens with their red blood.

"Ragnarok comes: I see it far in the days to be. Yet to me, the farseer, it is as if that day were now, and all that I see in the future is happening before me now. I see it, and I tell you what I see and hear as it rises about me until Future and Present seem as one.

"For I see the Wolf Skoll who in that far day swallows the Sun, and the Moon is swallowed also, while the stars are quenched with blood. Now the earth shakes, the trees and the rocks are torn up and all things fall to ruin.

"Away in Jotunheim the red cock Fialar crows loudly; and another cock with golden crest crows over Asgard. Then all bonds are loosened: the Fenris Wolf breaks free; the sea gushes over the land as Jormungand the Midgard Serpent swims ashore. Then the ship Naglfar is loosened: it is made of dead men's nails—therefore when a man dies, shear his nails close so that Naglfar may be long in the building. But now I see it moving over the flood, and the giant Hymir steers it. Fenris advances with open mouth, and Jormungand blows venom over sea and air: terrible is he as he takes his place beside the Wolf Fenris.

"Then the sky splits open and the Sons of Muspell come in fire: Surt leads them with his flaming sword, and when they ride over Bifrost the bridge breaks behind them and falls in pieces to the earth. Loki also is set free and comes to the Field of Vigrid; he and Hymir lead the frost giants to the battle. But all Hel's champions follow Loki: Garm the Hell Hound bays fiercely before the Gnipa Cave, and his jaws slobber with blood.

"Now I hear Heimdall in the Gate of Asgard blowing upon the Giallar Horn. Its notes sound clear and shrill throughout all worlds: it is the Day of Ragnarok. The Æsir meet together; Odin rides to Mimir's Well for the last time. Yggdrasill the World Tree trembles, and nothing shall be without fear in heaven or in earth.

"Now I see the Æsir put on their armour and ride to the field of battle. Odin rides first in his golden helmet and his fair armour; Sleipnir is beneath him and he holds the spear Gungnir in his hand. He rides against the Fenris Wolf, and Thor stands at his side, shaking Mjollnir: yet he cannot help Odin, for all his strength is needed in his own battle with Jormungand.

"Now Frey fights against Surt; the struggle is long, but Frey falls at the last. Ah, he would not have died had he his sword in his hand:

but that sword he gave to Skirnir. Oh, how loudly Garm bays in the Gnipa Cave! Now he has broken loose and fights against Tyr: had Tyr two hands it would go hard with Garm, but now they slay and are slain the one by the other.

"Thor slays the Midgard Serpent, and no greater deed was ever done. He strides away from the spot; nine paces only, and then he falls to the earth and dies, so deadly is the venom which Jormungand has poured upon him.

"Odin and Fenris still fight together: but in the end the Wolf has the victory and devours Odin. But Vidar strides forward to avenge his father, and sets his foot on the lower jaw of Fenris. On that foot is the shoe made of the scraps of leather which men cut from their toes or heels: therefore should men cut often and fling away if they desire to help the Æsir. Vidar takes the Wolf by the upper jaw and tears him apart, and that is the end of Fenris.

"Loki battles with Heimdall, and in their last struggle each slays the other and both fall.

"Now Surt spreads fire over the whole earth and all things perish. Darkness descends, and I can see no more."

The voice of Haid the Vola faded away into silence. But still she sat rigid and still gazing beyond the distance, gazing into the future with wide, unseeing eyes.

Very slowly, as he stood behind her, it seemed to Odin that her power was creeping into him. His own eye grew misty—grew dark —and then on a sudden he was looking out with two eyes, with her eyes and not his own.

At first he saw only a great waste of water, tossing and tumbling over all the world. But as he watched, a new earth rose out of the sea, green and fruitful, with unfading forests and pleasant meadows smiling in the light of a new sun. Then the waters fell away, making wide rivers, and sparkling falls and a new blue sea about the land.

Then, on Ida's Plain where Asgard had stood before, he saw Vidar and Vali, the two of the Æsir who had survived through Ragnarok. Thor's two sons, Magni and Modi, came to join them, bearing Mjollnir in their hands. After this the earth opened and back from Helheim came Balder the Beautiful, holding his brother Hoder by the hand.

They sat down and spoke together concerning all that had happened, of the passing of Fenris and Jormungand, and other evils. Then, shining among the grass and flowers, they saw the ancient golden chessmen of the Æsir, and collecting them began to play once more on the board of life.

Presently Hoenir came to them out of Vanaheim, bringing great wisdom to the new Æsir. At his bidding new halls rose on Ida's Plain, glittering palaces waiting for the souls of dead men and women from Midgard.

For in Midgard also life came again. In the deep place called Hoddminir's Holt a man and a woman had escaped from Surt's fire. Now they awoke from sleep, Lif and Lifthrasir; and for food they found the morning dew was all they needed. From them were born many children so that Midgard was peopled anew. And there were children also in the new Asgard which was called Gimli the Gem Lea, where the halls were thatched with gold. There the blessed among men mingled with the new race of the Æsir, and the new Sun shone brightly, and the new world was filled with light and song.

Then Odin wept with joy, and as the tears coursed down his face, the vision faded into the greyness of the cold Northern world where Ragnarok is yet to come. The wind moaned over the chill plains, the wolves howled in the lonely mountains, and across the sea stole forth a longship hung with shields in which Viking men went out to harry and slay and burn.

The old sibyl sat alone by her cave, chanting the words of the *Volo-spa*, the poem of prophecy, the finest of all the old Northern poems which are still known among men.

But Odin threaded his way quietly across Midgard to Bifrost Bridge, up its gleaming arch where Heimdall stood on guard, and so brought his good news to the Æsir.

For now he knew the meaning of the mysterious word which he had whispered into Balder's ear as his dead son lay upon the funeral ship: the word "Rebirth" which was to bring comfort and hope to the Men of Midgard as well as to the Gods of Asgard.

228

Retellings and Translations

Norse Myths

COLUM, PADRAIC. *The Children of Odin.* Harrap, London, 1922.

DASENT, GEORGE WEBBE (translator). *The Prose or Younger Edda.* Stockholm, 1842.

ELTON, OLIVER (translator). *Saxo Grammaticus: Gesta Danorum.* D. Nutt, London, 1894.

*GREEN, ROGER LANCELYN. *Myths of the Norsemen* (first published as *The Saga of Asgard*). Penguin, Harmondsworth, 1960.

GUERBER, H. A. *Myths of the Norsemen.* Harrap, London, 1908.

HOBHOUSE, ROSA. *Norse Legends.* J. M. Dent, London, 1930.

HOSFORD, DOROTHY. *Thunder of the Gods.* Henry Holt, New York, 1952, and The Bodley Head, London, 1964.

*KEARY, ANNIE. *The Heroes of Asgard and the Giants of Jötunheim.* Macmillan, London, 1857.

MABIE, HAMILTON WRIGHT. *Norse Stories.* Grant Richards, London, 1902.

*PICARD, BARBARA LEONIE. *Tales of the Norse Gods and Heroes.* Oxford University Press, London, 1953.

*TAYLOR, PAUL B., AUDEN, W. H. (translators) and SALUS, PETER H. *The Elder Edda.* Faber, London, 1969.

THOMAS, EDWARD. *Norse Tales.* Clarendon Press, Oxford, 1912.

WILMOT-BUXTON, E. M. *Told by the Northmen.* Harrap, London, 1908.

Germanic Heroic Legends

*ALEXANDER, MICHAEL (translator). *Beowulf.* Penguin, Harmondsworth, 1973.

*CROSSLEY-HOLLAND, KEVIN (translator). *Beowulf.* With an introduction by Bruce Mitchell. Macmillan, London, 1968. Reissued by D. S. Brewer, Cambridge, 1977.

GUERBER, H. A. *Myths and Legends of the Middle Ages.* Harrap, London, 1919.

*HATTO, A. T. (translator). *The Nibelungenlied.* Penguin, Harmondsworth, 1965.

HOSFORD, DOROTHY. *Sons of the Volsungs.* Henry Holt, New York, 1949.

MORRIS, WILLIAM. *The Story of Sigurd the Volsung and the Fall of the Niblungs.* Ellis and White, London, 1877.

*NYE, ROBERT. *Beowulf the Bee Hunter.* Faber, London, 1968.

*PICARD, BARBARA LEONIE. *German Hero-Sagas and Folk-Tales.* Oxford University Press, London, 1958.

*SUTCLIFF, ROSEMARY. *Beowulf.* The Bodley Head, London, 1961.

*SYNGE, URSULA. *Weland: Smith of the Gods.* The Bodley Head, London, 1972.

WEBER, HENRY, JAMIESON, R. and W. S. [Walter Scott] (translators). *Illustrations of Northern Antiquities.* Edinburgh, 1814. (In this book Germanic material predominates, but there are also translations from Icelandic, including the passage by Walter Scott included in this anthology.)

Icelandic Sagas

DASENT, GEORGE WEBBE (translator). *The Story of Gisli the Outlaw.* Edinburgh, 1866.

GATHORNE-HARDY, G. M. (translator). *The Norse Discoverers of America: The Wineland Sagas.* Oxford University Press, London, 1921.

HAUGEN, EINAR (translator). *Voyages to Vinland.* A. A. Knopf, New York, 1942.

*JONES, GWYN (translator). *Eirik the Red and other Icelandic Sagas.* Oxford University Press, London, 1961.

KERSHAW, N. (later Chadwick) (translator). *Stories and Ballads of the Far Past.* Cambridge University Press, Cambridge, 1921.

LAING, SAMUEL (translator). *The Heimskringla, or Chronicle of the*

Kings of Norway. Longmans, London, 1844. (*Part One: The Olaf Sagas.* Revised by Jacqueline Simpson. J. M. Dent, Everyman's Library, London, 1964. *Part Two: Sagas of the Norse Kings.* Revised by Peter Foote. J. M. Dent, Everyman's Library, London, 1961).

MAGNUSSON, MAGNUS and PÁLSSON, HERMANN (translators).
  *King Harald's Saga. Penguin, Harmondsworth, 1966.
  *Njal's Saga. Penguin, Harmondsworth, 1960.
  *The Vinland Sagas. Penguin, Harmondsworth, 1965.

*PÁLSSON, HERMANN and EDWARDS, PAUL (translators). *Gautrek's Saga and other Medieval Tales.* University of London Press, London, 1968.

*SCHILLER, BARBARA. *Hrafkel's Saga.* The Seabury Press, New York, 1972.

*SIMPSON, JACQUELINE (translator). *The Northmen Talk.* J. M. Dent, London, 1965.

In this very short bibliography I have confined myself to retellings and translations that still have some life in them and have altogether omitted curiosities and bundles of bones. Those books marked with an asterisk are in print.

The best introduction to the religious beliefs of the Norsemen, the Anglo-Saxons and their contemporaries is *The Gods and Myths of Northern Europe* by Hilda Ellis Davidson (Penguin, Harmondsworth, 1964) and the most lavishly illustrated is the same author's *Scandinavian Mythology* (Paul Hamlyn, London, 1969). *The Lost Gods of England* by Brian Branston (Thames and Hudson, London, 1957) is a work of imaginative scholarship, often exciting in the way it relates past and present. The most scholarly study of the subject is *Myth and Religion of the North: The Religion of Ancient Scandinavia* by E. O. G. Turville-Petre (Weidenfeld and Nicholson, London, 1964).

Index of Names and Subjects